THE JOLLIEST SCHOOL

OF ALL

ANGELA BRAZIL

THE JOLLIEST SCHOOL OF ALL

CHAPTER I

Off to Italy

In a top-story bedroom in an old-fashioned house in a northern suburb of London, a girl of fourteen was kneeling on the floor, turning out the contents of the bottom cupboards of a big bookcase. Her method of doing so was hardly tidy; she just tossed the miscellaneous assortment of articles down anywhere, till presently she was surrounded by a mixed-up jumble of books, papers, paint-boxes, music, chalks, pencils, foreign stamps, picture post-cards, crests, balls of knitting wool, skeins of embroidery silk, and odds and ends of all kinds. She groaned as the circle grew wider, yet the apparently inexhaustible cupboards were still uncleared.

"Couldn't have ever believed I'd have stowed so many things away here. And, of course, the one book I want isn't to be found. That's what always happens. It's just my bad luck. Hello! Who's calling 'Renie'? I'm here! Here! In my bedroom! Don't yell the house down. Really, Vin, you've got a voice like a megaphone! You might think I was on the top of the roof. What d'you want now? I'm busy!"

"So it seems," commented the fair-haired boy of seventeen, sauntering into his sister's room and taking a somewhat insecure seat upon a fancy table, where, with hands in pockets, he regarded her quizzically. "Great Scott, what a turn out! You look like a magician in the midst of a magic circle. Are you going to witch the lot into newts and toads? Whence this thusness? You won't persuade me that it's a fit of neatness and you're actually tidying. Doesn't exactly seem you, somehow!"

"Hardly," replied Irene, with her head inside a cupboard. "Fact is, I'm looking for my history book. I can't think where the wretched thing has gone to. School begins to-morrow, and I haven't touched my holiday tasks yet; and what Miss Gordon will say if I come without those exercises I can't imagine. I'm sure I flung all my books into this cupboard, and, of course, here's the chemistry, which I don't want, but never so much as a single leaf of the history. Don't grin! You aggravate me. I believe you've taken it away to tease me. Have you? Confess now! It's in your pocket all the time?"

Irene looked eagerly at the bulging outline of her brother's coat, but her newly formed hopes were doomed to disappointment.

"Never seen it! What should I want with your old history book? I've finished for good with such vanities, thank the Fates!"

"Don't rub it in. It's a beastly shame you should be allowed to leave school while I must go slaving on at Miss Gordon's. Ugh! How I hate the place! The idea of going back there to-morrow! It's simply appalling. A whole term of dreary grind, and only a fortnight's holiday at the end of it. Miss Gordon gives the stingiest holidays. If my fairy godmother could appear and grant me a wish I should choose never, never, never to see St. Osmund's College in all my life again. I'd ask her to wave her magic wand and transport me over the sea."

Irene spoke hotly, flinging books about with scant regard for their covers. Her slim hands were dusty, and her short, yellow hair as ruffled as her temper. There was even a suspicion of moisture about the corners of her gray eyes. She rubbed them surreptitiously with a ball of a handkerchief when her head happened to be inside the cupboard. She did not wish Vincent to witness this phase of her emotions.

"Every girl ought to be provided with a decent fairy godmother," she gulped. "If mine did her duty she'd come to rescue me now. Yes, she would, and be quick about it too!"

How very seldom in the course of an ordinary life such wishes are granted! Not once surely in a million times! Yet at that identical moment, almost as if in direct answer to her daughter's vigorous tirade, Mrs. Beverley entered the room. There was a sparkle of excitement in her eyes, and her whole atmosphere seemed to radiate news. She ran in as joyously as a girl, clapping her hands and evidently brimming over with something she was about to communicate.

"Why, Mums! Mums—darling! What's the matter?" asked Irene. "You look as if you'd had a fortune left you. Tell us at once."

"Not quite a fortune, but next best to it," said Mrs. Beverley, sitting down on the end of the sofa. "Daddy says I may tell you now, bairns. It has all happened so suddenly, and has been arranged in a rush. You remember Dad mentioning a few weeks ago that Mr. Southern, the firm's representative in Naples, was very ill? Well, Mr. Fenton has decided to send Dad to Italy to take his place, for a year at any rate, and perhaps longer. We're to start in a fortnight."

Such a stupendous announcement required a little realizing. Vincent removed his hands from his pockets.

"You don't mean to say we're all going?" he inquired. "Jemima! Leaving London fogs and toddling off to Italy? Materkins, you take my breath away! How's the whole business to be fixed up so soon?"

"Quite easily. We shall let this house, just as it is, to Mr. Atherton, who will come from the Norfolk branch to fill Father's post in London. We are to rent Mr. Southern's flat in Naples, while he takes a voyage round the world to try to regain his health. Dad means to put you into his office in Naples, Vin. Don't look so aghast! It's high time you started, and it will be a splendid opening for you. And as for Renie—of course she's too young to leave school yet——"

"Mums! Mums!" interrupted an agonized voice, as Irene took a flying leap over her circle of books and, plumping herself on the sofa, clutched tightly at her mother's sleeve. "You're not going to leave me behind at Miss Gordon's? You couldn't! Oh, I'd die! Mums darling, please! If the family's going to jaunt abroad I've got to jaunt too! Say yes, quick, quick!"

"What a little tempest you are! Cheer up! We'd never any intention of deserting you. We'll stick together for a while at any rate, though when we

4

arrive in Naples you'll be packed off to a boarding-school, Madam, so I give you fair warning."

"An Italian school?"

Irene's gray eyes were round with horror.

"No, an Anglo-American school for English-speaking girls. Do you remember that charming Mr. Proctor who stayed with us last year on his way from New York to Naples? His daughter is at this school, and he strongly recommended it. It seems just exactly the place for you, Renie. It will solve a great problem if we can educate you out there. It would have complicated matters very much if we had been obliged to leave you in England. As it is you'll be quite near to Naples, and can come home for all your holidays."

"Hooray! Then I'm not to go to Miss Gordon's again?"

"As we start in a fortnight it's not worth while your beginning a fresh term at St. Osmund's."

"Then I needn't bother to find the hateful old history book. I'm so glad I didn't do those wretched holiday tasks — they'd just have been sheer waste. Mums, I'm so excited! May I begin and pack for Italy now? I can't wait."

For the next two weeks great confusion reigned in the Beverley household. It is no light matter to decide what you need to take abroad, what you wish to lock up at home, and to leave your establishment in apple-pie order for the use of strangers. Inventories of furniture, linen, blankets, and china had to be written and checked, a rigorous selection made of the things to be packed, and the luggage cut down to the limits prescribed by the railway companies. Poor Mrs. Beverley was nearly worn out when at last the overflowing boxes were fastened, the bags and hold-alls were strapped, and the taxis, which were to take them to the station, arrived at the door. Tears stood in her eyes as she crossed the threshold of her own house.

"It's a tremendous wrench!" she fluttered.

"Never mind, Mums!" consoled Irene, linking her arm in her mother's. "It's an adventure, and we all want to go. You'll love it when we're once off. No, don't look back: it's unlucky! Your bag's in the cab; I saw Jessie put it in. Hooray for Italy, say I, and a good riddance to smoky old London! In another couple of days we shall be down south and turning into Romeos and Juliets as fast as we can. You'll see Dad learning a guitar and strumming it under your balcony, and serenading you no end."

"Hardly at his time of life!" said Mrs. Beverley; but the joke amused her, she wiped her eyes, and, as Irene had hoped and intended, stepped smiling into the waiting taxi, and left her old home with laughter instead of with tears.

In her fourteen years of experience Irene had traveled very little, so the migration to Italy was a fairy journey so far as she was concerned. To catch the boat express they had made an early start, and they breakfasted in the train between London and Dover. It was fun to sit in comfortable padded armchairs, eating fish or ham and eggs, and watching the landscape whirling past; fun to see the deft-handed waiters nipping about with trays or teacups; and fun to observe the occupants of the other tables in the car. There was a fat, good-natured Frenchman who amused Irene, a languid English lady who annoyed her, an elderly gourmand who excited her disgust, and a neighboring party, one member of which at least aroused her interest and caused her to cast cautious side glances in the direction of the next table. This center of attraction was a small girl about eight or nine years of age, a dainty elfin little person with bewitching blue eyes and a mop of short, flaxen curls. She was evidently well used to traveling, for she would lift a tiny finger to summon the waiter, and gave him her orders with all the savoir-faire of an experienced diner-out. Perhaps her clear-toned treble voice was a trifle too high-pitched for the occasion, and would have been better had it been duly modulated, but her parents seemed proud of her conversational powers and allowed her to talk for the benefit of anybody within ear-shot. That she excited comment was manifest, for many looks were turned to her corner. The criticisms on her were complimentary or the reverse. "Isn't she perfectly sweet?" gushed a young lady at Irene's left. "Sweet? She ought to be in the nursery instead of showing off here!" came a tart voice in reply, from some one whose face was invisible but whose back and shoulders expressed an attitude of strong disapproval. "Hope we shan't be boxed up with her in the same carriage to Paris! I vote we give her a wide berth at Calais."

Irene laughed softly. The little flaxen-haired girl attracted her; she felt she would have gravitated towards her compartment rather than have avoided her. But traveling companions were evidently more a matter of chance than choice, for the crowd that turned out of the train at Dover became mixed and mingled like the colored bits of glass in a kaleidoscope. Irene realized that for the moment the one supreme and breathless object in life was to cling to the rest of her family, and not to get separated from them or lost, as they pushed through narrow barriers, showed tickets and passports, traversed gangways, and finally found themselves on board the Channel steamer bound for France. Father, who had made the crossing many times, scrambled instantly for deck-chairs, and installed his party comfortably in the lee of a funnel, where they would be sheltered from the wind. Mrs. Beverley, who had inspected the ladies' saloon below, sank on her seat, and tucked a rug round her knees with a sigh of relief.

"It will be the 'Black Hole of Calcutta' downstairs," she remarked. "I'd rather stay on deck however cold it is. The mother of the wee yellow-haired lassie is lying down already, evidently prepared to be ill. The stewardess says we shall have a choppy passage. She earns her tips, poor woman! Thanks, Vincent! Yes, I'd like the air-cushion, please, and that plaid out of the hold-all. No, I won't have a biscuit now; I prefer to wait till we get on terra firma again."

Irene, sitting warmly wrapped up on her deck-chair, watched the white cliffs of Dover recede from her gaze as the vessel left the port and steamed out into the Channel. It was the last of "Old England," and she knew that much time must elapse before she would see the shores of her birthplace again. What would greet her in the foreign country to which she was going? New sights, new sounds, new interests—perhaps new friends? The thought of it all was an exhilaration. Others might seem sad at a break with former associations, but as for herself she was starting a fresh life, and she meant to get every scrap of enjoyment out of it that was practically possible.

The stewardess had prophesied correctly when she described the voyage as "choppy." The steamer certainly pitched and tossed in a most uncomfortable fashion, and it was only owing to the comparative steadiness of her seat amidships that Irene escaped that most wretched of complaints, mal de mer. She sat very still, with rather white cheeks, and refused Vincent's offers of biscuits and chocolates: her sole salvation, indeed, was not to look at the heaving sea, but to keep her eyes fixed upon the magazine which she made a pretense of reading. Fortunately the Dover-Calais crossing is short, and, before Neptune had claimed her as one of his victims, they were once more in smooth waters and steaming into harbor.

Then again the kaleidoscope turned, and the crowd of passengers remingled and walked over gangways, and along platforms and up steep steps, and jostled through the Customs, and said "Rien à déclarer" to the officials, who peeped inside their bags to find tea or tobacco, and had their luggage duly chalked, and showed their passports once more, and finally, after a bewildering half-hour of bustle and hustle, found themselves, with all their belongings intact, safely in the train for Paris. Irene had caught brief glimpses of the child whom she named "Little Flaxen," whose mother, in a state of collapse, had been almost carried off the vessel, but revived when she was on dry land again: a maid was in close attendance, and two porters were stowing their piles of hand-luggage inside a specially reserved compartment. "The cross lady won't be boxed up with them at any rate," said Irene. "I saw her get in lower down the train."

It was dark when they arrived in Paris, so Irene had only a confused impression of an immense railway station, of porters in blue blouses, of a babel of noise and shouting in a foreign language which seemed quite different from the French she had learned at school, of clinging very closely to Father's arm, of a drive through lighted streets, of a hotel where dinner was served in a salon surrounded by big mirrors, then bed, which seemed the best thing in the world, for she was almost too weary to keep her eyes open.

"If every day is going to be like this we shall be tired out by the time we reach Naples," she thought, as she sank down on her pillow. "Traveling is the limit."

Eleven hours of sleep, however, made a vast difference in her attitude towards their long journey. When she came downstairs next morning she was all eagerness to see Paris.

"We have the whole day here," said Mrs. Beverley, "so we may as well get as much out of it as we can. Daddy has business appointments to keep, but you and I and Vin, Renie, will take a taxi and have a look at some of the sights, won't we?"

"Rather!" agreed the young people, hurrying over their coffee and rolls.

"I wouldn't miss Paris for worlds," added Vincent; "only don't spend the whole time inside shops, Mater. That's all this fellow bargains for."

"We'll compromise and make it half and half," laughed Mother.

A single day is very brief space in which to see the beauties of Paris, but the Beverleys managed to fit a great deal into it, and to include among their activities a peep at the Louvre, a drive in the Bois de Boulogne, a visit to Napoleon's Tomb, half an hour in a cinema, and a rush through several of the finest and largest shops.

"It's different from London—quite!" decided Irene, at the end of the jaunt. "It's lighter and brighter, somehow, and the streets are wider and have more trees planted in them. It's a terrible scurry, and I should be run over if

I tried to cross the street. The shops aren't any better than ours really, though they make more fuss about them. The little children and the small pet dogs are adorable. The cinema was horribly disappointing, because they were all American films, not French ones; but that light that falls from the domed roof down on to Napoleon's tomb was worth coming across the Channel to see. Yes, Mummie dear, I thoroughly like Paris. I'm only sorry we have to leave it so soon."

The train for Rome was to start at nine o'clock in the evening, and immediately after dinner the Beverleys made their way to the station. It would be a thirty-eight hour journey, and they had engaged two sleeping compartments, wagon-lits as they are called on the Continental express. Mrs. Beverley and Irene were to share one, and Mr. Beverley and Vincent the other. The beds were arranged like berths on board ship, and Irene, who occupied the upper one, found, much to her amusement, a little ladder placed in readiness for her climb aloft.

"I don't need to use that!" she exclaimed, scrambling up with the agility gained in her school gymnasium. "How silly of the conductor to put it for me."

"How could the poor man tell who was to occupy the berth! You might have been a fat old lady for anything he knew!" replied Mrs. Beverley, settling herself on the mattress below.

It was a funny sensation to lie in bed in the jolting train, and Irene slept only in snatches, waking frequently to hear clanking of chains, shrieking of engines, shouting of officials at stations, and other disturbing noises. As dawn came creeping through the darkness she drew the curtain aside and looked from the window. What a glorious sight met her astonished gaze! They were passing over the Alps, and all around were immense snow-covered mountains, great gorges full of dark fir forests, and rushing streams of green glacier water. It was very cold, and she was glad to pull her rug up, and later to drink the hot coffee which the conducteur made on a spirit-lamp in the corridor and brought to those who had ordered it overnight.

Irene never forgot that long journey on the Continental express. The sleeping compartments became sitting-rooms by day, for the berths turned into sofas, and a table was unfolded, where it would have been possible to write or sew if she had wished. She could do nothing, however, but stare at the landscape; the snow-capped mountains and the great ravines and gorges were a revelation in the way of scenery, and it was enough occupation to look out of the window. Switzerland and Northern Italy were a dream of wild, rugged beauty, but she woke on the following morning to find the train racing among olive groves and orange trees, and to catch glimpses of gay, unknown, wild flowers blooming on the railway banks. Here and there were stretches of the blue Mediterranean; and oxen and goats in the fields gave a vivid foreign aspect to the country. Everything—trees, houses, landscape, and people—seemed unfamiliar and un-English, yet strangely fascinating. The bright land with its sunshine appeared to be welcoming her.

"I shall like it! I shall like it! I shall like it!" said Irene to herself, hanging out of the open window of their compartment and watching some picturesque children who were waving a greeting to the train. "I know I shall like it!"

"Put your hat on and strap up your hold-all," said Father's voice in the corridor outside. "Everybody else has luggage ready, and in another ten minutes or so we shall be in Rome."

CHAPTER II

The Villa Camellia

The Beverleys did not break their journey in Rome, but merely changed trains and pushed on southward. Irene was sorry at the time not to see the imperial city, but afterwards she was glad that her first impression of an Italian town should have been of Naples. Naples! Is there any place like it in the whole world? Irene thought not, as she stood on her veranda next morning and gazed across the blue bay to where Vesuvius was sending a thin column of smoke into the cloudless sky. Below her lay the public gardens, in which spring flowers were blooming, though it was only the end of January, and beyond was a panorama of white houses, green shutters, palm trees, picturesque boats, and a quay thronged with traffic. To that harbor and that blue stretch of sea she was bound this very day, for Father and Mother had arranged to take her straight to her new school, and leave her there before they established themselves in their flat.

"We haven't any time for sightseeing at present, dear," said Mrs. Beverley, when Irene begged for at least a peep at the streets of Naples. "We must put off these jaunts until the Easter holidays. The term has begun at the Villa Camellia, and you ought to set to work at your lessons at once. Don't pull such a doleful face. Be thankful you're going to school in such a glorious spot. We might have left you at Miss Gordon's."

"I'd have run away and followed you somehow, Mums darling! I don't mind being a few miles off, but I couldn't bear to feel the Channel and the whole of France and Switzerland and Italy lay between us. It's too far."

"Yes, our little family quartette is rather inseparable," agreed Mother. "It's certainly nice to think that we're all 'within hail.'"

The school, recommended to Mr. and Mrs. Beverley by their American friend, Mr. Proctor, was situated at the small town of Fossato, not far from Naples. The easiest way of getting there was by sea, so Irene's luggage was wheeled down to the quay, and the family embarked on a coasting

12

steamer. Father and Mother were, of course, taking her, and Vincent accompanied them, because they could not leave him alone in a strange city.

"It will be your last holiday though, young man," said Mr. Beverley jokingly, "so make the most of it. To-morrow you must come with me to the office and start your new career. I don't know whether the Villa Camellia observes convent rules, and whether you will be admitted. If not, you must wait outside the gate while we see Miss Rodgers."

"Oh, surely she wouldn't be so heartless?"

"That remains to be seen. In a foreign country the regulations are probably very strict."

The Beverleys were not the only British people on board the steamer. Parties of tourists were going for the day's excursion, and as much English as Italian or French might be heard spoken among the passengers. Two groups, who sat near them on deck, attracted Irene's attention. The central figure of the one was a girl slightly taller than herself—a girl with a long, pointed nose, dark, hard, bright eyes, penciled eyebrows, beautiful teeth, and a nice color. She was talking in a loud and affected voice, and laying down the law on many topics to several amused and smiling young naval officers who were of the party. An elder girl, like her but with a sweeter mouth and softer eyes, seemed to be trying to restrain her, and occasionally exclaimed, "Oh, Mabel!" at some more than ordinary sally of wit; but the younger girl talked on, posing in rather whimsical attitudes, and letting her roving glance stray over the tourists close by, as if judging the effect she was making upon them.

"She's showing off," decided Irene privately. "Is that 'Villa Camellia' on the label of her bag? I hope to goodness she's not going to school with me. Hello! Who's that talking English on the other side? Why, Little Flaxen for all the world! What's she followed us down here for?"

The small, fair-haired girl, whom they had seen in the train to Dover, was undoubtedly claiming public notice on their right. Her high-pitched, childish voice was descanting freely about everything she saw, and people smiled at her quaint questions and comments. Her mother, still very pale and languid, made no effort to silence her, and her father seemed rather to encourage her, and to exploit her remarks for the entertainment of several gentlemen friends.

A little bored by the evident self-advertisement of these rival belles, Irene moved away with Vincent to a quieter corner of the deck. She was to see more of them soon, however. They both disembarked when the steamer reached Fossato, their luggage was piled upon the carriages, and she watched them drive away up the steep, narrow road that led into the town.

The Beverleys had decided to have an early lunch at the hotel by the quay before taking Irene to school. It was their last meal together, so she was allowed to choose the menu, and regaled the family on hitherto unknown Italian dishes, winding up with coffee, ices, and chocolates.

"I'm glad you don't cater for us every day, Renie, or I should soon be ruined," said Father, as the waiter brought him the bill. "Now are you ready? If we don't hurry and get you up quickly to school we shall miss the boat back to Naples. Another package of chocolates! You unconscionable child! Well, put it in your pocket and console yourself with it at bedtime. The concierge says our vetturino is waiting—not that any Italian coachman minds doing that! All the same, time is short and we had better make a start."

In that first drive through the narrow, steep, stone-paved streets of Fossato Irene was too excited to take in any details except a general impression of rich, foreign color and high, white walls. Afterwards, when she came to know the town better, she realized its subtler points. She felt as one in a dream when the carriage turned through a great gate, and passed along an avenue of orange trees to a large, square house, color-washed pink, and approached by a flight of marble steps. What happened next she could

14

never clearly recall. She remembered the agony of a short wait in the drawing-room until Miss Rodgers arrived, how the whole party, including Vincent, were shown some of the principal rooms of the house, an agitated moment of good-by kisses, then the sound of departing wheels, and a sudden overwhelming sensation that, for the first time in her life, she was alone in a foreign land. Foreign and yet familiar, for the Villa Camellia was a skillful combination of the best out of several countries. Its setting was Italian, its decorations were French, and its fifty-six pupils were all unmistakably and undoubtedly Anglo-Saxon. Irene was assured on this point immediately, for Miss Rodgers, calling to a girl who was passing down the corridor, gave the newcomer into her charge with instructions to take her straight to the senior recreation room.

"Our afternoon classes begin at 2.30," she remarked, "but you will have just ten minutes in which to be introduced to some of your schoolfellows. Elsie Craig will show you everything."

Elsie made no remark to Irene — perhaps she was shy — but, starting off at a quick pace, led her down a long passage into a room on the ground floor. It was a pleasant room with a French window that opened out on to a veranda, where, over a marble balustrade, there was a view of an orange garden and the sea. Round a table were collected several older girls, watching with deep interest a kettle, which was beginning to sing, upon a spirit-lamp. They looked up with surprise as Elsie ushered in the new pupil.

"Hello! You don't mean to tell us there's another of them!" exclaimed a dark girl with a long pigtail. "We've had two already! Why are they pouring on us to-day, I should like to know? It's a perfect deluge."

"I hate folks butting in when the term has begun," said another grumpily.

"We shall be swamped with 'freshies' soon," grunted the owner of the spirit-lamp. "If they expect coffee I tell them beforehand they just won't get it."

"She says her name's Irene Beverley," volunteered Elsie Craig, in a perfunctory voice, as if she were performing an obvious duty and getting it over.

"Oh, indeed!"

"Well, now we know, so there's an end of it."

It could hardly be called a flattering reception. The general attitude of the girls was the reverse of friendly. The kettle was suddenly boiling, and they were concentrating their attention upon the making of the coffee, and rather ostentatiously leaving the stranger outside the charmed circle. Irene, used to school life, knew, however, that she was on trial, and that on her present behavior would probably depend the whole of her future career. She did not attempt to force her unwelcome presence upon her companions, but, withdrawing to the window, pretended to be utterly absorbed in contemplation of the scenery. She kept the corner of her eye, nevertheless, upon the group at the table. The girl with the long pigtail had made the coffee and was pouring it into cups. A shorter girl nudged her and whispered something, at which she shook her head emphatically. But the short girl persisted.

"I'm superstitious," affirmed the latter aloud. "One's for sorrow, two's for joy, and three's for luck! She's the third to-day and she may be a mascot."

"I'd rather have chocolates than mascots," said an injured voice from behind a coffee-cup.

The chance remark gave Irene the very opportunity she needed. She suddenly remembered the chocolates her father had handed her before she left the hotel, and, producing the package, she offered its contents. After a visible moment of hesitation the girl with the long pigtail accepted her hospitality, and passed the delicacies round. Instantly all were chumping almonds, and the icy atmosphere thawed into summer. Everybody began to talk at once.

"There's a spare cup here if you'd like some coffee. Yes, Rachel, I shall offer it!"

"I suppose you're over fourteen?"

"We may make coffee after lunch if we're seniors, but the kids aren't allowed any."

"You've just one minute to drink it in before the bell rings."

"Hustle up if you want to finish it."

"I'll bet a cookie you're a real sport."

"There's the bell! Don't choke or you'll blight your young career."

"We've got to scoot quick!"

"Come along with me and I'll show you where."

Irene, taken in tow by a girl with a freckled nose, was hurried along the corridor and up the stairs to the classrooms. Although she had scarcely spoken a word she had undoubtedly gained a victory, and had established her welcome among at least a section of her schoolfellows. She did not yet know their names, but names are a detail compared with personalities, and with some members of the coffee-party she felt that she might ultimately become chums.

"Don't I bless Dad for those chocs!" she thought as she took her seat at a desk. "They worked the trick. If I'd had nothing to offer that crew I might have sat out in the cold forevermore. The dark pigtail is decent enough, but if it comes to a matter of chumming give me 'Freckles' for choice."

The Villa Camellia was a high-class boarding-school for English-speaking girls whose parents were residents, permanently or temporarily, in the neighborhood of Naples. It was generally described as an Anglo-American college, for the arrangements were accommodated to suit the customs of both sides of the Atlantic. Miss Rodgers and her partner, Miss Morley, the two principals, came respectively from London and New York; one teacher had been trained in Boston, and another at Oxford, while the British section

17

of the community included girls from South Africa, Australia, and New Zealand. Pupils belonging to other European races were not received, the object of the college being to preserve the nationality of girls who must of necessity be educated in a foreign land, and whose parents did not wish them to attend Italian schools. The arrangements were of course modified by the climate and by the customs of the country. Outwardly the Villa Camellia resembled a convent. Its garden was surrounded by immensely high walls edged with broken glass, and the only entrance was by the great gate, which was solemnly unlocked by old Antonio, the porter, who inspected all comers through a grille before granting them admittance. Small parties in charge of a teacher were taken at stated times for walks or excursions in the neighborhood, but no girl might ever go out unless escorted by a mistress or by her parents. The Villa Camellia was a little world in itself, and as much retired from the town of Fossato as the great, gray monastery that crowned the summit of the neighboring mountain.

Fortunately the grounds were very large, so there was room for most of the activities in which the girls cared to indulge. Tennis and netball were the principal games. There were several courts, and there was a gymnasium, where the school assembled for exercise on wet days. From two flagstaffs on the roof floated the Union Jack and the Stars and Stripes respectively. It was an understood fact that here Britannia and Columbia marched hand in hand with an entente cordiale that recognized no distinctions whatsoever.

Miss Rodgers and Miss Morley, who respectively represented the interests of Britain and America, were tremendous friends. Miss Rodgers was fair and rather plump and rosy-faced and calm, with a manner that parents described as "motherly," and a leaning towards mathematics as the basis of a sound education. Miss Morley, on the contrary, was thin and dark and excitable, and taught the English literature and the general knowledge classes, and was rumored—though this no doubt was libel—to dislike mathematics to the extent of not even adequately keeping her own private accounts. The pair were such opposites that they worked in absolute

18

harmony, Miss Rodgers being mainly responsible for the discipline of the establishment, and acting judge and court of appeal in her study, while Miss Morley supplied the initiative, and kept the girls interested in a large number of pursuits and hobbies which could be carried on within the walls of the house and garden.

As regards the fifty-six British and American maidens who made up this brisk little community we will leave some of them to speak for themselves in the next chapter.

CHAPTER III
Hail, Columbia!

Irene, finding herself in her new form, looked round inquiringly. A few of the girls with whom she had taken coffee were seated at desks in the same room, but the rest of the faces were unfamiliar. Her teacher entered her name on the register, and seemed to expect her to understand the lesson which was in progress, but the subject was much in advance of what she had hitherto learned at Miss Gordon's, and it was very difficult for her to pick up the threads of it. She grew more and more bewildered as the afternoon passed on, and though Miss Bickford gave her several hints, and even stopped the class once to explain a point, Irene felt that most of the instruction had been completely over her head. It was with a sense of intense relief that she heard the closing bell ring, and presently filed with the rest of the school into the dining-room for tea. Her place at table was between two girls who utterly ignored her presence, and did not address a single remark to her. Each talked diligently to the neighbor on either side, but poor Irene seemed an insulator in the electric current of conversation, and had perforce to eat her meal in dead silence. She was walking away afterwards in a most depressed condition of mind, when at the door some one touched her on the arm.

"You're wanted in the senior recreation room," said a brisk voice. "Rachel has convened a general meeting and told me to tell you. So hurry up and don't keep folks waiting. We want to get off to tennis."

Marveling why her actions should hinder the tennis of the rest of the community, Irene obeyed the message, and presented herself in the room where she had been introduced on her arrival. It was now full of girls of all ages, some sitting, some standing, and some squatting on the floor. Rachel Moseley, the owner of the long dark pigtail, seemed in a position of command, for she motioned Irene to a vacant chair, then rapped on the table with a ruler to ensure silence. She had to tap not once but several times, and finally called:

"When you've all done talking I'll begin." There was an instant hush at that, and, though a few faint snickers were heard, most of the audience composed itself decently to listen to the voice of authority.

"I've called this meeting," began Rachel, "because to-day an unusual thing has happened. Three new girls have arrived, although the term is well under way. By the rules of our society they must give some account of themselves, and we must explain what is required from them. Will they kindly stand up?"

Blushing considerably Irene rose to her feet, in company with the dark-eyed damsel who had crossed in the same steamer with her from Naples, and the fair-haired child whom she had privately christened Little Flaxen.

"Name and nationality?" demanded Rachel, pencil and note-book in hand. She wrote down Irene Beverley, British, without further comment; the fact was evidently too obvious for discussion. At "Mabel Hughes, Australian, born in Patagonia," she demurred slightly, and she hesitated altogether at "Désirée Legrand."

"That's not English!" she objected. "We don't reckon to take Frenchies here, you know!"

"But I'm not French," came the high-pitched voice of the little, fair-haired girl. "I'm as English as anybody. I am indeed!"

"Then why have you got a French name?"

"Legrand isn't French — we come from Jersey."

"Very much on the borderland," sniffed Rachel. "What about Désirée? Not much wholesome Anglo-Saxon there at any rate."

"I was called Désirée because I was so very much desired. Mother says it just fits me."

An indignant titter went round the room and Rachel frowned.

"I'm afraid you won't find yourself so much desired here," she said sarcastically. "I'll enter you British, though I have my doubts. Now come

21

along, all three of you, and lay your hands on this book. You've got to take an oath of allegiance. I'll repeat the words, and you must say them after me:

"'I hereby promise and vow that being of Anglo-Saxon birth I will uphold the integrity of Great Britain and her colonies and of the United States of America, and strive my utmost to maintain their credit in a foreign land.' Now then, do you understand what your oath means?"

Her eyes rested on Irene as she asked the question. That much embarrassed damsel stuttered hesitatingly:

"We're not to trouble our heads about learning foreign languages?"

A delighted chuckle came from several members of the audience at this interpretation of the vow. Rachel hastily condescended to explain.

"Oh, no! You'll have to study French and Italian, but what we mean is for goodness' sake don't stick on all the airs and graces that some of these foreign girls do. Remember we're plain, wholesome, straightforward Anglo-Saxons, who play games and say what we mean, and call a spade a spade and have done with it. Whatever Italian friends you may make during the holidays please forget them during term-time, and try and imagine that the Villa Camellia stands in Kent or Massachusetts. Do you understand my drift now?"

"Oh, yes!" sighed Mabel languidly. "Anglo-American patriotism, crystallized in a nutshell, I suppose! I'm not going to offend your prejudices, I'm sure!"

"You'd better not, or you'll hear about it," said Rachel, looking at her sharply. "Well, girls, that's the wind-up. The three freshies are admitted and you've witnessed their vows. Just jolly well take care they keep them, that's all. Juniors are due now at netball practice, and any seniors who want the tennis courts — — "

22

But Rachel's sentence went unfinished for her listeners were tired of sitting still, and the second they found themselves dismissed had jumped up and fled from the room.

"Now that that ordeal's over I guess you may smooth out the kinks in your forehead, honey!" said a serene voice at Irene's elbow.

Turning quickly she saw the short girl who had braved Rachel's possible wrath and had offered her coffee on her arrival. It was a pleasant face that gazed into hers, not exactly beautiful, but with a charm that eclipsed all mere ordinary prettiness; the sparkling gray eyes were dark-fringed, the cheeks were like wild roses under their freckles, the tip-tilted little nose held an element of audacious sauciness, and dimples lay at the corners of the wide, smiling mouth.

"I'm Priscilla Proctor, called Peachy for short. Oh, yes, I knew all about you beforehand, although you happen to be the newest girl. Dad wrote me a whole page—wonderful for him!—and said he'd stayed at your house in London, and I was to tack myself on to you and show you round, and see you didn't fret and all the rest of it. Are you wanting a crony, temporary or otherwise? Then here I am at your service. Link an arm and we'll parade the place. I guess by the time we've finished there's not much you won't know about the Villa Camellia."

"Have you been here long?" asked Irene, accepting the proffered arm with alacrity, and submitting to be led away by her cicerone.

"Just a year. Cried myself to a puddle when I first came, but I like it now. I didn't realize who you were when you first arrived, or I'd have given you a tip or two straight away. Thank goodness you're fairly in favor with Rachel at any rate. Any one who starts by offending her has a bad term. I don't envy Mabel Hughes. That girl will get a few eye-openers before she's much older, and serve her right. She rooms with you? Well, I'm sorry for you. I wish there was a spare bed in our dormitory, but we're full up to overflowing. Now then, I've brought you out by the side door to show you what we consider the best view of the garden. Ah, I thought it would make your eyes pop out! It's some view, isn't it?"

The garden of the Villa Camellia was certainly one of the greatest assets of the school, and to Irene, who had been transported straight from the desolation of a London suburb in January, it seemed like a vision of a different world. The long terrace, with its marble balustrade, edged a high cliff that overtopped the sea, while at present the setting sun was lighting up the white houses of the distant outline of Naples, and was touching the purple slopes of Vesuvius with gold. Pillars and archways formed a pergola, from which hung roses and festoons of the trumpetflower; from the groves near at hand came the sweet strong scent of orange blossoms, and the little favorites of an English spring, forget-me-nots, pink daisies, and pansies, lifted contented heads from the border below. In the basin of the great marble fountain white arum lilies were blooming, geraniums trailed from tall vases, and palms, bamboos, and other exotics backed the row of lemon trees at the end of the paved walk. Here and there marble benches were arranged round tables in specially constructed arbors.

"These are our summer classrooms," explained Peachy. "When it's blazingly hot we do lessons here early in the mornings, and it's ripping. No, we don't use them at this time of the year, because the marble is cold to sit upon, and the garden is damp really, although it looks so jolly. You should see it in a sirocco wind! You wouldn't want to have classes outside then, you bet! It's luck you're in the Transition form. If you'd been one of Miss Rodger's elect eleven, or one of Miss Brewster's lambs, I'd have had to chum with you by stealth. I'd have managed it somehow, of course, to please Dad, but it isn't done here openly. School etiquette is like the law of the Medes and Persians. We keep to our own forms. Hello! There's Sheila Yonge. Sheila! If you can find any Camellia Buds that aren't playing tennis bring them along right here for a little powwow with Irene."

"Is she a 'buddy' yet?" whispered Sheila.

"Of course not! She's only been here a few hours. What a dear old silly you are. Hunt up some of that crew all the same, and I'm yours forever. Don't you understand the situation? Well, Irene's folks entertained Dad in London and were just lovely to him—nursed him when he was sick and took him round the shows when he got well. He's been bursting with gratitude ever since, and he wrote and told me Irene was coming here and I must pay her out—no, pay her back—pour coals of fire on her head— Great Scott, I'm getting my similes mixed! I mean give her a right down good time as far as I can, and make her think the Villa Camellia is a dandy place. Twiggez-vous, chérie?"

"I twig!" laughed Sheila. "I'll beat up all I can muster," and she ran lightly away along the terrace.

"A decent girl, though a little hard of comprehension," Peachy nodded after her. "Doesn't she look adorable in that blue tam-o'-shanter?"

"She's awfully pretty!" agreed Irene readily.

"She'd be the beauty of the school if she'd any idea how to use her advantages," sighed Peachy. "Give me her complexion and that classical nose and—well, I guess I'd blaze out into a cinema star before I'd done with life. I hope she won't be all day raking a few girls together. She's not what you'd call quick. I've misjudged her. Here she comes with half a dozen at least—and, oh, no, Sheila! You don't mean to say you've brought candy? Well, you are a sport! Let's squat under the mimosa tree and hand it round."

The little group of Peachy's favorite friends who settled themselves under the yellow mimosa bush to suck taffy and watch the flaming sunset were all afterwards intimately bound up with Irene's school career. Each was such a distinct personality that she sorted them out fairly accurately on that first evening, and decided the particular order in which they would rank in her affections.

There was Jess Cameron, a jolly Scottish lassie. She rolled her r's when she spoke, and was a trifle matter-of-fact and practical, but was evidently the dependable anchor of the rest of the scatter-brained crew, the one who made the most sensible suggestions, and to whom—though they teased her a little and called her "Grannie"—they all turned in the end for help and advice. Jess was slightly out of her element in a southern setting. Her appropriate background was moorland and heather and gray loch, and driving clouds and a breeze with fine mist in it, that would make you want to wrap a plaid round your shoulders and turn to the luxury of a peat fire. Quite unconsciously she suggested all these things. Peachy once described her as a living incarnation of one of Scott's novels, for she was steeped in old traditions and legends and superstitions, and could tell tales in the gloaming that sent eerie shivers down the spines of her listeners, or would recite ballads with a swing that took one back to the days of wandering minstrels. She was not a girl to make a fuss over anybody, and she did not greet Irene with the least effusion, but her plain "If you're a friend of Peachy's I'm glad to see you," was genuine, and better than any amount of gush. Jess undoubtedly had her faults; she was what her chums called "too cock-sure," and she was apt to be severe in her judgments, flashing into the righteous wrath of one whose standards are high, but her very imperfections were "virtues gane a-gley," and she was a considerable force in the molding of public opinion at the Villa Camellia.

If Jess, calm, canny, and reliable, stood for the spirit of the North, attractive, persuasive, fascinating little Delia Watts represented the South. She came from California, and was as quick and bright as a humming-bird, constantly in harmless mischief, but seldom getting into any serious trouble. Her highly strung temperament found school restrictions irksome, and she was apt to blaze out into odd pranks which in other girls might have met with sterner punishment. But Miss Morley had a soft corner for Delia, and, though she did not exactly favor her, she certainly made allowances for her excitability and her strongly emotional disposition.

"Delia's like a marionette—always dancing to some hidden string," the teacher remarked once to Miss Rodgers. "She mayn't be strong-minded but she's immensely warm-hearted, and if we can only pull the love-string she'll act the part we want. You can't force her into prim behavior; she's as much a child of nature as the birds, and if you clip her wings altogether you take away from her the very gift that perhaps God meant her to use. Let me have the handling of the little sky-rocket, and I'll do my best to keep her within bounds, but she's not the disposition to 'be made an example of' or to be set on the 'stool of repentance.' Five minutes with Delia in private is worth more than a long public admonition. You've only to look at her face to know her type."

And Miss Rodgers, who stood no nonsense from really naughty and turbulent girls, yielded in this case, and left the exclusive management of Delia in the hands of her partner.

Of the seven damsels who sat under the yellow feathery flowers of the mimosa bush, three of them—Peachy, Jess, and Delia—talked so hard and continuously that none of the others had a chance to chip in with anything more than an occasional yes or no. Irene realized in a vague way that Esther Cartmel was plain and stodgy looking, but that every now and then a world of light suddenly flashed into her eyes, and transfigured her for the brief moment; that Sheila Yonge giggled at all Peachy's remarks, and that Mary Fergusson was a pale and weak copy of Jess, and slavishly followed her lead in everything. It was the seventh member of the little party, however, who particularly attracted her attention. Lorna Carson was quiet, probably from sheer lack of opportunity to speak, but her pale face was interesting and her dark eyes met Irene's with a curious questioning glance. It was almost as if she were asking "Have we known each other before?" Irene could not help looking at her, and ransacking the side cupboards of her memory to try to light upon some forgotten clew as to why the face should seem half familiar.

"Have I seen her in London? Or is she like some one else? No, I can't fix her at all. Surely I must have dreamed about her," mused Irene, while aloud she said, almost as if compelled to speak:

"Have you been long at school here? Are you English, or American, or colonial, or what?"

"A little bit of anything you like," smiled Lorna. "Rachel gets very muddled about me. I've such a sneaking weakness for Naples that I believe she thinks I'm an Italian at heart. That's a crime Rachel absolutely can't forgive. 'Foreign' is the last word in her vocabulary."

"So I gathered when she made me take that oath. I suppose she's head girl and that's why she rules the roost? Is she decent or does she keep you petrified? I don't know whether I'm expected to say 'Bow-wow,' or to listen in respectful humility when she deigns to notice me."

"You'd better not have any 'bow-wows' with Rachel," broke in Peachy, "though you just jolly well have to wag your tail the way she wants. She's not bad on the whole, but rather a tyrant, and it would do her all the good in the world if some day somebody had the courage to knock sparks out of her. We do what we can in a mild way," (here the other chuckled) "but she's got the ears of both Miss Rodgers and Miss Morley, and if you go on the rampage against her you only land yourself in a scrape. Of course, for purposes of protection the Transition girls have to unite and——"

"Peachy! Take care!" exclaimed Jess warningly.

Peachy blushed crimson under her freckles.

"I wasn't telling anything!" she retorted. "I suppose Irene——"

"Do shut up!"

"Well Agnes said herself——"

"It doesn't matter what Agnes said."

"She's fixed——"

"Peachy Proctor, if you blab like this you'll be tarred and feathered. Girl alive, can't you keep a still tongue in your head? If you'd lived in the Middle Ages you'd have ended your days in a dungeon!"

Jess spoke hotly, and, by the general scandalized look on the faces of the others, Irene judged that luckless Peachy must have been on the verge of betraying some secret. She tactfully turned the conversation with a remark upon the beauty of the sunset, and the clanging of the garden bell opportunely broke up the gathering, and sent the girls hurrying helter-skelter along the terrace in the direction of the house. Irene paused for a moment to look back at the sea and the sky, and the distant twinkling lights, and to curtsy to the crescent moon that hung like a good omen in the dome of blue. There was a scent of fragrant lemon blossoms in the air, and she trod fallen rose petals under her feet. Suddenly a remembrance of the desolation of Miss Gordon's garden in a February fog swept across her mental vision. Whatever trials she might encounter here—and she did not expect her new life to be absolute Paradise—the environment of this school in the south was perfect and would make up for many disadvantages.

"Give me sunshine and flowers and I'll always worry on somehow," she murmured, plucking a little crimson rose, and tucking it into her dress for a mascot, then ran with flying footsteps under the orange trees to catch up with her companions, who were already mounting the marble steps that led to the Villa Camellia.

CHAPTER IV

A Secret Sorority

The dormitories at the Villa Camellia were among the main features of the establishment, and were a source of considerable pride and satisfaction to the principals, Miss Rodgers and Miss Morley. They were always shown to parents as the very latest and newest development of school arrangements. Some of them were on the second story and some were on the third, but all had French windows opening onto long verandas on which were placed large pots of geraniums or oleanders. The walls were covered with striped Italian papers, the frieze being color-washed and decorated with designs of flowers or birds, the woodwork was white, the beds were enameled white, and the blankets, instead of being cream or yellow as they are in England, were all of a uniform shade of pale blue, with blue eider-downs to match. The whole of the house was heated by radiators, so that the dormitories were always warm, and were used as studies by the older girls, who did most of their preparation there. A table with ink-pots stood in the middle of each room, and a large notice enjoining, "Silence during study hours" hung as a warning over every fireplace.

Irene was given a vacant bed in No. 3 on the second floor, and found herself in company with Elsie Craig, Mabel Hughes, and Lorna Carson. For the first two she felt no attraction, but the last excited her interest and curiosity. There was an air of mystery about Lorna; she asked questions but gave little information in return on the subject of her own concerns. Her bright dark eyes were unfathomable, and she "kept herself to herself" with a reserved dignity not very common among schoolgirls of her age. Irene, who loved to chatter, found Lorna a ready listener, and, although the confidence was not reciprocated and in consequence the friendship seemed likely to be rather one-sided, it was a friendship all the same from the very start. At the end of the week, moreover, something important happened to cement it.

For the first seven days of her residence at the Villa Camellia Irene had felt herself "goods on approval." Peachy Proctor and her chums had indeed given her a welcome, but afterwards they had held back a little as if testing her before offering further intimacy. There seemed to be some secret bond amongst them, some alliance carefully hidden from the general public. She caught nods, signs, mysterious words, and veiled allusions, all of which were instantly suppressed when her presence was noticed. On the eighth day after arrival she found a note inside her desk. It was marked —

PRIVATE

This must be opened in absolute seclusion

and

its contents must be treated with the

Strictest Confidence

A crowded classroom, with inquisitive form-mates ready to peep over her shoulder, did not seem the congenial atmosphere for the opening of the missive, so Irene was obliged to curb her curiosity until mid-morning "interval," when she gulped her glass of milk hastily, took her portion of biscuits, and, avoiding conversation, hurried down the garden to the seclusion of a stone arbor. Here she tore open the envelope, and drew forth a large sheet of exercise paper. On it was printed in bold black letters:

"You are elected a member of the Sorority of Camellia Buds. Please present yourself for initiation to-night at 8.10 prompt in No. 13. Strictest secrecy enjoined."

There was no signature, but Irene gave a smile of comprehension. Dormitory No. 13 was shared by Peachy Proctor, Jess Cameron, Delia Watts, and Mary Fergusson. There was, therefore, little doubt but that she was to be received into the secret society of whose existence she had already gathered some hints.

"I'll be there at 8.10," she whispered to Peachy, as they trooped into the French class.

"Right-o!" replied that light-hearted damsel. "Just one warning—don't be scared at anything that happens; it's all in fun! Don't say I told you, though. No, I can't explain. I'm not allowed. You'll soon find out."

Peachy shook off Irene's company as if in a hurry to get rid of her before she asked any more questions, so there was nothing to be done but wait in patience until the evening. Supper was at 7.30, and from 8 till half past the girls did as they chose. Those who wished to study might take the extra time for preparation, but work was not obligatory, and it was an understood thing that in the interval between supper and "set recreation" visits might be paid to other dormitories, and that so long as no noise reached the ears of the prefects, anybody disposed to be frivolous might indulge in a little harmless fun.

Irene's wrist-watch was not a reliable timepiece, having bad habits of galloping and then suddenly losing, so to-night she did not trust to it, but sat in the hall with her eyes on the big white-faced clock. At exactly nine and a half minutes past eight she ran upstairs and tapped at the door of dormitory 13. There were sounds of scuffling inside and an agitated voice squealed:

"Wait a minute."

But after a few moments quiet reigned and somebody else called:

"Come in!"

Feeling rather as if she were awaiting initiation into some Nihilist association Irene entered the room. As she did so a bandage was clapped over her eyes and she was led forward blindfolded. It was only after an impressive pause that the handkerchief was removed.

It was well she had been warned beforehand, or the sight which met her gaze might have caused her to emit a yell loud enough to attract the attention of a passing prefect. The Villa Camellia was admirably supplied with electric light, but on this historic occasion the apartment was illuminated solely by a couple of candle-ends stuck in a pair of vases. Their flickering flame revealed a solemn row of nine dressing-gowned figures, each of which wore a black paper mask with holes for her eyes. The general effect was most startling and horrible, and resembled a meeting of the Inquisition, or some other society bent on torture and dark doings. Repressing her first gasp, however, Irene bore the vision with remarkable equanimity, and advancing towards the dread figures waited obediently until she was addressed. Evidently she had done the right thing, for the spokeswoman, clearing her throat, began in impressive accents:

"Sister Irene Beverley, you are admitted here to-night to be made a member of our Sorority. Are you willing to join and to take the pledges?"

"Yes, thanks, but please what's a sorority?" ventured Irene meekly.

Two or three distinct snickers were heard from underneath the black masks, but a voice murmured, "Order!" and the sounds promptly ceased.

"A sorority is a secret sisterhood," explained the President, "just the same as a fraternity is a brotherhood. We call ourselves 'The Camellia Buds,' and we're members of the Transition who have banded ourselves together for the purposes of mutual protection. It's a great honor to be elected. There are only nine of us so far, and we've waited ever so long to choose a tenth. I hope you appreciate the privilege?"

"I do indeed!"

"You're ready to take the vow? Then the initiation may proceed. Sword-bearers, guard the door, please."

There was a Masonic quality about the proceedings. Two dark figures, armed with rulers, placed themselves at the threshold, prepared to settle all intruders, and to preserve the absolute secrecy of the ceremony.

"Will you give your word of honor to be a loyal member of the Sorority of Camellia Buds, and never to do a dirty trick so long as you remain at this school?" asked the President.

"I promise!" replied Irene.

At that somebody switched on the electric light, and the members, pulling off their black masks, disclosed their laughing faces.

"You stood it A-1. I was quite prepared for you to start hysterics and had the sal volatile bottle ready right here," chirruped Delia gayly.

"We call it our 'strength of mind' test," explained President Agnes, blowing out the guttering candles.

"If I had screamed what would have happened?" inquired Irene.

"Probation for another week till you got your nerves. We'd a business with Sheila just at first; she's rather fluttersome. Well, anyway, you've got through the ordeal, and now you're a full-fledged 'bud.' Aren't you proud?"

"Rather! Is the society limited to ten?"

"Sorority, please, not society. It's limited because there isn't anybody else in the Transition who's worth asking to join. Most of them are a set of utter sneaks. They may take Rachel's oath about preserving their nationality and all the rest of it, but if they're to be counted specimens of Anglo-American honor it makes one blush for one's mother country whichever side of the ocean it happens to be on. Oh, you don't know most of them yet! Wait till you find them out."

"You'll be glad then you belong to us."

"Not that we're perfect, of course."

"We don't set up as Pharisees."

"On the whole we're rather a lot of lunatics."

"We just have a little sport among ourselves to keep things humming."

"Well, now Irene understands, we'd best get her fixed up with a 'buddy' and close the meeting."

"But I don't understand. What, for goodness' sake, is a buddy, and why must I have one?" demanded Irene tragically.

"Sit down there, child, and let Grannie talk to you," replied President Agnes. "If you haven't heard of a buddy yet it's time you did. They're the latest out. They had them at all the camps last summer, in England as well as in America. A buddy is a chum with whom you're pledged to do everything, and who's bound to support you. For instance, when the bathing season is on you must never swim unless your buddy is swimming with you; if you go on an excursion you stick to each other tight as glue, and if one of you is lost the other is held responsible. You're as inseparable as a box and its lid, or the two blades of a pair of scissors, or a bottle and its cork, or any other things you happen to think of that ought to go together, and aren't any use apart."

"We only realized buddies last term," explained Peachy, "but the idea caught on no end. We all went simply crazy over it. I don't mind guessing that every girl in this school who's worth her salt has got her buddy. She mayn't let it be known outside her own sorority, but we aren't blind."

"Are there other sororities in the school then besides the Camellia Buds?" asked Irene.

"Bless your innocence! I should think there are. There's a rival one in the Transition. I rather fancy they've snapped up Mabel already. I gave Winnie a hint she wasn't to tackle you, because you'd come to school with an introduction to me, so I ought to have first innings. The prefects have a sorority all to themselves, and the seniors have one, and as for the juniors, silly little things, they're as transparent as glass, with their signaling and their grips and their cypher letters. Any one can see through them with half an eye. But we're wasting time. We've got to fix you up with a buddy, and we must be quick before the bell rings."

"May we choose?" asked Irene, and her eyes fell longingly on Peachy.

"No, we mayn't!" said President Agnes firmly. "We have to take what the fates send us. It's Kismet. Every time we elect a new member we draw lots again for buddies. It's a kind of general shuffle. If we're an uneven number somebody of course has to be odd man out."

"I was the 'old maid' last draw, and I haven't had a buddy this term," remarked Sheila plaintively.

"Never mind, ducky! You're bound to find a partner now," consoled Delia. "It might even be my little self, so live in hope."

"No such luck," groaned Sheila. "I'll probably get Joan, and you know she always uses me as a door-mat."

Agnes meantime was writing ten names on ten separate pieces of paper and folding them in identically the same fashion. Peachy offered the loan of a hat, and into this treasury they were cast and shuffled.

"The newest member draws," murmured Agnes, and the others pushed Irene forward. She chose two folds of paper at a venture, and twisted them together, then performed the like service for another pair, until all the ten were assorted. The thrill of the ceremony was when Agnes opened the screws of paper and read out the names. Fate had mixed the Camellia Buds together thus:

Whether the members of the secret sorority felt satisfied or otherwise with the result of the shuffle, etiquette forbade them to show anything but polite enthusiasm. Each took her buddy solemnly by the hand and vowed allegiance. Peachy then produced what she called "the loving cup," a three-handled vase of brown pottery brought by Jess from Edinburgh and with the motto "Mak' yersel' at hame," on it in cream-colored letters. It was usually a receptacle for flowers, but it had been hastily washed for the occasion and filled with lemonade, a rather bitter brew concocted by Peachy and Delia from a half-ripe lemon plucked in the garden and a few lumps of sugar saved from tea. This was passed round, and the Camellia Buds gulped it heroically as a pledge of sisterhood.

"The password is Thistle-down," decreed Agnes, as the members, trying not to pull sour faces, consoled themselves with candy and broke up the meeting. "Any one who can think of a stunt for next time please bring along propositions. We're always open to new ideas and ready for a startler."

As a direct result of her admission to this select sorority Irene found herself flung by Fate into the arms of Lorna Carson. Had any individual choice been allowed she would have selected Peachy, Jess, Delia, or even Sheila in preference, but the lot once cast she must abide by it and be content. She had a very shrewd suspicion that when the buddies got tired of each other they elected a fresh member and so necessitated a general reshuffle of partners, and that her admission to the society had been welcomed as the pretext for such a change. Here she was, however, pledged to intimate friendship with Lorna, a girl who half fascinated and half repelled her, and who, though she might possibly turn out trumps in the future, was for the present at least most difficult to understand.

CHAPTER V

Fairy Godmothers, Limited

Irene Beverley, when she first left the shores of her native land, was a particularly light-hearted, jolly little Britisher, not at all bookish, and not accustomed to worry her head over any of the deep affairs of life, but ready to have a royal time with anybody of similar tastes and inclinations. In her first letter home she summed up the results of a week's experience.

"THE VILLA CAMELLIA.

"MUMMIE DARLING,

"This is to tell you I am still alive! I'm a little surprised, because I thought math would kill me. Miss Bickford is mosthorribly conscientious and insists upon finding out whether I really understand or not, and it is generally 'not.' I suppose I was born with a thick head for figures, anyway, she seems amazed at my ignorance. I lay the blame on St. Osmund's. Is that mean of me? It's my only way of paying out Miss Gordon for past scores.

"I don't mind admitting I have warm times in school over some of the classes, but the rest of the life is lovely. Miss Bickford is often a big thorn, but Peachy is a rose. As for Lorna she's like one of those tropical flowers that Uncle Redvers grows in his conservatory. How does Vin like being at the office? Are you straight yet at the flat? Come and see me as soon as ever you can, because I'm a little bit lonesome and wanting my home folks, though I wouldn't confess it to any of these girls for the world.

"Heaps of love to Dad and Vin and your dear self.

"From

"RENIE."

If Irene, who had found her niche in a congenial set at the Villa Camellia, was capable of feeling the pangs of homesickness, that unpleasant malady exhibited itself with far more serious symptoms in the case of another new girl who had entered the school upon the same day. Désirée Legrand could not settle down among the juniors. She was used to the society of grown-up people, and did not take kindly to young companions. In the excitement of her own affairs Irene had hardly given the child a thought since her arrival, but one afternoon, when enjoying a solitary ramble round the garden, she suddenly came face to face with Little Flaxen. She was shocked at the change in her; the once pink cheeks were white and pasty, and her eyelids were red and swollen as if with perpetual crying.

"Hello! Whatever have you been doing to yourself?" exclaimed Irene. "You look rather a bunch of misery, don't you? What's the matter?"

Désirée, squatting forlornly on the steps that led to the upper tennis courts, produced a lace-bordered pocket-handkerchief and mopped her eyes.

"Nobody loves me here!" she blurted out dramatically. "I'm just wr-r-r-etched! They all laugh and call me Frenchie! I'm not French, and I w-w-ant to be l-l-oved!"

Irene looked at her and shook her head.

"That's not the way to go about it I'm afraid. I'm sorry, but you know you'll just invite teasing if you carry on like this. Can't you brace up and be sporty? Pretend you don't mind anything they say and they'll soon stop."

"But I do mind!" sobbed the tragic little figure on the steps. "I mind d-d-dreadfully! Why are they all so horrid to me? People have always been so nice till I came here!"

"That's exactly the reason," said Irene, grasping the situation and explaining it truthfully. "You've been accustomed to be petted by everybody, and after all why should the other girls in your form pet you? You don't pet them, do you?"

"N-n-o!"

Désirée's eyes were round with amazement.

"Well, can't you see school's a matter of give and take? If you do something for the rest they'll possibly like you, but they won't fall on your neck just out of sheer good nature. Why don't you write home for a box of chocolates and offer them round your form?"

"I never thought of it. I had some chocolates—but—I ate them!"

"There you are! You expected to get all the attention and give nothing. Sorry if I seem brutal, but it's the solid truth. You take my advice and cheer up instead of continually sniveling. I've been at school myself since I was seven, and I know a thing or two. If a girl's popular there's generally some reason behind it. Look here, I'll help you if I can. Those kids over there are doing nothing. I'll get them to come and play rounders, choose you for a partner, and I'll back our side to win. Here's Peachy! Perhaps she'll join in too. I'll ask her."

Irene rapidly explained her philanthropic intentions, and enlisted both Peachy and Delia in her team. The juniors, amazed and flattered at an invitation from older girls, were ready enough for a game. Irene insisted upon the innovation of what she called "hunting in couples," that is to say, dividing the company into partners who made the course hand in hand. She took good care to choose Désirée for her "running-mate," and as they were both fleet of foot they scored considerably. By the time the bell rang they had beaten the records.

"Look here!" said Irene, addressing the juniors before they scooted away, "you kids are missing a chance. Why don't you make Désirée train for the sports? She can run like a hare! With the start she'd get as a junior she might win you a trophy. Hadn't it ever entered your silly young noddles to see what she could do for your form? Well, you are a set of slackers! That's my opinion of you. We manage our affairs better in the Transition."

"Oh, thank you! Thank you!" gasped Little Flaxen, lingering a moment or two behind the others. "You've been just great! I'll write to Dad to-night to send me some chocs, and I won't eat a single one myself. They shall have them all. They shall really!"

With scarlet cheeks and shining eyes she was a different child from the weeping Niobe who had sat and sobbed on the steps.

"Now if I'd simply coddled her and sympathized she'd have cried a few gallons more and have been no better off," mused Irene, as her protégée danced away. "I fancy those juniors have been fairly nasty to her, though I wouldn't tell her so. Something ought to be done about it, but the question is 'what?' I want to have a talk with Peachy when I can wedge in ten minutes of spare time."

All evening remembrance of Little Flaxen's red eyes and white cheeks haunted Irene. She felt it ought not to have been possible for the child to be so lonely and neglected. Granted that her unpopularity might be partly her own fault, boycotting was nevertheless hard to bear. It was clearly somebody's business to have looked after her, and that duty ought not to have devolved upon a newcomer like herself, who only realized the necessity by the merest chance.

"What's the use of the prefects?" Irene asked herself, but she gave up the answer, and appealed to Peachy at breakfast-time instead.

That cheery young American took the matter more seriously than Irene expected. There was a very kind little heart hidden under her bubbles of fun.

"I'll call a meeting of the Camellia Buds right now," she declared. "I guess we don't want any of those poor babes crying their eyes out. Talk of homesickness! You should have seen me my first week here. I brought four dozen pocket-handkerchiefs to school with me and I used them all. It's not good enough! Prefects, did you say? Humph! I don't call Rachel exactly laid out for this job. Bring your biscuits to the 'Grotto' at interval, and we'll have a powwow about it."

There was a twenty-minute mid-morning break between classes, during which the girls ate lunch and amused themselves as they pleased in the house or grounds. The biscuits, three apiece, were laid out in rows on the dining-room table together with each pupil's glass of milk. As Irene ran in to take her portion she heard a scrimmage going on at the other end of the room. Several small girls were quarreling loudly, and above the noise came Désirée's piping, high-pitched voice:

"I haven't had a biscuit for days and it isn't fair."

"What's all this about?" asked Irene, striding into the crowd just in time to see Mabel and another member of the Transition pass, laughing, through the lower door.

There was a babel in reply.

"Those big girls come and grab our biscuits!"

"It's a shame of them!"

"There ought to be three apiece!"

"And there never are!"

"It's something if you get two!"

"Nancy's taken both mine!"

"Honest injun, I haven't!"

"I tell you I'm famished!"

"Help! Don't all shout at once," decreed Irene. "Let's have a biscuit parade. Each hold out what she's got. Here, Audley, hand one of yours over to Francie. Effie, break that one in half and share with Chris. Désirée, you may have mine this morning, but this business mustn't happen again. I've no time to stop now, but I'll inquire into this, you bet!"

Leaving an only partially satisfied group of small girls behind her Irene sped to her tryst in the garden. She took a short cut, and ran through the orange grove, where the half-ripe oranges were beginning to turn yellow on the trees, then shamelessly jumping over a flower border of stocks and primulas, crossed under the rose-pergola, turned down a creeper-covered side alley, and found herself in a neglected portion of the grounds. Here there was a very dilapidated little arbor, built sixty or seventy years ago when the Villa Camellia had been owned by an Italian count with a weakness for the fine arts. The roof leaked, and a riot of jessamine almost hid the door; the window-sill had fallen, and the floor was a mass of dead leaves. The plastered walls were painted with frescoes — faded and moldy now — of a country château with cypress trees, and three ladies in big plumed hats riding on white horses, and a gentleman in shooting costume and tall boots, who wore side whiskers, and carried a gun, and had four hunting dogs standing in a row behind him. All these were rather stiff and badly painted, yet gave an air of neglected grandeur to the grotto. There were marble seats, and a rickety marble table, and a little broken statue of Cupid in the corner, and the floor under the rubbish was of blue glazed tiles, so that the building, though fallen on evil days, still showed some remnants of its former glory. As it was in an out-of-the-way spot and far from the tennis courts, it was not often visited, and had therefore been appropriated by the Camellia Buds as a suitable place for the secret meetings of their sorority.

The nine were all assembled here waiting impatiently for Irene. She brushed through the jessamine-covered doorway, took her seat, and breathlessly explained the reason of her delay.

"Would you have believed such meanness?" she ended.

Peachy nodded solemnly.

"I told you some of our precious Transition would make you blush. Was it Bertha? I thought so! I knew she had got hold of Mabel. I believe they're buddies, and a charming pair they'll be! We shall have to tackle them somehow. This certainly can't be allowed to go on."

"Isn't it a case for the prefects?" asked Irene, addressing the President.

Agnes's forehead was drawn into a series of puckers.

"We hate telling," she sighed. "The fact is the prefects in this school aren't quite what they ought to be. They think they do their duty, but they're too aloof and high-handed and bossing, and the consequence is they're not popular, and the girls would as soon complain to a teacher as to Rachel or Sybil or Erica. It simply isn't done. Yet those kids need a champion. There are several abuses among them that I've noticed myself."

"Guess we've got to take it on then and 'champ'," murmured Delia.

"Poor little souls, it's a shame to steal their 'bikkies'; we'll have to stand over them and act as fairy godmothers," said Sheila.

Peachy bounced suddenly in her seat.

"Sheila Yonge, you've given me an idea—yes, an absolute brain-throb. What the Camellia Buds ought to do is to turn the sorority into an Amalgamated Society of Fairy Godmothers, and each of us take over a junior to look after and act providence to. It's what those kids are just aching for—only they mayn't know it. What good are prefects to them except as bogies? They skedaddle like lightning if they see so much as Rachel's shadow. They each ought to have one older girl whom they can count on as a friend."

"A kind of buddy?"

"Something of the sort, but more like a foster-mother."

"I vote we ask them all to a candy party, and each adopt one," suggested Delia warmly.

"There are ten of us, and there are nineteen juniors," calculated Jess. "How's it going to work out?"

"Why, some of us must take twins or even triplets," decreed Peachy. "I'm bursting to begin. Let's have that candy party right away. Can anybody raise a lira or two?"

"We'll give you our subscriptions back in the house, if you'll act treasurer and wheedle Antonio. Fairy Godmothers, Limited! It's a brainy notion. When shall you ask those kids? You bet they'll buzz in like bees."

The loud clanging of the garden bell, which seemed to punctuate life at the Villa Camellia, broke up the meeting in a hurry and scattered its members in the direction of their classrooms. At the first opportunity, however, Irene unlocked her cash-box and took out a contribution towards the candy party. She was not yet used to the Italian paper money, and had only a vague idea of its value, but she judged that two lire was the expected amount, and carried it accordingly to Peachy's dormitory.

"You white angel! It's a bountiful 'contrib.' I've squared Antonio. He'll leave the parcel inside the grotto. What we should do without that dear old man I can't imagine. I've told the juniors, and they're simply crazy to come. I've fixed it up for directly after tea."

Antonio, the old concierge who had charge of the gate, was absolutely faithful to his duties as porter, and guarded the Villa Camellia as zealously as a convent, but he was lenient on one point—he was willing sometimes to smuggle sweets, and those girls who knew how to coax could induce him to make an expedition to the confectioner's and fetch them a small private store of what delicacies they fancied. He had his own ideas of how much was good for them, and would never be responsible for more than a limited allowance; neither would he undertake more than one commission per week for any single girl. It was a matter of favor, and to some of the pupils he would only grunt a refusal. Peachy, however, was a champion wheedler; she had a certain command over the Italian language, and could persuade Antonio, in his native tongue, of the absolute necessity of her demands. He was quite generous on this occasion, and slipped a fair-sized parcel of mixed Neapolitan bonbons into the sanctuary of the deserted summer-house.

Nineteen interested juniors, bidden to an unwonted entertainment, dodged their prefect after tea, evaded a basket-ball practice, scattered themselves in the grounds, met in the long pergola, and proceeded to the jessamine-covered arbor, where they were received politely by their ten hostesses. It was, of course, impossible to accommodate them inside, but the grotto was close to the place where Paolo, the gardener, chopped wood for the stoves, so there were plenty of logs lying about that served as seats. In a very short time the guests were settled, hospitality was handed round, the colored papers were removed from the goodies, and there was a general abandonment to sticky satisfaction. Between the first and second distributions Agnes, as President of the Sorority, addressed the meeting.

"We've a proposition to make to you all," she began. "There are some things in this school that aren't always quite what they ought to be, and it's rather hard for juniors to fight their own battles. Sometimes you squabble among yourselves — oh, I know! — and sometimes you get it hot from the seniors or the Transition. Well, we're going to help you. Each of us means to take on one or more of you and be a sort of fairy godmother to you, and responsible for seeing you're decently treated. I understand there's been a little trouble about your lunch biscuits?"

"It's Bertha!"

"And Mabel!"

"They're real mean!"

"They simply grab them!"

"Oh, do please stop it!"

"And we haven't had our turns at the tennis courts!"

"And Winnie borrowed my paint-box and won't give it back!"

Agnes held up a hand to stop the general clamor.

"That'll do!" she decreed. "I'm going to sort you out and give you each to your fairy godmother, and you may pour your woes into her ears, and she'll try her level best to right your wrongs. No, you mayn't say whom you'd like to have. It's we who'll do the choosing, thanks! Anybody who's not satisfied can walk off and she won't get a champion at all or any more candy either. I mean what I say."

Such an awful threat reduced the juniors to order, and they submitted quite peaceably to be apportioned among their various benefactresses. Irene secured Little Flaxen, Lorna had a pair of solemn-eyed sisters, Peachy pounced upon the liveliest trio and proclaimed them as her triplets, and Delia adopted the two youngest as twins.

"You can come to us at a pinch," explained Agnes, "but please remember we're Fairy Godmothers, Limited. We'll fight any just crusade, but we're not going to write your exercises for you, or pull you out of scrapes when you don't deserve it. That's not our function. There, you understand? Hand the candy again, somebody. There's another piece each all round at least, and if there are any over I'll throw them up and you shall scramble for them."

The immediate effect of this mission of the Camellia Buds was a decided improvement in the conditions of the juniors. Next morning, at lunch-time, a stern-faced contingent mounted guard over the biscuits, and when Bertha and Mabel, plainly bent on piracy, sauntered down the room, they were told certain unpalatable home truths, and ignominiously put to rout.

"Stop that instanter!" commanded Peachy.

"We're here to see fair play!" snarled Jess.

"Be content with your own portions!" flared Delia.

"Well, really! Who asked you to boss us?" retorted Bertha angrily.

"Nobody; but we're going to stop your mean tricks, so we give you warning. You two are a disgrace to the Transition. I don't know what flags you class yourselves under, but I'm sure neither America nor Britain would be proud to own you — you biscuit-snatchers!"

Peachy's eyes were snapping sparks, and the matter might have waxed even warmer had not Rachel reëntered the room for a pencil she had dropped. The head prefect pricked up her ears at the sound of the disturbance, whereupon Mabel and Bertha, who knew they would receive short shrift if she demanded an explanation, made a hasty exit, merely murmuring to Jess and Peachy as they pushed past them:

"We'll pay you out for this!"

"Just you wait!"

CHAPTER VI

Among the Olive Groves

Quite by accident as it seemed, the Sorority of the Camellia Buds had turned itself from a society instituted for mutual protection and fun into a Crusaders' Union, pledged, like Spenser's Red Cross Knight, to avenge the wrongs of distressed damsels in the junior forms. The ring of battle certainly added a spice of excitement to their secret. It was much more interesting to interfere personally on behalf of their protégées than to place debatable matters before the prefects. If war were involved with another sorority it could not be helped. And war there undoubtedly was. Bertha and Mabel, too clever to court open ignominy, desisted for the present from biscuit-snatching, but sought other means of retaliation. It was unfortunate for Irene and Lorna that Mabel had been apportioned to them as a roommate. Both she and Elsie were members of the rival sorority, so there was division in No. 3 dormitory. Sometimes the opposing factions would not speak to one another at all. Elsie was more stand-off than actively disagreeable and kept herself to her own cubicle, but Mabel was openly annoying. She transgressed every rule of dormitory etiquette, dashed for the bathroom instead of waiting her due turn, dumped her belongings on to other people's chairs, spread the center table with her papers, fidgeted during study hours, and in various ways made herself objectionable.

Irene and Lorna, as sworn buddies, cemented yet more firmly the bond between them, and supported one another on every possible occasion. Irene was really growing fond of Lorna. Though the latter might be reserved it was something to find a ready listener and sympathizer. As a rule we can't deliberately choose our soul-friends. Fate just seems to send them along and we must accept them with all their faults or go without. It certainly does not do to be too particular, or we may soon find ourselves chumless in the world. Irene was rather lovelorn for Peachy, but that bright little American, besides being in an upper dormitory, was before-appropriated by other "heart-to-hearties," and, though she held out the palm of good fellowship, was too staunch a character to desert old friends for new.

"She's just sweet to me, but I don't count first," decided Irene. "Well, it's no use being jealous. If you can't have the moon you must be content with a star, that's all. It's a vast amount better than nothing."

Lorna might more aptly be described as a planet than a star, for her thoughts had started to revolve round Irene in a fixed orbit. As regards her half of the bargain she was absolutely content. She adored her buddy, and blessed the lot that had coupled their names together. She had not before made a real friend, and Irene's happy-go-lucky, affectionate, confiding disposition appealed to her. She began to try to protect her and look after her. It was really something of the mother instinct cropping out. She had never possessed a sister or anything little of her own to love, and it was a new experience to find a girl, rather small and younger than herself, who clung to her and seemed actually fond of her. Life, which had hitherto been chilly and self-centered, suddenly grew warm. She had been used to pose as one who disliked school, but with this fresh interest her views on the subject underwent a change.

Any girl must indeed have been hard to please who was not satisfied with the Villa Camellia and its beautiful Italian garden. All through the month of February flowers were in bloom there which in England only peep out timidly in April or May, and often will not brave a northern climate at all. The front of the house was covered with a glorious purple bougainvillea, violets bloomed under the orange and lemon trees, and the camellias, from which the villa took its name, flourished in profusion, growing as great trees ten or twelve feet high and covered with rose-colored, white, or scarlet blossoms. Iris, freesias, narcissus, red salvias, marguerites, pansies, pink peonies, wallflowers, polyanthus, petunias, stocks, genistas, arbutula, cinerarias, begonias, and belladonna-lilies kept up a brave display in the border, and, though they would be more beautiful and luxuriant later on in the season, they nevertheless dispelled the idea of winter. The general temperature at Fossato resembled an English April, the sunshine was warm, but the wind was apt to be chilly, and at night-time it was quite cold, though never frosty. The central heating apparatus was kept going in the school, and the girls, though they might run about without coats in the sunshine, were always required to have a warm jersey at hand, for the wind at this season could be treacherous, and those unused to the climate, deceived by its brightness and wealth of flowers, were very liable to catch chills and to be laid up with feverish colds as the result of their own imprudence. Sometimes indeed a bitter sirocco wind would blow, and bring torrents of rain to turn the blue sea and sky to a leaden gray and to blot out the view of Naples and Vesuvius, but it seldom lasted more than a few days, and in a land of drought was welcomed to refresh the gardens and to fill the cisterns and water-tanks.

It has been mentioned in a previous chapter that the Villa Camellia was of necessity run somewhat on convent lines. In Italy young girls do not walk about unchaperoned as in England and America, but are always very closely escorted by older people, and it was advisable to keep to the customs of the country. The pupils obtained most of their exercise inside their own garden. On Sundays they paraded to the British church, but otherwise they did not very often go into Fossato. Once a week, if the weather were fine, a limited number were taken for an expedition, but Irene had been at school for some weeks before this good fortune fell to her lot. One lucky Wednesday, however, she found her name and Lorna's written on the list of "exeats" on the notice-board, and flew to announce the glad tidings to her chum.

"Twelve of us, with Miss Bickford and Miss Parr as leaders. Won't it be ripping? It says Monte Pellegrino. Where's that? The big hill over there? Oh, great! I love a climb! I'm just dancing to go! I feel as if I had been boxed up inside these big walls for years and years. I only wish Peachy and Delia had been on the list too."

"But we are!" exclaimed Delia's excited voice behind her. "Stella and Marjorie both have colds, so we've swapped places with them, and they'll go next time instead. Isn't it fine!"

"I'm tingling right down to my toes," agreed Peachy, her jolly little freckled face one wide grin. "It's going to be an afternoon of afternoons."

"If it doesn't rain," said Lorna, eyeing the sky suspiciously.

"Oh, don't be a wet blanket! It's no use courting trouble, honey, as Willy Shakespeare says somewhere. Oh, well, if it wasn't Willy Shakespeare it was somebody else who said it, and it's just as true anyway. Take your umbrella and wait till the rain comes down before you grumble. I've got an exeat and I didn't expect it, and I'm going off my head a little. That's all! Don't worry yourselves about me. I'm sane at the bottom."

With Peachy and Delia prancing about and hardly able to regulate their satisfaction the expedition promised to be a lively one, though the harum-scarum pair calmed down in the presence of Miss Bickford, and assumed a deportment of due decorum. The favored twelve were half seniors and half Transition, the remaining pair of the latter consisting of Bertha Ford and Mabel Hughes. The Camellia Buds exchanged eloquent glances at the sight of their arch-enemies, but wisely forbore to make any provocative remarks; Delia indeed even murmured something pleasant about the excursion to which Bertha grunted a reply, so the party started off in apparent harmony.

Antonio, with his big key, unlocked the great gate, they filed through into the eucalyptus-shaded road, and in ten minutes they had left the quiet school behind them, and were down in the gay little town of Fossato. It was new and wonderful to Irene. The wide main street with its intense brilliant sunshine contrasting with the deep shade of the narrow side streets, the open shop-fronts with their displays of picturesque wares, the stalls of fruit and vegetables sold by quaint country vendors, the balconies full of flowers, the kindly, dark-eyed, smiling people, the pretty peasant children clattering about in heelless wooden shoes, the brightly painted carts and the horses decorated with flowers and feathers as if for a perpetual May Day, all made up a scene that was more like a portion of a play than a piece of real life, and made her almost able to imagine herself upon the stage of a theater. They had reached a great square, where leafless trees were covered with a beautiful purple blossom, something like mezereon. From a marble fountain bareheaded women, with exquisitely arranged dark tresses and bright handkerchiefs folded shawl-wise round their shoulders, were drawing water in brass pitchers, and chattering the soft southern dialect with the pretty tuneful Neapolitan voices that speak like singing and sing like opera. An equestrian statue of Garibaldi stood on a pedestal in the midst of a flowerbed of gay geraniums, and below, in the shadow, a military officer, with a gorgeous pale blue cloak draped over one shoulder, was talking to two Italian soldiers whose plumed hats were adorned with shining cocks' feathers.

Miss Bickford, in the van of the Villa Camellia queue, strode on, taking no notice, beyond a firm shake of the head, of the various interruptions that met her path—the drivers who offered their carriages for hire, the smiling women who thrust forward baskets of oranges for sale, the beguiling children who held out little brown hands and begged for soldi (halfpennies), and the post-card vendors who spread out sets of colored views of the neighborhood. It was a good thing that Miss Parr was at the rear of the procession to keep order, or the girls would have succumbed to some of these temptations and have broken rank, an unpardonable offense in the eyes of the school authorities, who wished to keep up the prestige of their establishment in the estimation of the town, and to emulate the convent school on the hill, whose pupils marched along the high street as demurely as young nuns.

Turning out of the piazza they walked alongside a deep natural gorge which divided Fossato from the open country. This immense ravine was a fearsome place, with a sheer descent of many hundreds of feet; its jagged rocks were clothed with bushes and creepers, and clefts and the openings of caves could be seen amongst the greenery. The girls leaned on the low wall and shuddered as they gazed down the precipice.

"Antonio and Dominica say that dwarfs live in the caves down there," remarked Peachy. "Half the people in the town believe in them, but they're too afraid to go and see because the dwarfs have 'the evil eye,' and would bring them bad luck."

"What superstitious nonsense!" laughed Rachel. "How can they make up such stuff?"

"Not altogether such nonsense as you think," corrected Miss Bickford, who was a student of archæology; "indeed I find it intensely interesting. It's a case of survival of tradition. A few thousand years ago no doubt a race of little short dark Stone Age men actually lived in those caves, and took good care to avenge themselves on any of the taller, stronger tribes who interfered with them and tried to push them out of their territory. The remembrance of them would be handed down long after they had become extinct, and, of course their doings were exaggerated, and their cunning tricks were set down to magic. Just as the prehistoric monsters lingered as dragons and firedrakes, so the small early inhabitants of Europe have passed into dwarfs and brownies and pixies. If anybody cared to dig in those caves I dare say flint weapons might be found. It's a chance for the local antiquarian society if they'd only take it."

Leaving the gorge the party turned up a steep and very narrow alley between walls nine or ten feet high. At the tops of these walls were raised gardens planted with orange and lemon trees, whose fruit, in all stages of green, gold, and yellow, overshadowed the path. Across some of them were erected shelters of reeds or plaited grass, to prevent too quick ripening, but in some of the orchards the crop was ready, and workers were busy with ladders and baskets gathering their early harvests. It was a picturesque route, for the sides of the deep walls were covered with beautiful maidenhair ferns, and over the tops hung geraniums or clumps of white iris or purple stocks or clusters of little red roses. Here and there, at a corner, was a wayside shrine with a faded picture of the Madonna, and a quaint brass lamp in front, and perhaps some flowers laid there by loving hands; dark-eyed smiling little children were playing about and giving each other rides in home-made hand-carts, and at one point the girls stood aside to let pass a donkey so loaded with tiny bamboo trees that it looked a mere moving mass of green.

At length the deep alley between the orange orchards gave way to a different scene. They had been climbing steadily uphill, and now found themselves above the fruit zone and among the olive groves. The high walls had disappeared, and the path ascended by a series of steps. Gray olive trees were on either side, and on the bordering banks grew lovely wild flowers, starry purple anemones, jack-in-the-pulpit lilies, yellow oxalis, moon-daisies, and the beautiful genista which we treasure as a conservatory plant in England. As it was country the girls were allowed to break rank, and keenly enjoyed gathering bouquets; they scrambled up the banks, vying with one another in getting the best specimens. The view from the heights was glorious: below them stretched the gray-green of the olive groves, broken here and there by the bright pink blossoms of a peach tree; the white houses of Fossato gleamed among the dark glossy foliage of its orange orchards, and beyond stretched the beautiful bay of Naples, with its sea a blaze of blue, and old Vesuvius smoking in the distance like a warning of trouble to come.

It was at this point of the walk that Irene, foolish, luckless Irene, made a fatal mistake, and, as Miss Bickford afterwards told her, "wrecked the whole excursion and spoiled everybody's pleasure." She beckoned Lorna and ran up a hill to obtain a higher vantage ground, then, instead of descending by the route she had come, she insisted upon taking a short cut to rejoin the path and catch up with the rest of the party. Now neither Lorna nor Irene was aware that the mountain was a network of many paths leading to little vineyards and gardens, and that when they ran down the opposite side of the slope they were striking a fresh alley, altogether different from the one along which Miss Bickford was leading her flock. For quite a long way the two girls walked on, thinking they were in advance of the others and had stolen a march upon them. Then they sat down and waited, but nobody came. It was a considerable time before it dawned upon them that they were separated from the rest of the party.

"We've come wrong somehow," said Lorna, in much consternation.

"What had we better do?"

"I don't know."

"Perhaps they're not far off. I'll try if I can make them hear."

"I wouldn't shout," objected Lorna, but she was too late, for Irene was already letting off her full lung power in a gigantic coo-e-e. It had a totally different effect from what she anticipated. No schoolgirls with Villa Camellia hats made their appearance, but some rough looking Italian youths scrambled over a fence and came sniggering towards them. Their manner was so objectionable and offensive that the girls turned and ran. They pelted down the path anywhere, quite oblivious of the direction they were taking, and, as a matter of fact, branching yet farther away from their original route. They could hear footsteps and giggling laughter behind, and they were growing extremely terrified when to their immense relief they saw in front of them an elderly peasant woman coming from the town. She had a bright yellow handkerchief round her neck and carried on her head a big basket containing flasks of oil, loaves of bread, and some vegetables. She stopped in some astonishment as Lorna and Irene rushed panting up to her, then glimpsing the lads she seemed to grasp the situation, and called out angrily to them in Italian, whereupon they promptly and rapidly disappeared. As she had reached the gateway of her own garden she motioned the girls to enter, and they gladly availed themselves of the opportunity to seek sanctuary. A large archway led into a paved courtyard, on one side of which was a little brown house, and on the other a small chapel, quite a picture with its quaint half-Moorish tower and two large bells. Their new friend seemed to be the caretaker, for she escorted them inside to show them, with much pride, an altar-piece attributed to Perugino and some ancient faded frescoes of haloed saints. She gave them a peep into her housetoo, and they were deeply interested to see the unfamiliar foreign home, not comfortable according to British or American ideas of comfort, but with a certain charm of its own. There was a big dark room on the ground floor with an orange press, various agricultural implements, and numberless baskets for gathering fruit; there was a bare kitchen with a wood fire and a table spread with cups and dishes; then up a winding stair was a bedroom with walls colored sky blue, and a veranda that looked down over a glorious orange orchard.

"Oh, I'd adore to go out there!" said Irene, pointing to the path that led between the fruit-laden trees, and their hostess evidently divined her meaning, for she not only led her guests into the garden, but fetched a ladder, climbed a tree, and plucked each of them a whole cluster of oranges surrounded by a bunch of leaves.

The girls were so delighted with their entertainment in this Italian cottage that they hardly wished to tear themselves away, yet a vision of Miss Bickford's reproachful face began to hover before their eyes, and Lorna at last suggested that they must be moving.

"I hope those abominable boys aren't waiting about anywhere outside," shivered Irene.

The same thought seemed to have struck their hostess, for she called an elderly man, evidently her husband, who was pruning vines, and began a catechism as to where her visitors lived. Lorna replied as well as her knowledge of Italian allowed, and at the mention of the Villa Camellia the pair nodded in comprehension. After a brief conversation with his wife in an undertone the old man offered himself as guide, and undertook to escort the truants safely back to school again, a proposal which they thankfully accepted. It would indeed have been difficult for them to find their own way among the various interlacing paths, and they were particularly glad to have his protection against possible ragazzi. There was tremendous trouble waiting for them at the Villa Camellia. Poor Miss Parr had collapsed almost into hysterics, and Miss Bickford with two other teachers had returned to the hillside on a further search, while Miss Rodgers was communicating by telephone with the Fossato police station, and offering a reward for any news of their whereabouts. Irene had thought the principal could be stern, but she never knew how her eyes could flash before that interview in the study. Both girls came out quaking like jellies and weeping for all to hear.

"Did you catch it hot?" inquired Peachy, sympathetically linking arms with the truants.

"Rather! It isn't the punishments so much, it's that she made us so ashamed."

"Our parole won't be trusted till after half-term."

"We didn't mean to run away."

"It was really quite an accident."

"Cheer up!" consoled Peachy. "Miss Rodgers cuts like a steel knife, but she doesn't bear grudges. I will say that for her. With some teachers you'd never hear the last of it, but once you've worked off your impositions you'll be quite in favor again. Whatever possessed you to go and do it though?"

"Just our wretched bad luck, I suppose," said Irene, rubbing her eyes as she turned up the passage and deposited her confiscated cluster of oranges, as directed, in the pantry.

CHAPTER VII

Lorna's Enemy

For the next two weeks Irene and Lorna were strictly "gated," a great deprivation, for it would have been their turns to go shopping with Miss Morley, and Irene at least was anxious to sample some of the quaint wares spread forth so temptingly in the Fossato stores. With the exception of church-going they did not have a chance to step outside the grounds of the Villa Camellia. The Sunday expedition came as a welcome relief to break the monotony. The school liked the little British church at Fossato. It was so utterly different from anything to which they had been accustomed in England or America. To begin with it was not an ecclesiastical building at all, but simply a big room in the basement of the Hôtel Anglais. The walls had been exquisitely decorated by a French artist with conventionalized designs of iris in purple and gold, and through the windows there was a gorgeous peep over the bay. The girls used to exercise much maneuvering to secure the seats with the best view, and somehow that bright stretch of the Mediterranean seemed to blend in as part and parcel of all the praise and thanksgiving that was being offered.

Punctually at twenty minutes to eleven on Sunday mornings the fifty-six pupils and the seven mistresses would leave the great gate of the Villa Camellia and march into the town, along the esplanade under the grove of palm trees, then through the beautiful sheltered garden of the Hôtel Anglais, where many exotic flowers and shrubs were blooming and the white arum lilies were like an Easter festival, to the doorway, under the jessamine-covered veranda, that led to the Eglise anglaise et américaine. The school practically made half the congregation, but there were visitors from the various hotels, and a sprinkling of British residents who had houses at Fossato. When the service was over there followed a very pleasant quarter of an hour in the piazza of the hotel; the clergyman and his wife would speak personally to many of the girls, and any of the pupils who met friends were allowed to talk to them. Fossato was a popular week-end resort from Naples, so relatives often turned up on Sundays and there were many joyous reunions. Kind little Canon Clark and his small bird-like wife were great favorites at the Villa Camellia. They were always invited to school functions, and each term the girls, in relays of about ten at a time, were offered hospitality at the "Villa Bleue," a tiny dwelling that served as parsonage for the British chaplain. To go to tea at the dear wee house—color-washed blue, and with pink geraniums in its window-boxes—was considered a treat, and Irene and Lorna looked very glum indeed when Miss Rodgers kept severely to their punishment, and substituted Agnes and Elsie for themselves in the next contingent of guests.

"You'll go later on," consoled Peachy. "Miss Rodgers is really very decent in that way. She'll see that you get your turn once in a term at any rate. Last time I went we had hot brown scones and molasses. Oh, they were good! There! I oughtn't to have told you that when your turn's off. Never mind. It will be something to look forward to. We always play paper games there, and they're such fun. There I am again! Well, if you went to-day it would be over and done with by to-morrow, and it's still all to come. That's one way of taking it."

"Oh, it's all very well to moralize!" grumped Lorna, who was feeling thoroughly cross. "It's easy enough to count up other people's blessings. I'm a blighted blossom!"

quoted Peachy with an extra wide grin. "Cheer up! Don't you realize it's only ten days to half-term? Oh, do, for goodness' sake, look less like a statue of melancholy! Do you know, child, that you're getting permanent wrinkles along that forehead of yours, and it makes you more like fifty than fifteen. You're too sedate. That's what's the matter with you, Lorna Carson! It's a fault that ought to be overcome. Copy Delia and me. We know how to enjoy ourselves. There—my lecture is over and now let's talk of earthquakes."

"It's all very well for you, you've got everything you want," murmured Lorna bitterly under her breath. "Some people haven't half the luck, and it's hard to be content with a short allowance and pretend you're the same as every one else. It can't always be done."

She turned away as she said it, so Peachy only caught the sound of a grumble and did not hear the actual words. Had she done so she might possibly have exhibited more sympathy, for she was a very kind-hearted girl. Neither she nor anybody at the Villa Camellia understood Lorna in the least. So far their classmate had been somewhat of a chestnut-bur, and nobody in the Transition had ever penetrated her husk of reserve. There is generally a reason for most things in life, if we could only know it, and poor Lorna's morose and hermit attitude at school was really the result of matters at home. To get into her innermost confidence we must follow her to Naples on her half-term holiday and see for ourselves the peculiar circumstances amid which she had been placed, and the disadvantages that had caused her to differ from other girls.

Lorna's family was the smallest possible, for it consisted only of her father. Nobody at the Villa Camellia had ever seen Mr. Carson — not even Miss Rodgers. He had communicated with her by writing when he wished to place his daughter at the school, but he had never paid a single visit to Fossato. He pleaded stress of business as the excuse for this remissness, but Lorna herself knew only too well that he had no intention of coming. Except to the office at which he was employed he never went to any place where he would be likely to meet English visitors. The furnished rooms where he lived were in the strictly Italian portion of Naples, and not in the vicinity of the big hotels. Secretly Lorna dreaded her holidays. There was nothing for her to do while her father was at the office. She was not allowed to go out alone, and unless she could induce fat Signora Fiorenza, their landlady, to be philanthropic and chaperon her to look at the shops, she was obliged to amuse herself in the house during the day as best she could. In the evening things were certainly better. Her father would take her to dine at an Italian restaurant, and would sometimes treat her to a performance at a theater or cinema close at hand, or would escort her for a lamplight walk along the streets, but these brief expeditions were evidently made out of a sense of duty, and Mr. Carson was plainly unhappy until he was once more ensconced in his own sitting-room with his favorite books and his reading-lamp. He had seen so little of his daughter during the five years they had lived at Naples that, though in a sense he was fond of her, she was more of an embarrassment to him than an asset. Lorna realized this only too keenly. Her sensitive disposition shrank away from her father. She was shy in his presence, and never knew what to say to him. She seemed always aware of some enormous shadow that hung over their lives and darkened the daylight. What this was she had no means of guessing, but it was emphatically there. She had learned, by bitter experience, never to ask to be taken to the fashionable portions of the city; she knew that the sound of a voice speaking English at a neighboring table was enough to cause her father to finish his meal in a hurry and leave the restaurant. They never went to the British Church, and even such cosmopolitan spots as the aquarium or the museum were equally taboo.

Long and often did Lorna puzzle over this idiosyncrasy of her father. She retained vague memories of her early childhood, when he had surely been utterly different and would come into the nursery to romp with her. It had not been altogether her mother's death; that had happened when she was only six years old, and there were bright memories after it of happy times together. No—it was when she was ten years old that the unknown catastrophe must have occurred which had ruined her father's life. She could remember plainly the visit of several gentlemen, and of loud angry voices talking inside the drawing-room; she was standing on the stairs as they came out into the hall, and her father had told her roughly to run away. Then had followed a hasty removal, and they had left their comfortable home in London and had come to live in Naples. After a dreary time in a second-rate Italian boarding-house she had been sent to the Villa Camellia, and all link with England was lost and broken. No aunt or cousins ever wrote to her, and the earlier portion of her life seemed a period that was utterly ended.

So far Lorna had never had the courage to make any inquiries into the why and wherefore of this unsatisfactory state of affairs. If a question rose to her lips the sight of her father's forbidding face effectually curbed her curiosity. That some tragedy had been concealed from her she was positive. The suspicion, nay the absolute certainty, was sufficient to place a division between herself and other girls. She would hear her schoolfellows discussing their homes, relations, and friends, and when she contrasted their gay doings with her own barren holidays she shrank into her shell, and would make no allusion to her private affairs.

"Lorna's an absolute oyster, you can get nothing out of her," was the universal verdict of her form.

But if she said little she thought a great deal. She would listen jealously to the accounts of other people's fun, and a bitter feeling had grown in her heart. Why should her life be so shadowed? She had as much right to happiness as the rest of the school. Why should she seem singled out by a vindictive fate and separated from her companions?

In justice to the girls at the Villa Camellia it is only fair to say that any separation was entirely of Lorna's own making. Had she been more expansive she would have readily enough found friends. No one knew of the misery of her home life, and she was simply judged as what her schoolfellows thought her—a queer-tempered crank who refused to join in the general fun of the place, and in consequence was left out of most things.

Irene, pleasant and hail-fellow-well-met with all comers, had at once noticed this attitude of the others towards Lorna. At the drawing of lots in the sorority she had somehow realized that everybody was extremely thankful to have escaped having her unpopular chum as a buddy. Chance remarks and slight allusions, hardly noticed at the time, but remembered later, had confirmed this.

"They're not exactly unkind, but they're down on that girl," she had concluded. "I haven't made up my mind yet whether I altogether like her, but I'm going to be decent to her all the same."

As the very first who had treated her on a real equality of girlhood Irene had been placed on a pedestal in Lorna's empty heart. The separation between the two added to the loneliness of the latter's brief half-term holiday. She had never missed school so much before, or hated her surroundings so entirely. The long week-end dragged itself slowly away. Sunday was wet and they stayed all day in the little sitting-room, Mr. Carson reading as usual, and Lorna trying to amuse herself with Italian magazines and fidgeting as much as she dared. Towards evening the rain cleared a little and her father went out, refusing, however, to allow her to accompany him. At the end of an hour he returned and flung himself heavily into his chair. He was in a state such as she had never witnessed before, violently excited, with glaring eyes and twitching hands.

"Lorna!" he exclaimed in quick panting accents, "I have met my enemy. The man who ruined me! Yes, the man who deliberately blackened and ruined me!"

Lorna turned to him half frightened.

"What is it, Father?" she asked. "Have you an enemy? You've never let me know before. Oh, I wish you'd tell me! I'm fifteen now, and surely old enough to hear. It's so horrible to feel there's something you're always keeping from me."

"I suppose you'll find out some time, so I may as well tell you myself," replied Mr. Carson grimly. "I'm a wronged, ruined man, Lorna, suffering for the sin of another who goes scotfree. The world judged me guilty of embezzlement, but before God I am innocent! I never touched a penny of the money. Do you believe me innocent? Surely my own daughter won't turn against me?"

"No, no, Father! Indeed I believe you innocent. Tell me how it happened. Was it when we left London? I seem to remember the trouble there was then, though you never explained. We had a different name then, hadn't we?"

"You were too young at the time to understand, and it wasn't a subject I wished to revive. Briefly, a big sum, for which I was responsible, disappeared. The head of the firm believed me guilty, but for the sake of old associations he would not prosecute; he simply told me to go. I consulted my lawyer, and, if there had been the slightest chance of clearing myself, I'd have fought the matter to a finish, but he told me my case hadn't a leg to stand on, and that, if I were foolish enough to bring it into court, I should certainly be convicted of embezzlement, and sent to penal servitude; that it was only the clemency of my chief's attitude that saved me, and that he advised me to go abroad while I could. So I left England in a hurry, a disgraced man, disowned by his family and his friends. I changed my name to Carson, and through the kindness of a business acquaintance I was offered a clerkship in an Italian counting-house in Naples, which post I have kept ever since. How I should otherwise have made a living God only knows! It's always my haunting fear that some one in Naples will recognize me and tell them at the office who I am. If that old story leaks out I may once more be ruined."

"But who did it, Father?" asked Lorna. "Had you no clew at all?"

"Not enough to convict, only a strong suspicion, so strong that it is practically a certainty. The man who ruined me was once my friend. Now for five long years, he has been my bitterest enemy. We were both heads of departments in the firm of Burgess and Co. Probably he's a partner now, as I ought to have been. I've never heard news of him since I left London, but to-day I saw him in the Corso. I saw him plainly without any possibility of mistake. What is he doing in Naples? Has he come here to ruin me again?"

"No, no, Dad, surely not! Perhaps he doesn't know you're in Italy. Probably he's only taking a holiday and will go back to England soon," faltered

Lorna, suddenly realizing that in her father's excited nervous condition she ought to offer consolation and soothe him instead of adding to his agitation. "It's very unlikely that he would find you out. Dad, don't grieve so, please!"

She went near to her father's chair and laid a timid hand on his shoulder. An immense gush of pity for him flooded her heart. If she had known this story before, she would have understood, and instead of thinking him unkind and misanthropic she would have tried to be a better daughter to him. The new-found knowledge illuminated all the past and seemed to draw them closely together.

"Mother would have believed in you, Dad," she ventured to say.

"Thank God she never knew! She was spared that at any rate. I raged against Providence when I lost her, but afterwards I felt she had been 'taken away from the evil to come.' Her relations thought me guilty. I went to them and explained, but they practically told me I was lying. When I went abroad I never sent them my address. I just wished to vanish. I don't suppose they have ever troubled to inquire for me. Who cares about a ruined and disgraced man?"

"I care, Dad," said Lorna. "I'm only fifteen and I can't understand everything, but if you'll let me the least little bit take Mother's place, may I try? I'm not much, but perhaps I'm better than nobody, and we two seem all alone in the world."

For the first time in five years the barrier between them was down, and Lorna was hugging her father as in the old happy childish days. To know all is to forgive all, and her resentment against his treatment of her turned into a deep pitying love. She would never be frightened of him again. A new impulse seemed to have come to her. If she could in any way comfort him for what he had suffered, it would be something to live for.

"He's my father, and I'll stick to him through thick and thin," she said to herself fiercely, as she went to bed that night. "I don't know who this enemy is, but if ever I meet him I'll hate him and all belonging to him. I say it, and I don't go back on my word. I'll be my own witness as nobody else is present. Lorna Carson, you've taken up a feud and you've got to carry it through. May all the bad luck in the world come down upon you if you break your oath."

CHAPTER VIII

At Pompeii

Lorna returned to Fossato feeling as if she had passed through a great crisis. The short week-end and its revelation seemed to have added years to her life. She had never been a typical specimen of "sparkling girlhood," but her new knowledge made her more sedate than ever. It brought her both gain and loss: gain in the fact that she now shared her father's confidence, and could help him to bear his heavy burden, and loss in the sense of a yet wider division between herself and her schoolmates. She realized now, only too bitterly, why her father so persistently shunned all English people. It would surely have been better to have placed her at an Italian school than among girls of her own nationality. Lorna, naturally morbid and over-sensitive, shrank yet deeper into her shell, and became more sphinx-like than ever. Her one bright spot at the Villa Camellia was her devotion to her buddy. Half a dozen other girls had at various periods tried to "take Lorna up," but all had promptly dropped her, declaring that they could not get any further, and that she was a solitary "hermit-crab." Irene, after one or two ventures, realized that Lorna was utterly reserved and uncommunicative, but was content to continue the friendship on a one-sided basis, giving confidences, but receiving none in return. She was a little laughed at in certain quarters on the subject of her chum.

"Hope you like crab sauce."

"We're tickled to bits at the pair of you."

"It won't last long."

"Shall we give you an oyster-opener for a birthday present?"

"You've got the champion chestnut-bur of the school—aren't you full of prickles?"

"Go on!" smiled Irene calmly. "I've been teased all my life by my brother, so I'm pretty well bomb-proof. Say just what you like. I'm sure I don't care."

It really did not trouble Irene that Lorna should cling to this habit of closeness. She had so many affairs of her own in which to be interested. She had spent a glorious half-term holiday with her family in their flat at Naples, and was delighted to describe every detail of her experiences. She chatted about her relations till Lorna knew Mr. and Mrs. Beverley and Vincent absolutely well by hearsay, though she had never met them in the flesh. The accounts of their doings gave her a peep of home life such as she had not hitherto realized.

"Lovely to be you," she ventured once.

"You must come and see us," replied Irene impulsively. "I'll get Mother to ask you some day. Don't look so scared. They wouldn't eat you. Don't you like paying visits? Oh well, of course, if you don't want to come I won't worry you. No, I'm not offended. Why should I be? Let everybody please herself is my motto. Oh, don't apologize, for it really doesn't matter in the very least! I'd far rather people were frank and said what they thought."

"I'm going with you to Pompeii to-morrow at any rate," said Lorna. "I'm glad they've put us both down together for that excursion."

It was part of the educational scheme of Miss Rodgers and Miss Morley that the girls should be taken to certain places of interest in the neighborhood. They were carefully prepared in class beforehand, so that they should thoroughly understand what they were going to see. All the school studied Greek and Roman history, and since Christmas there had been special lectures by Miss Morley on the buried city of Pompeii, illustrated by lantern-slides. But photography, however excellent, is a poor substitute for reality when the latter can be obtained. Had the Villa Camellia been situated in England or America no doubt the pupils would have considered those views a tremendous asset to their history class, but being in the near neighborhood of Naples they were able to "go one better," and have actual expeditions to Pompeii itself. A dozen of the girls, personally conducted by Miss Morley, were to start on Thursday, take their lunch, and make a day of it. Most of those chosen were comparative newcomers to the school, or for some reason had not done the excursion before, so it would be a fresh experience to nearly all of them. Six seniors and six members of the Transition made up the party, with little Désirée Legrand tagged on at the last as a mascot, because Stella and Carrie had pointed out that twelve pupils and one mistress would make thirteen at table if they had tea together, and though Miss Morley had scoffed at such ridiculous superstition, she took Désirée all the same to break the possible bad luck. They had the satisfaction of assembling in the hall for the start exactly as their companions were filing into classrooms.

"Got your nose-bag?" asked Delia, indicating her lunch satchel. "It wouldn't do to leave those behind. I always feel famished when I'm out sightseeing. Hope I shan't eat my lunch before the picnic. Renie, it's no use lugging that camera with you. You won't be allowed to take any photos inside the ruins, so I warn you."

"Miss Morley's taking hers," objected Irene, loath to relinquish the object in question.

"Miss Morley has a special government permit to sketch or photo in Pompeii. Nobody may take the slightest snap-shot or drawing without. I've been once before, so I know, Madam Doubtful. You'll see ever so many officials will ask to look at Miss Morley's ticket. Why? Because the place would get choked up with artists I suppose. And also they want to sell their own photos. You'll be pestered to buy post-cards outside the gates."

"I'd adore to get just one or two snaps," persisted Irene. "I won't take this big camera, but I'll slip my wee one inside my pocket, and see if I find a chance."

"Are you ready, girls?" came Miss Morley's voice from the porch, and the waiting thirteen formed into double line and marched.

They were to go by the electric tram from Fossato to Castellamare, from which it was only a comparatively short drive to Pompeii. The jogging, jolting, little tramcar ran along the coast, linking up several towns and villages and conveying people intent on either business or pleasure. There were many visitors anxious to make the excursion to-day, but the contingent from the Villa Camellia had posted themselves by the statue of Garibaldi in the square, and scrambled for the car as soon as it arrived, boarding it with three hatless Italian girls, two women with orange baskets, a sailor carrying a little boy, and a stout old padre, who apologized prettily for pushing.

"We did those folks from the Hotel Royal," chuckled Delia, sitting on Irene's knee for lack of further accommodation. "Did you ever see a tram fill up quicker? I'm afraid I'm heavy. I know I'm an awful lump. We'll take it in turns, and I'll nurse you after a while. I call this rather priceless.Everybody's good-tempered even if they do hustle. They don't seem to mind people treading on their toes. It's infectious. I catch myself smiling, and I'd jolly well frown as a rule if any one yanked a basket into my back."

"I think it's the climate," remarked Irene. "In a London tram most faces don't look too cheerful, but with this sky overhead people are simply chirping like crickets. It's like a perpetual summer holiday."

The car was rattling along the steep coast road through miles of glorious scenery. On the left was an ultramarine sea, with white-sailed boats, and to the right lay cliffs and olive groves. Some of the trees were covered with catkins, and others had already burst into green leaf; gorgeous yellow genistas clothed the hillsides, and the banks were dappled with blue borage and marigolds. There were so many things to look at from either window of the tram; goats were feeding along the crags, and a gray businesslike battle-ship was wending its way across the harbor in the direction of Naples. They passed through several small towns or villages, getting a vivid impression of the lives of the inhabitants, who, on sunny days, seemed to do much of their domestic work out of doors, and to peel potatoes, wash salads, cook on charcoal braziers, sew, mend shoes, make lace, and pursue many other vocations on the pavements in front of the houses, and so far from being disturbed by onlookers, would smile and even wave friendly hands at the strangers on the tramcar.

"That darling old soul in the green apron blew me a kiss," chuckled Delia. "She looks as happy as a queen, though she's probably living on about ten cents a day."

"Did you see them dressing the baby on the pavement?" squealed Stella. "They were winding it round and round in yards of bandages exactly like old Italian pictures. I didn't know it was done nowadays."

"Oh! Look at the carts drawn by bullocks."

"And the lamb with its fleece all combed out and tied with blue ribbons."

"That's because it's Mid-Lent."

"Don't you see the baby donkey? There! Quick!"

In her efforts to watch everything at once Delia craned her neck through the window of the car and away went her school hat, sailing over a bridge and down into a deep ravine below, lost forever so far as she was concerned, as the tram certainly would not stop and wait while she searched for it.

"You've come down a peg in life, old sport, that's all," laughed Carrie. "In Italy wearing a hat is a sign of gentility. No work-girl ever has one on her head even on Sundays. I offered a cast-off of mine to the bonne at a hotel once, and she eyed it longingly, but said she daren't wear it if she took it, her friends would think it such swank."

"What do they have on in church then?" asked Delia.

"Handkerchiefs, of course. Every Neapolitan has one handy to slip round her head at the church door. It must save millinery bills."

"And they all have the most beautiful hair. Hello! Here we are at the terminus. What a crowd of beggars. They look like brigands waiting to pounce on us. Help!"

Once out of the shelter of the tramcar the girls made the unpleasant discovery that in Italy begging is not forbidden, but quite a recognized profession with certain of the poorer classes. They were immediately surrounded by a ragged rabble, some of whom exhibited sores or other unsightly afflictions to compel compassion, and all of whom held out dirty hands and persistently clamored for money. The blind, the halt, and the maimed were there, evidently regarding tourists as their legitimate prey, and bent upon claiming all the charity they could get.

"Don't give them anything," commanded Miss Morley, anxiously keeping her little flock in tow, and shepherding them towards the piazza where the carriages could be hired. "Just say Niente, and shake your heads. Hold a safe hand on your purses and stick together. Don't get separated on any account."

With considerable difficulty they forced their way across the square, and thankfully took refuge in several waiting landaus, whose drivers, feeling sure of their patronage, promptly raised their terms high above the ordinary tariff. It was only after much bargaining on the part of Miss Morley that they consented to fix a reasonable sum for the excursion to Pompeii.

"Miss Morley talks Italian like a native, so they can't 'do' her," rejoiced Stella proudly. "Aren't they the absolute limit? No, I don't want to buy a comb, or corals, or brooches, or post-cards, or anything. They seem to think we're made of money. Why can't they let us alone? There, thank goodness, we're off at last and can leave the whole persuasive crew of them behind us!"

The five-mile drive from Castellamare was part of the fun of the excursion, but Pompeii was, of course, the main object, and there was much excitement when they at last drew up at the great iron gate. Miss Morley bought tickets for the party, and they were assigned a guide, a smiling Italian of superlative politeness, bearing a badge with the number 24 upon it.

"I asked for one who could speak English, but they're all out with other visitors," explained Miss Morley. "Never mind. It's a good opportunity of testing your Italian, and I can interpret if you don't understand."

In spite of the lantern-slides which they had previously been shown, the girls had come with varying expectations of what they were to see. Some imagined they would walk into a Roman city exactly as it stood when buried by the ashes of the great eruption of A.D. 79; others thought there would be a few interesting things peeping up here and there amid mounds of cinders. None had imagined it would be so large.

As a matter of fact the remains are simply the bare ruins of a town destroyed by burning ashes, which have been extricated from the rubbish accumulated during more than seventeen centuries. The paved streets and the roofless and broken walls of the houses still remain, with here and there some building that by a fortunate chance escaped, either in whole or in part, the general catastrophe, and suffice to show the general style and beauty of the Græco-Roman architecture of the first century. The guide marshaled his party along, pointing out to them the various objects of interest that had been excavated, the beautiful marble drinking-fountain, the marble counters of the shops, identical with those still used in Southern Italy, the wine jars of red earthenware, the hand-mills for grinding corn, the brick ovens, or the vaults where wine had been stored. They went into the site of the ancient market, and the Forum and several temples, and walked up long flights of steps and admired rows of broken columns, and saw the public swimming-baths with their tasteful wall decorations and the niches where the bathers had placed their clothes, and they admired the law-courts, and marveled at the great theater that had been wont to hold five thousand spectators.

The general impression was one of utter desolation. The mighty ruins lay in the bright Italian sunshine, and, close above, Vesuvius frowned over the scene, as if still watching the result of his deadly handiwork. Who had lived in those blackened fire-swept houses, and walked in those grass-grown streets? It was difficult to imagine the busy thronging crowds that once must have peopled all these silent haunts, where the only signs of life were the little green lizards that darted over the crumbling walls.

Certain of the best houses were railed round and kept carefully locked, and inside these could be seen what was left of the domestic life of civilized Pompeii. The girls enjoyed looking at the rooms in the Casa Dei Vettii, with the exquisite paintings of cupids still left upon the scarlet walls, they laughed at the quaint mosaic of the chained dog with its warning Cave Canem (Beware of the dog!), and they went into ecstasies over the lovely little statue of the Dancing Faun and some terracottas of Venus and Mercury. One link with the past was left in the fact that a few of the houses still preserved the names and even the portrait-busts of their former owners.

"My! Doesn't he look boss of the place still? I wonder if I ought to leave my visiting card for him," declared Delia, staring at the green marblerepresentation of Cecilius Giscondis, a banker by profession.

The others laughed. They had all been feeling rather oppressed, and were glad to break the ice.

"I'm so tired, I should think we must have walked miles," groaned Lorna.

"And I'm on the point of famishing," protested Irene, slapping her lunch-bag with a resounding smack.

Miss Morley turned round at the sound, and possibly caught the remark, for she spoke hastily to the guide, then suggested that the girls should sit in a row on a fallen column and consume their provisions.

"You all need a rest and something to eat now. Then we'll go on with our sightseeing, and have tea at the restaurant when we've finished," she decreed.

Never were ham sandwiches and oranges so acceptable. Viewing ruins may be extremely interesting, but it is a highly fatiguing occupation, and Delia at least had reached the stage of the over-burdened camel.

"I guess I don't like anything B.C. It's too depressing. Give me Paris!" she declared tragically.

"Cheer up, old sport!" consoled Irene. "I'm going to take a snap-shot of some of us when the guide isn't looking. You shall be in it. You'd like to send some prints to your friends in America, wouldn't you?"

"Rather! They'd burst with envy to see me photographed inside Pompeii. Where are you going to take us? I've finished my lunch. Let's get busy quick, before the guide comes round the corner."

Delia was prancing with eagerness. She flitted about like a butterfly, bent on choosing the best position for the desired snap-shot. Blanche, Mabel, and Elsie came hurrying up anxious to join the group, and fixed themselves in elegant poses.

"Oh, I can't put in such a crowd," objected Irene. "You block out the whole of the view. I only want Delia and Lorna, and yes, I'll have Désirée, but nobody else. Please clear out of the way."

"Well, really!"

"You mean thing!"

"We don't want to be in your old photo!"

Irene had felt cross and was possibly impolite, but she was not prepared for the Nemesis that descended upon her head. She had just congratulated herself that Blanche, Mabel, and Elsie had beaten a retreat and that she had been able to take her snap-shot so successfully, when who should make his unwelcome appearance but the guide, catching her in the very act of winding on her film. He sighed sorrowfully, and spread out his hands with a dramatic Italian gesture.

"Signorina! Non e permesso!" he objected.

"I'm awfully sorry. I won't do it again, really," murmured Irene, cramming the little camera back into her pocket.

But this apology did not content No. 24. He very courteously, but quite firmly, insisted upon temporarily confiscating the prohibited article. Miss Morley, who hurried up at the sound of the altercation, took the side of the authorities.

"Who brought a camera? Irene! You knew it was not allowed. Yes, you must let the guide have it. He'll give it back to you at the gate. I hope there won't be any trouble about it. I believe you can be fined. It was very naughty of you to do such a thing."

Much crestfallen Irene retired into the rear of the party, and bewailed the fate of her snap-shots.

"It was hard luck the guide should pop round the corner that exact minute," she groaned.

"Mabel fetched him," squeaked Désirée. "I could see over the railing, and I watched her go. She was mad that you wouldn't put her in the photo."

"What a sneaking trick to play. She's the meanest girl. I wouldn't have told about her. I hope No. 24 won't take the spool out of the camera, because there are three undeveloped snaps of the Villa Camellia on it, and I shall be wild if I lose them. He couldn't be so heartless. If I only knew Italian better I'd try and coax him."

The guide had obligingly waited while the girls ate lunch, but he now waxed impatient, and hurried his party on to the House of Pansa. This must have been quite a palatial residence, and showed such perfect examples of the arrangement of the various rooms in a Roman mansion that they lingered a long time looking at the atrium, the tablinum, the peristyle, and the kitchen with its curious mosaics of snakes. Now, though it was all very interesting, it was certainly tiring, and some of the girls grew weary of listening to the guide's descriptions in Italian or Miss Morley's explanations.

"I'm bored stiff," confessed Delia, in a whisper, linking on to Irene's arm. "If I have any more information crammed into my head it will burst. I know quite enough about ancient customs already. All I can say is I'm thankful I'm living now instead of then. Renie, if you love me, take me out of ear-shot of Miss Morley and let me chatter and frivol."

"Poor old sport!" laughed Irene. "Let's slip away and take another turn round the garden while the guide finishes haranguing. I'm out of friends with him since he stole my camera. He doesn't deserve anybody to listen to him. I've a few chocs left in this package. You shall have some to cheer you up. They're modern at any rate."

"You mascot!" murmured Delia. "Stella says I'm a Goth, but why need I like old things? Did the Pompeians take their schoolgirls to look at buriedGreek cities, or were they satisfied with their own times? How soon do you think we shall have tea? These chocs have saved my life, but I'm longing for bread and butter and buns."

"Why, we haven't finished lunch very long."

"I ate more than half of mine in the carriage, so I hadn't much left. Hello! Where have the others been? I didn't know there was a way up there."

The rest of the party were clattering down a flight of wooden steps with many expressions of admiration for what they had seen at the top.

"Perfectly beautiful! The finest view of all," purred Miss Morley. "Renie and Delia, didn't you go up? You silly girls. You've missed a treat. No, I'm afraid we can't wait now. The guide is anxious to take us on. We haven't seen the House of Sallust yet or the Street of Tombs. I want to ask him whether they've been doing any more excavations near the Herculaneum Gate."

Miss Morley, deep in conversation with No. 24, passed on, in the full belief that all her flock were following behind her. Irene and Delia, however, were determined to have just one peep at the view from the top of the wall, so both made a dash up the wooden staircase. From here there was a glorious prospect of the entire city with its arches and columns and broken temples, its cypress trees, and its somber background of smoking mountain. They could see exactly the way they had come from the entrance, and could tell which was the Street of Fortune and which the Street of Abundance. It was so fascinating that they lingered rather longer than they intended.

"They'll be waiting for us," ventured Irene at last.

"Oh, bother! So they will," exclaimed Delia, rushing down prepared for a scolding.

But the others had not waited. They had all simply walked on, and the custodian had locked the gate behind them. It was fast closed, and no amount of shaking would move it.

"We're shut in," gasped Irene. "Where's the porter? He ought to be somewhere about with the key."

The custodian, quite oblivious of the fact that anybody had been left inside the House of Pansa, was reading a newspaper and eating bread and garlic under his wooden shed farther down the street, where he would remain till the next guide came along with a party and requested admission. So he did not hear, though the girls thumped and called and made a very considerable noise. They were both horribly frightened.

"Shall we have to stay here all night?"

"I'd be scared to death."

"Think of the spooks!"

"Why the whole place must be simply chock-full of ghosts after sunset."

"Couldn't we jump from the wall?"

"I wish I'd never come. Oh, I hate things B.C.! I shall have fits in a minute."

Fortunately for Delia's nerves they were not kept long in durance vile. Lorna very soon discovered the loss of her buddy, drew Miss Morley's attention to the matter, and the whole party hastened back to look for them. The custodian was fetched from his wooden shelter and unlocked the door, loudly disclaiming any responsibility on his part, and blaming the guide.

"It's your own fault," scolded Miss Morley. "You really must keep with the party. I can't have any of you wandering off alone. You can't expect me to count you every time we come out of a building. I put you on your parole not to get separated again."

"We won't indeed, indeed! We don't like being lost," promised the delinquents earnestly.

Everybody, including the Principal, was very tired by this time, and not altogether sorry when the guide finished his tour of the ruins, and conducted them safely back again to the entrance.

"It's glorious, but you want days to see it in, instead of only a few hours," sighed Phyllis.

"And cast-iron backs and legs," agreed Sybil. "I shall enjoy thinking it over when I'm home, but I'm ready to drop at the present moment."

"What about my camera?" asked Irene anxiously.

The guide had not forgotten it; he produced it from his pocket, and — perhaps in consideration of the tip he had received from Miss Morley — he did not confiscate the spool, but handed it over intact with a polite gesture and a cryptic smile.

"Grazie molto — molto!" murmured Irene, which meant "Thanks awfully," and was one of the very few Italian phrases which she knew.

Everybody was extremely glad to adjourn to the restaurant, where tea had been ordered for their party, and a table reserved for them. The big room was full of visitors and rather noisy; a band of musicians in the center rendered Neapolitan songs to an accompaniment of mandolins and guitars, and occasionally the audience joined the choruses. The performance was not of the highest quality, but it was tuneful and interesting to those who had not before heard the folk-songs of Southern Italy. After tea the girls made a rush to buy post-cards and other mementoes of Pompeii, which were on sale in a room next to the restaurant, and would have spent half an hour over their purchases had not Miss Morley collected her flock and insisted on a homeward start. Poor little Désirée slept all the way back in the tramcar, with her head on Stella's shoulder, and most of the party were in much more sober spirits than when they had started. All felt, however, that it was a never-to-be-forgotten experience.

"I'd adore to go again sometime," ventured Lorna, clasping a model of a Pompeian lamp, which her chum had given her for a souvenir.

"So would I," agreed Irene. "Miss Morley calls this 'part of our education,' and I think it's a very sensible way of teaching things. I hope she'll take us to other places."

"You'll get Vesuvius if your conduct sheet is all right."

"Oh, lovely! I'd rather go there than even to Pompeii."

"The same this child," chipped in Delia. "Renie, I guess you and I will have to shake ourselves up and reform for a week or two. We were in Miss Morley's black book to-day, and if we don't take care we shall be left out of the next excursion."

"I'll be an absolute saint," promised Irene. "You'll see me sprouting wings. I'm going to draw a physical map of the world and mark in all the principal volcanoes, and then show it to Miss Morley. She'll think it so brainy of me and be so glad I'm interested in the subject. She'd really feel I ought to see Vesuvius after that."

"You schemer! It's not a bad idea though, and perhaps I'll do the same, though I hate drawing maps. Hello! Is this the piazza? I'd no idea we'd got back to Fossato so soon. Yes, it's been a 'happy day,' but I feel all I want now is supper and bed."

CHAPTER IX

Reprisals

It was immediately after this that Peachy, who was always doing imprudent things and running risks, went a little too far and caught a severe chill. She was moved into the sanatorium, a room at the top of the house, and spent three quite happy days in bed, reading books and magazines, and drinking hot lemonade, which was Miss Rodgers' favorite remedy for a cold. When she was certified as free from any infection, a few of her special chums were allowed to visit her. She petitioned specially for Jess, Delia, and Irene. They found her propped up with pillows, and looking very charming in a pale pink dressing-jacket and her hair tied back with a broad ribbon.

"Thanks very much. I'm sitting up and taking nourishment," she grinned, in reply to their commiserations. "I'm going to have some more fun before I pop off! Joking apart, I've had the time of my life here. It's been blissful just reading and resting, with a big jug of lemonade at my elbow."

"We've been talking about you downstairs. Didn't your ears burn?" asked Jess.

"Not more than usual. What were you saying about poor little me?"

"We had a special meeting of the Camellia Buds, and passed a vote of sympathy, for one thing. I suppose I ought to 'convey' it to you in the orthodox fashion."

"Highly gratified, I'm sure," chirped Peachy. "How do I return thanks, please? I can't get up in bed and bow. What next?"

"Well, the next is that nobody can think of anything original for the Transition to do at the carnival, and everybody said 'Ask Peachy,' so we've come to you for a suggestion."

"Whew! That's a big order," groaned the invalid. "We've had almost every kind of stunt that's practically possible. What are the seniors getting up this time?"

"Something musical, to judge from the practicing we hear. It sounds like operetta. And the juniors are having a fairy play. Miss Morgan is teaching them. What we want is something utterly and entirely different."

"Exactly!" agreed Peachy, taking a drink of lemonade.

"If you don't have a brain-throb we shall have to descend to an ordinary concert."

"Or a scene from Shakespeare."

"Or a tableau vivant."

"And those have been done simply dozens of times."

"I know," frowned Peachy. "We had 'The Trial Scene' from The Merchant of Venice ourselves last carnival. We couldn't give the same stunt again. Oh, don't bother me! Let me think. How can I get ideas when you're all talking at once?"

Peachy put her fingers in her ears and buried her head temporarily in the pillow, from which she appeared to draw inspiration, for in a few moments she sprang up with a bounce of rapture.

"Got it!" she announced cheerily. "Let's do a toy-shop. You shall all be dressed up as toy animals and be wound up to work. Oh, I see ever such possibilities. The seniors never had that at any rate."

"Good!"

"It sounds prime!"

"What a mascot you are."

"Don't breathe a word outside the form," warned Peachy. "I'll plan it all out and we'll have a rehearsal when I'm downstairs again. I guess we'll give them a surprise. Hand me my writing-pad, somebody, and a pencil. I want to get busy sketching costumes. I can see the whole thing in my mind's eye and it ought to be great."

Every year in the month of March the pupils at the Villa Camellia celebrated a carnival of their own. It coincided with a local festival at Fossato, on which occasion the inhabitants were wont to make merry, dressing themselves in fantastic costumes, parading the streets, and letting off fireworks. Originally the girls had been taken to see the gay doings, but the town was often so rough that Miss Rodgers had decided it was an unsuitable entertainment for young ladies, and, to prevent disappointment, made the happy suggestion that they should keep the festival in their own grounds. So each spring the three divisions of the school vied with one another in producing some fresh surprise, and had a very interesting and amusing afternoon in the garden or gymnasium, and were too busily occupied to feel any regret at being deprived of the sight of what was going on in Fossato.

Canon and Mrs. Clark and a few of Miss Rodgers' and Miss Morley's friends, who lived in the neighborhood, were generally invited to swell the audience of teachers. The juniors were given a little assistance by their form mistresses, but the seniors and the Transition managed their own affairs. Now it was a most unfortunate circumstance that at present the two sororities in the Transition were in direct opposition. Each was, of course, aware of the other's existence, but each society kept its own secrets. The Camellia Buds did not even know the name of their rival, though they could guess at its list of members. Peachy, recovered from her cold, came downstairs bubbling over with plans for a due celebration of the festival. She submitted them gleefully to the assembled girls, after French class. Much to her surprise about half of the form demurred.

"We're going to do something of our own," announced Bertha airily. "We don't want your stunt."

"Of our own? What d'you mean?" asked Peachy, her gray eyes snapping.

"I mean what I say. Some of us have arranged a little private performance—we're going to keep it to ourselves."

"And leave out the rest of us?"

"You can have one of your own."

"Well, I like that!" flamed Peachy. "You're dividing the form into two stunts. We've never done that before. Besides, who sent up a message asking me to think of something fresh and original? I certainly understood it was from all of you."

Peachy, in huge indignation, glared into several conscious and guilty faces, while her allies backed up her arguments by cries of "Shame!" Bertha turned rather red but bluffed the matter out.

"We changed our minds. We can't always do everything all in a lump. As I said before, we've got our own stunt, and you Camellia Buds can have yours."

Camellia Buds! If Bertha had dropped a bomb in the classroom she could not have caused greater consternation among the opposition. So the rival society knew the name of their sorority. A suppressed "O-o-h!" arose here and there. Evidently much enjoying their confusion Bertha and her confederates retired, leaving the poor Camellia Buds to hold an indignation meeting. Everybody talked at once.

"How did they find out?"

"Has anybody sneaked?"

"It's the absolute limit!"

"I couldn't have believed it!"

"It gives me spasms!"

"Of all mean things!"

"It makes me tingle!"

Then Jess, who was practical, made a suggestion.

"I vote we take an oath of every member that she hasn't betrayed us."

"'O wise young judge!'" quoted Agnes. "That's the best thing anybody's said yet. Let's stand round in a row and swear 'Honest Injun.'"

If the Camellia Buds sustained doubts of one another's integrity these were absolutely dispelled by the fervency with which each pleaded her innocence.

"Somebody must have been eavesdropping at one of our meetings, I suppose," sighed Agnes gloomily. "It's horrid to think they know our secrets and we don't know theirs. I'd give worlds to get even."

"Where do they meet?" asked Delia. "I've never been able to find out."

"They're very clever in hiding themselves."

"Yes, I expect they keep watch, and scoot whenever they see one of us."

"That's it, of course," said Irene. "Well, what we've got to do is to catch them off their guard. I vote we get the kids to help us. They detest Bertha and Mabel. They'd just adore to track them for us. We needn't exactly tell them why."

"Good for you, Renie Beverley. Those kids will do a turn for their fairy godmothers. We'll call another candy party and put them on the scout. I've a box of peppermint creams that will just go round. One apiece ought to be enough for them to-day."

The juniors were fond of peppermints, and even a limited candy party was in their opinion better than none at all. They had never received sweets of any description from Bertha or Mabel; indeed they regarded them as arch-enemies. The idea of keeping a watch over their movements appealed to them.

"We'll shadow them, you bet!" grinned little Jean Hammond. "There isn't much going on in the school that we don't know."

"I'm afraid there isn't. You're rather imps. But you'll be doing a good deed if you find this out for us. The first who brings news shall have two chocolates."

The Camellia Buds felt no more compunction in employing the juniors on this quest than a government that organizes a secret service department. The enemy had betrayed them shamelessly and deserved reprisals. It was Désirée after all who won the chocolates. She haunted house and garden with the persistency of a small ghost, and at last proudly made the announcement:

"They've called a meeting by the big Greek jar to-day at five. I heard Ruth tell Callie. What are you going to do about it?"

That was exactly the question which puzzled the Camellia Buds. It was one thing to obtain information and quite another to act upon it. If they went and interrupted the rival meeting they would have the satisfaction of routing the enemy but would be none the wiser. It was Peachy's diplomacy that pointed out a way.

"The Greek vase!" she said meditatively. "Yes, it's enormously big and I think I can manage it. Now, my dearies, don't you want to be real philanthropic this afternoon and give up your turns at the tennis courts to other folks? Why? Because I've a little scheme on hand. I want to keep those girls well away from the lemon pergola until it's time for their precious meeting. Then they'll run up all unsuspecting, poor innocents, and find – –"

"What will they find?"

"'A chiel amang them takin' notes!'" chuckled Peachy. "In other words yours truly will be hiding inside the big jar."

"Peachy! You can't!"

"Can't I? Great Scott! Do you think I'm going to let this beat me? You can just bet your last nickel I shall. Renie and Jess shall help to hide me, and the rest of you must watch the coast's clear till I'm safely inside. I tell you I'm crazy to try it. It'll be the frolic of my life."

There was certainly no plan too madcap for Peachy to undertake. She revelled in anything venturesome or bizarre. The Camellia Buds did as shedecreed, and resigned the courts that afternoon to Bertha, Mabel, Elsie, Ruth, Rosamonde, Winnie, Monica, and Callie, who fell readily into the trap prepared for them. Leaving this double set busy at tennis they fled to the opposite end of the garden.

The lemon pergola was a sheltered walk that led down a flight of marble steps to a small fountain. There was a shady nook here with bushes of bamboo, and a tree with a sweet flower like honeysuckle, and little red roses, and a border of Parma violets, and a seat made of bright green tiles — altogether a very retired and pleasant and suitable spot in which to hold a committee meeting. Exactly behind the seat stood an enormous jar of terra-cotta, colored red, and decorated with Greek figures in black silhouette, rather blurred and rubbed off, but still distinguishable. No doubt its original use had been to store water, wine, or olive-oil, but nowadays it was merely an ornament to the garden. A plant pot full of scarlet geraniums rested on its head, and an arbutula twined up the sides.

Peachy climbed up the bank behind, and with the help of Jess removed the pot of scarlet geraniums; then very cautiously and carefully she let herself down inside the jar. It was just big enough to contain her, and she lay concealed like one of the forty thieves in the story of Ali Baba. She had one advantage, however, over the famous brigands. There was a little round hole broken in the front of the jar, and by putting her eye to this she had an excellent view of her surroundings.

"Are you all right?" asked Irene anxiously.

"Fixed splendidly, thanks. Stick that flower-pot back on the top and nobody'll ever guess I'm inside. Now scoot, quick, for it won't do for them to see you haunting round. The place must look absolutely innocent when they arrive."

"We won't go too far. Shout for us if you get so you can't bear it any longer," said Jess, putting the geraniums on like a stopper, and dragging Irene away.

Peachy's position was certainly not one of comfort, squatting at the bottom of the great jar, and she was relieved that she had not long to wait before the rival sorority arrived to hold its meeting. The girls came scurrying, flushed after their games of tennis, and flung themselves down, some on the marble steps and some on the tiled seat. Bertha, as the Camellia Buds had suspected, was evidently the high priestess, and opened the ceremony without delay.

"Members of the Starry Circle," she began hurriedly, "repeat your oath."

"We vow to be loyal to one another and to our President, and never to reveal the secrets of our society," recited seven voices in reply.

("Aha!" chuckled Peachy to herself, in the depths of the gigantic jar. "Got the name of your precious sorority slap-bang off!")

"We've met together this afternoon," continued Bertha, "to settle finally what parts we're going to take at the carnival. Ruth, just look round, please, and be sure none of those wretched Camellia Buds is anywhere about."

Bertha paused, while Ruth made a tour among the bushes, and seemed slightly puzzled when the latter reported:

"Coast clear."

"It's a funny thing," commented the President, "but I declare I can smell that particular strong lily-of-the-valley scent that Peachy is so fond of. I suppose it's only fancy?"

"I can smell it too," confirmed Elsie, sniffing the air.

"Are there any lilies-of-the-valley out anywhere near?" asked Mabel.

"No, it's too early for them."

"Then somebody else must have the same scent, or have picked up Peachy's mouchoir by mistake."

A general examination of handkerchiefs followed, but each girl disclaimed all responsibility for the delicate odor.

"Queer! I can't understand it. However, let's get to business. Our waxworks are absolutely going to take the shine out of their stupid old toy-shop. The only trouble is how we're going to get hold of the right costumes. There's Queen Elizabeth now—I can manage her skirt, but I want something for her farthingale. What can we raise?"

"Peachy has a lovely flowered silk dressing-gown," remarked Mabel. "It would be just the thing."

"Suppose she uses it herself though."

"I won't give her a chance. I'll take it out of her cubicle the night before and hide it."

"O-o-h! You will! Will you?" exploded a voice from the interior of the Greek jar. "We'll just see about that."

The fact was that Peachy's crouching position had grown intolerable. She was bound to move and reveal herself, and her indignation at Mabel's cool suggestion flamed forth through the peep-hole.

The Circle sprang up in much alarm, and some of them squealed as the pot of geraniums fell with a crash from the top of the big jar, and Peachy's pink face and fluffy hair appeared instead. Her flashing gray eyes certainly held no love light in them.

"You mean things!" raged Peachy. "Call yourselves stars, do you? I can't see anything very star-like about you. Have your old waxworks if you like, but I can tell you beforehand you won't take the shine out of us. You've copied my idea shamelessly, and if you're going to steal our properties too—yes, you may well scoot. Don't ever dare to show your faces to me again."

For the members of the Starry Circle had broken up their meeting, and were running away down the lemon pergola in the direction of the house, immensely upset to find there had been a secret listener in their midst. Once they were out of sight Peachy cooeed for Jess and Irene, who appeared bursting with laughter and demanding details, having witnessed the rout of the enemy from a distance.

"I'll tell you presently if you'll help me climb out of this wretched thing," said Peachy, who found it a far more difficult matter to extricate herself from the jar than it had been to drop into it. "How'm I going to manage? Oh, don't pull my arms so, you hurt!"

It was indeed somewhat of a problem, and Peachy was beginning to feel seriously alarmed, when, fortunately, one of the gardeners came to the rescue, and tilted the jar over so as to allow her to crawl out.

"I feel like a released Slave of the Lamp, or a freed dryad, or something fairy-taley or mythological," she declared. "It was worth it, though, to see those girls' faces. Thank you, Giovanni! I'm ever so much obliged. Sorry if I've spoilt your bed of violets. Is that Delia calling us? Coming, dearie. Where are the rest of the Camellia Buds? I may as well tell my story to the whole bunch of you together. Then you'll see the sort of thing we're up against. They've taken our idea, and they're trying to beat us on our own ground. That's what it's all about."

CHAPTER X

The School Carnival

The Camellia Buds considered that they possessed a real grievance. The difference between an animated toy-shop and waxworks was so slight as to be immaterial. In both the figures would require to be wound up, after which they would perform various antics. The idea had certainly originated with Peachy, and the Starry Circle had merely copied it. Their stunt was in fact a shameless plagiarism.

"Why couldn't they have joined with us and we'd have done the toy-shop all together?" demanded Agnes crossly.

"Oh, I don't know. It's just their perversity. It'll look so stupid to have two separate shows. Whichever comes last will seem so stale after the other."

"Why, of course, ours will come first! It must!"

"There'll be a fight for it."

"We can't squabble at the carnival with Miss Rodgers and Miss Morley looking on. We'd better have our battle beforehand and get it over."

"Tell the Stars we mean to have first innings?"

"They'll never agree!"

"Look here, it's no use coming to open war with them. I vote we try diplomacy. Has anybody thought of the programs yet?"

"I heard the seniors groaning over having to paint covers for them."

"Well, let's go to them privately and volunteer to help. Then we shall have the opportunity of telling them that the Transition stunt is to be in two divisions, and that Part I will be taken by ourselves."

"Quite a brain-throb!"

"Renie, I'm beginning to admire you!"

"Peachy can paint beautifully!"

"So can Joan and Esther. Shall I go and say we offer to do six programs? Right-o! Come with me, Peachy. You're our champion wheedler."

The two delegates started at once on their diplomatic mission. They felt indeed that there was no time to be lost. They found several of the prefects collected in Rachel's bedroom, where possibly they were having a little private candy party, for there were sounds of a rustling of paper and a shutting of drawers before they were granted permission to enter the precincts. The Transition girls always envied the seniors' rooms. These were on the seaward side of the house, and their balcony had glorious views over the bay and the surrounding coast. The decorations were very tasteful. The walls were gray, with a stenciled frieze of hydrangeas, and there were soft-shaded Indian rugs on the polished wood floor. Rachel and her roommates had provided their own luxuries in the way of pretty cushions, table-covers, pictures, and flower-vases, and the general effect was of harmonious comfort.

"Well? What can I do for you?" inquired the head girl briefly, as Stella admitted the diplomats.

It was not a very encouraging reception. Possibly the prefects were annoyed at being disturbed in the midst of what they were doing.

Peachy, however, ignored Rachel's tone, and putting on her most winning smile inquired:

"We wonder if you're painting any program covers for the carnival?"

Rachel lolled back in her chair and retied the bow that terminated her long dark pigtail.

"Perhaps we are and perhaps we aren't," was her somewhat cryptic reply.

"The matter's in our hands entirely, of course," cooed Sybil, rocking to and fro on a cane sedia.

"I know," put in Irene, trying to be tactful. "We only thought that perhaps you might care to have a little help. Some of us would be ready to paint a few if you like."

This put a different complexion on the case. The seniors, always bristling for their privileges, resented idle curiosity—on the part of the Transition. But an offer of help was another matter.

"There certainly is a great number to be done," said Erica, with a beseeching look at Rachel.

The head girl thawed a little.

"Well, we shouldn't mind your taking a few off our hands," she conceded. "Half a dozen? Sybil, will you get those programs out of my drawer? Put anything you like on them—flowers, birds, figures, or landscapes. I'll lend you this to copy the printing from. Let me have them by Thursday if you can."

Rachel glanced meaningly at the door, as if she considered the interview might now with decency come to an end. Neither Peachy nor Irene took the hint, however. The main object of their mission had not yet been broached.

"You've not written the program inside yet," commented Peachy, opening one of the covers.

"We'll do that later."

"Shall we copy some for you?"

"Oh, no, thanks!"

Then Irene, growing desperate, blurted out what they had really come to say.

"The Transition stunt is to be in two parts this time. Bertha and Mabel are arranging one, and Peachy is getting up another. Do you mind putting ours down to come first?"

"Sorry, but I'm afraid it can't be done," yawned Rachel. "Bertha has been up and bagged first innings. I wrote it down, didn't I, Stella? Where's that list? Yes, here we are. The juniors are to come first, because Miss Morgan has trained them and she thinks they'll get the fidgets if they wait, and it's better to have their performance over. Then, of course, comes our stunt, and then the Transition."

"Could we possibly have our half of the Transition stunt before yours? It would make more variety."

"Most certainly not!"

Rachel's brow was puckered in a frown, and Sybil, from the depths of the rocking-chair, murmured, "Cheek!"

"We've got the program all fixed up, and we're not going to change it for anybody," chirped Erica.

"Any one who isn't satisfied needn't act," endorsed Rachel, with such a very decided glance at the door that the two delegates could no longer obtrude their presence, and were obliged to beat an unwilling retreat.

They walked along the passage very dissatisfied with the result of their mission.

"We've got all the fag of painting these wretched programs, and gained nothing at all," groused Irene.

"They might have told us first about Bertha. Isn't she an absolute Jacob — supplanting us like this?"

"Those seniors are most unsympathetic. I want to go back and tell Rachel what I think of her."

"She'd only say, 'How foreign' if you got excited. And it wouldn't be an atom of use either."

"They've taken the best place in the program for their stunt."

"Trust the prefects to do that."

"What's to be done about it?"

"It will need some thinking over."

Peachy's agile brains were rarely to be beaten. She slept upon the problem, and informed her friends afterwards that inspiration came to her at exactly 3 a.m.

"I know, because I heard the convent clock strike. I sat up in bed and laughed. I wonder I didn't wake the dormitory, but nobody stirred a finger. Listen, and I'll explain. The situation at present is this: Bertha and her Starry Circle have cribbaged our idea and forestalled us on the program, and are going to act their wretched waxworks first, and are congratulating themselves that their piece will take the shine out of ours."

"So it will, I'm afraid. The audience will have sat through the juniors' play, the seniors' stunt, and the waxworks. They'll be bored stiff to see our toy-shop straight away afterwards."

"Well, they shan't see it. That's my idea. Let's drop the toy-shop and do something quite different."

"Drop our toy-shop! O-o-h!"

"We'll do it some other time. But you see we've one advantage on the program at any rate. We come last."

"That's what we're raving against."

"I know! But if you think of it, it's a great opportunity. Suppose we do a splendid finishing tableau instead of animated toys? It would make a magnificent wind-up, and would be a surprise for everybody. Think of the amazement of the Starry Circle, when they're expecting us to do a pale copy of their own stunt, to see us posed as a tableau, and everybody clapping the roof off."

"It would be rather sporty."

"Only I did so want to dress up as a kangaroo," mourned Joan dolefully.

"You shall be Australia instead, and you'll look far nicer. I'll guarantee to make you ever so pretty. It's to be an Anglo-American pageant, to symbolize the school. We'll have Columbia and Britannia and all her colonies, in a sort of entente cordiale. You'll see it will please Miss Morley and Miss Rodgers no end. That Starry Circle will be just aching with envy. They'll wish they'd been in it. It will absolutely take the wind out of their sails and lay them flat."

"Peachy Proctor, there's a spice of genius in your composition," said Jess admiringly. "I could never have thought of that myself."

"Oh, fiddlesticks! Glad you approve though. Now what we've got to do is to hustle up and get busy over costumes. They'll take some contriving. Hide all your best things away from the Stars, or they'll be commandeering them. Mabel has no conscience. And be careful that not the least teeny-weeny hint leaks out. Let's talk openly about the toy-shop, and pretend we're still going on practicing for it. It will be all the bigger sell for them when they find out."

The Camellia Buds, having undertaken to paint six program covers, nobly did their duty and finished them in the prescribed time. Lorna offered to take them to Rachel's room, and met with quite a gracious reception from the head girl. So much so that she ventured to put forward a suggestion of her own.

"May Part I of the Transition stunt have a time limit?" she asked. "We want to have some idea when we're to come on."

"Certainly," agreed Rachel. "We can't let Part I go on ad infinitum. I hadn't thought of that. I shall tell Bertha she may have ten minutes and no longer. I shall ring the curtain bell if she exceeds. I see your point entirely. It's only fair."

"I was afraid if it was getting near tea-time the audience mightn't want to stay."

"Exactly. I'll take care your stunt isn't crowded out. Trust that to me. I'm not head girl here for nothing. And I'm not entirely blind either. My advice is to look after yourselves."

Lorna returned to the Camellia Buds feeling she had considerably scored over the Stars. Her previous acquaintance with school theatricals had taught her that audiences are human, that even teachers will not sit through too lengthy a performance, and that the lure of tea cannot be resisted by those who are accustomed to drink it daily at 4 p.m. As their own dormitory was half in possession of the enemy, Irene and Lorna adjourned to Peachy's bedroom to make preparations for their costumes, and held cosy sewing-bees in company with Delia, Jess, Mary, and any other chums who were able to join them. They kept their properties safely locked up inside one of the wardrobes in No. 13, and Peachy wore the key tied under her skirt with a piece of ribbon.

"Because you can't trust that sneaking Mabel not to come in and poke about," she explained grimly. "I know she wants my dressing-gown."

"We shall have to gallop with our costumes if we're to make anything of a show," said Sheila, hastily running seams in a creation of scarlet and blue, destined to clothe Canada.

"I know, but we'll wear them even if they've got raw edges and are fastened together with pins. I don't suppose the audience will be near enough to see the stitches. I hope not, at any rate. Mine are absolute cats' cradles."

By the day of the festival, however, the Camellia Buds were exactly ready. They had kept their secret strictly, and flattered themselves that their rivals the Stars were in complete ignorance of their change of program. The acting was to be in the gymnasium, not in the garden, for a sirocco wind was blowing and the overcast sky promised rain. It was a pity, for the pergola would have made such a beautiful background, and some enthusiasts even petitioned Miss Morley to keep to her original plan.

"And have you all wet through, and the guests shivering with cold?" she replied. "No, indeed! Be thankful we have such a large room as the gymto act in. Otherwise the fête would have been put off altogether."

The girls were allowed, however, to decorate the platform with flowers, and to hang up Chinese lanterns so as to give a festive appearance to the scene. The performers donned their costumes in good time, but wore waterproofs over them to conceal them. They wished to witness each other's stunts, yet did not want to reveal their own secrets too soon. There was quite a good audience assembled in the gymnasium. Miss Rodgers and Miss Morley had sent out many invitations, and some parents and friends had come over from Naples to combine a peep at the celebrated Fossato festival with a visit to the school. Irene's cup of joy was full when, to her utter amazement, she saw her own father, mother, and brother walk into the room.

"Well! You are a surprise package," she exclaimed, greeting them gleefully. "Why didn't you write and tell me you were coming?"

"We didn't know ourselves," said Vincent. "We never thought we could manage to get off, and we didn't want to disappoint you. When does your stunt come on?"

"Not till the end, so I can sit with you most of the time. Oh! It's simply too good to have you all turn up like this. Mother darling, there's a chair for you here, and I'll be in the middle between you and Daddy."

The entertainment began with a fairy play acted by the juniors. They looked very pretty in their gauzy garments, and little Désirée, in a gossamer robe of elfin green, made an attractive queen, so dainty and ethereal that the audience almost expected to see through her. "What a sweet child!" was the general comment, as she tripped back in response to a storm of clapping, to give an encore to her "Moonbeam Song."

The juniors retired, having covered themselves with glory, greatly to the satisfaction of Miss Morgan, who had spent much time in training them for their performance.

It was now the turn of the seniors. They had got up an operetta of Robin Hood, and appeared clad in the orthodox foresters' costume of Lincoln green, with bows, arrows, and quivers. Stella, as Maid Marian, and Phyllis, as the Curtle Friar, were especial successes; while Will Scarlett and Little John gave a noble display of fencing with quarter-staves, a part of the program which they had practiced in secrecy, under the instruction of the gymnastic mistress, and now presented as a complete surprise to the school. Their acting was so spirited that everybody was quite sorry when the short piece was ended, and would have liked certain scenes repeated, had not Miss Morley pointed to her watch and shaken her head emphatically to forbid further encores. Past experience had warned her not to allow one section of the school to monopolize an undue share of the time to the exclusion of others.

"It's the turn of the Transition now," she said. "We shall only just work through our program by half past four."

Even the Camellia Buds, though they watched with jaundiced eyes, could not deny that the members of the Starry Circle managed their waxworks very creditably. Elsie indeed, as Madame de Pompadour, was not convincing, but Mabel made a distinguished Sir Walter Raleigh, and Bertha surpassed herself as Queen Elizabeth. The rival sorority, after witnessing this triumph, was more and more thankful to have abandoned the idea of acting an animated toy-shop. It would certainly have seemed tame to continue on the same lines as the prior performance. As it was they chuckled with satisfaction behind the curtain, while they arranged themselves for the tableau.

"I guess it will make them sit up," purred Peachy, setting a curl straight with the aid of her pocket-mirror. "It will be frightfully hard to keep still, for I shall just want to stare round and see their faces, but don't alarm yourselves. I promise not to give so much as a blink. I wouldn't disgrace our stunt for the world. I'll be a rigid marble statue till the curtain drops."

"Sh! sh! Don't chatter so much," warned Jess. "Aren't you ready yet? Miss Morley's getting impatient."

"It's nearly half past four, and I expect everybody is longing for tea," put in Irene.

"They'll have to wait for it till we've done our stunt. We're not going to be left out," said Peachy, hurriedly taking her pose.

The allegorical scene in which the girls were grouped presented a pretty picture as the curtain rose.

In the center Agnes and Delia, dressed as Britannia and Columbia, supported the Union Jack and the Stars and Strips together with a bunch of camellias as a delicate compliment to the school; Jess, in plaid and tam-o'-shanter, stood for her native Scotland; Peachy, with fringed leather leggings and cowboy's hat, was a ranch-girl; Joan in a somewhat similar costume represented "the bush" in Australia; Sheila in a white coat trimmed plentifully with cotton wool made a pretty Canada; Irene was an Irish colleen; Mary, with bunches of mimosa, typified South Africa; and Esther, gorgeous in Oriental drapery and numerous necklaces, was an Indian princess. But perhaps the most successful costume of all was Lorna's. She had been chosen to take the character of New Zealand, and was dressed in a pale yellow wrapper decorated with beautiful sprays of tinted leaves. Round her head was a garland of orange blossoms, and in her arms she held great branches of oranges and lemons, to typify the fruits of the country she was impersonating. With Lorna's dark eyes and hair the effect was most striking. She kept her pose admirably, scarcely blinking an eyelid, though Mary palpably moved, and even Joan was guilty of a smile. The audience, immensely surprised and pleased with the tableau, clapped enthusiastically. It was felt to be a very fitting finish to the festival.

"You kept your secret well, girls," said Miss Morley, as she congratulated them afterwards. "I'm sure nobody had the least hint. It was charmingly thought out and arranged. Come along now and have some tea. It has really been a most successful afternoon."

Audience and performers, the latter in all the glory of their pretty costumes, mingled together now for conversation and tea-drinking. Irene quickly joined her family, and had much to say to them, and many questions to ask about their doings in Naples.

"I say, Renie," whispered Vincent, suddenly interrupting her, "tell me who's that lovely girl? She looked the best in the whole of your tableau."

Irene followed his glance to the yellow-clad figure handing the teacups which Miss Morley was filling.

"That's Lorna. One of my best chums. Yes, that costume suits her. I want to bring her to speak to Mother. Yes, Lorna, you must come. I simply shan't let you run away. Mummie darling, this is Lorna. We room together, you know."

Lorna, dragged forward much against her will to be introduced, stood shy and blushing, but her heightened color and evident confusion added to her attraction, and several heads were turned to glance at her among the guests in that quarter of the room. It was not until this occasion of the carnival that any one at the Villa Camellia had recognized Lorna as a budding beauty.

"You ought always to wear yellow," Peachy said to her afterwards. "It's quite your color. By the by, who chooses your clothes for you?"

"Miss Rodgers generally takes me to Naples and buys them."

"She's no taste. Her ideas run to a gym suit and a school panama and nothing beyond. I'll give you a tip. Next time you need an evening dress or a Sunday jumper, engineer it so Miss Morley does the shopping. She'll get you something pretty, I'll guarantee. She chose that blue crêpe de chine for Delia. Don't forget. And don't look so fearfully surprised. If you haven't

102

thought about your clothes before it's time you did. My dear, you'll pay dressing. Come close and I'll whisper to you: some of those Stars are just too jealous of you for words. I'm tickled to bits."

CHAPTER XI

Up Vesuvius

On a certain day towards the end of March, Miss Morley, who usually acted as cicerone and general guide, arranged to take a select little party up Vesuvius. Irene, Lorna, Peachy, and Delia were among the favored few, and congratulated themselves exceedingly. It is certainly not an every-day occurrence for schoolgirls to view a volcano, and this particular excursion, being long and difficult, was kept as a special treat, and was regarded as the titbit of the various expeditions from the Villa Camellia. Many of the girls had, of course, made it on former occasions, but to those whom Miss Morley was escorting to-day it was all new.

"I was to have gone last autumn," confided Peachy, "but the fact is I got into a little fix with Miss Rodgers, and she started on the rampage and canceled my exeat. I cried till I was simply a sopping sponge, but she was a perfect crab that day. Lorna, weren't you to have gone too once before?"

"Yes, and got toothache. Just like my luck. There the others were starting off, and I was sitting by the stove with a swollen face, dabbing on belladonna, and Miss Rodgers careering round telling me I must have it out. Ugh! My ailments always turn up when I'm going anywhere."

"Well, you're all right to-day at any rate," consoled Delia, rather unsympathetically.

"If I don't get seasick on the boat."

"Oh, buck up! You mustn't. We'll throw you overboard to the fishes if you do anything so silly. For goodness' sake don't any one start symptoms and spoil the fun. Where's Miss Morley? I'm just aching to be off."

The party left Fossato by the early morning steamer and went straight to Naples. They drove from the quay to the station, then took the little local train for Vesuvius. Italian railways generally provide scant accommodation for the number of passengers, so there ensued a wild scramble for seats, and it was only by the help of the conductor, whom she had judiciously tipped, that Miss Morley managed to keep her flock together, and settle them in one of the small saloon carriages. Here they were wedged pretty tightly among native Italians, and tourists of various nations, including some voluble Swedes and a company of dapper Japanese gentlemen, who were seeing Europe. After much pushing, crowding, shouting, and gesticulation on the part of both the public and officials, the train at last started and pursued its jolting and jerky way. It ran first through the poorer district of Naples, where dilapidated houses, whose faded walls showed traces of former gay pink, blue, or yellow color-wash, stood in the midst of vegetable gardens; then, the slums left behind, the line passed a long way among vineyards and orchards of almond, peach, and cherry that were just bursting into glorious lacy blossom. The railway banks were gay with the flowers which March scatters in Southern Italy, red poppies, orange marigolds, lupins, campanulas, purple snapdragons, and wild mignonette, growing anywhere among stones and rocks, with the luxuriance that in northern countries is reserved for June.

At Torre Annunziata the party from the Villa Camellia all crowded to the carriage window, for Miss Morley had something to point out to them.

"We're passing over the lava formed by the great eruption in 1906. The whole of the railway line and ever so many houses were buried then. Don't you see bits of them peeping out over there?"

"Why, yes, it looks like cinders," commented Lorna.

"They're great masses of crumbling lava turning into soil. Wait till we get farther on, then you'll see lava more in its raw stage. Very soon we shall be passing over the top of Herculaneum. The ancient city lies buried thirty feet below the surface."

"Aren't they ever going to excavate it like they did Pompeii?"

"The trouble is that the modern town of Pugliano is built over the top, and naturally the owners don't want their houses pulled down, whatever treasures in the way of Greek or Roman antiquities may lie buried underneath. Isn't the view of the Bay of Naples beautiful from here?"

"Yes, and the flowers. It's like fairyland."

At Pugliano the party left the train, and after a long and tiresome wait at the station changed to the light electric railway that was to take them up Vesuvius. The little carriage resembled a tramcar, and its wide glass windows afforded excellent views of the scenery en route. Up—up—up they went, gradually getting higher and higher. It was marvelous how the vegetation altered as they ascended. The cactuses, olives, almonds, and peach orchards gave way to hillsides covered with small chestnut, oak, or poplar trees, and the poppies and daisies were succeeded by broom bushes and clumps of rosemary. They were getting on to the region of the lava, and all the ground was brown, like newly turned peat. Men were busy digging terraces in the volcanic earth, to plant vines, working calmly as if the great cone above them had never belched forth fire and ashes.

"How dare they live here?" shuddered Peachy, pointing to the tiny dwellings which had been reared here and there. "When they see all the ruin round them, aren't they afraid? What makes them go back?"

"The ground is so rich," explained Miss Morley. "Nothing grows vines so splendidly as volcanic earth. The people get fatalistic, and think it worth risking their lives to have these fruitful little farms. They say the mountain may not be angry again for years, and they will take their chance."

"It's smoking now," said Lorna.

"I suppose it's safe?" asked Delia anxiously.

"Perfectly safe to-day or we shouldn't have been allowed to go up in the electric railway. Do you see that big building—the observatory? Careful investigations are made every day of the crater, and the results telegraphed down to Naples. If there were the slightest hint of danger the trains would be stopped and tourists turned back."

The journey was ever upwards, over great wastes of rough brown lava, which looked as if some giant, in play, had squeezed out the contents of enormous tubes of oil paint on to the mighty palette of the mountain side. The air had grown fresh and cold, for they were at an altitude approaching 4000 feet, and, but for the scenery, might have imagined themselves in Wales or Scotland.

The light railway ended at a small station, where there was the observatory and a hotel. All round were masses of enormous cinders, and above, a grim sight, towered the immense cone of Vesuvius. To scale the tremendous incline to the summit there was a funicular railway, to which our party now transferred themselves, sitting on seats raised one above another as in the gallery of a theater. It was here that, if the events of the day are to be truly chronicled, we must record a scrimmage between Irene and her chum, Peachy. The conductor of the light railway had gathered a bunch of rosemary en route, and he now approached the funicular and bestowed his offering upon Peachy, who happened to be sitting nearest to the end. She was immensely gratified at the attention, sniffed the fragrant nosegay, and handed it on for admiration to Lorna, who, after also burying her nose in it, passed it to Irene. The latter ought to have realized it was not her own property, but unfortunately didn't. She calmly appropriated the bunch, and distributed it in portions to those nearest her. Peachy's cheeks flamed. She was a hot-tempered little soul underneath her gay banter.

"Well! Of all cool cheek," she exploded. "That was my bouquet. It was given to me, not to you, Renie Beverley. Next time you start being charitable use your own flowers, not mine. You haven't left me a single piece."

"I'm sorry," blushed Irene, trying to collect some portion at least of her offerings to hand back to the lawful owner. "I thought they were given to me."

"No, you didn't, you simply bagged them," snapped Peachy. "I'm not friends with you, so don't talk to me any more," and Peachy turned a red offended face out of the carriage window.

Irene might have apologized further, but the funicular gave a mighty jerk at that moment, and the carriage started. Up—up went the little train, working on wire ropes like a bucket coming out of a well. Higher and higher and higher it rose up the terrific incline, over masses of cinders, towards the thick cloud of smoke that loomed above. It stopped at last at a big iron gate, which opened to admit the passengers on to the summit. Here the guides were waiting, and after some parleying in Italian, Miss Morley engaged a couple of them to escort her party. Led by these men, who knew every inch of the way, they started to walk to the crater of the volcano. A cinder path had been made along the edge of the cone, having on the left side a steep ridge of ashes, and on the right a sheer drop of many thousand feet. From this strange road there were weird and beautiful effects—for it was above the region of the clouds, which floated below, sometimes hiding the landscape, and sometimes revealing glorious stretches of country, with gleams of sunshine falling on the white houses of towns miles below, and blue reaches of sea with mountains beyond. Great volumes of smoke kept coming down from the summit, and blowing in a dense cloud, then clearing for a few minutes and forming again. There were booming sounds like the firing of cannons that seemed to issue from the smoke.

Very much awed by these impressive surroundings the party kept close together. The guides, in their gray uniforms and caps with red bands, were a comforting feature of the excursion. But for their encouragement the girls would have been too much scared to proceed. Delia was clinging to Peachy, and Lorna held Irene's arm tightly. Miss Morley, who had been before, kept assuring everybody that there was no danger, and after a few minutes they grew sufficiently accustomed to the scene to thoroughly enjoy the magnificent effects of the clouds circling below them. But the guides were calling "Haste," for the mist was clearing, and it would be possible to get a view of the crater. They all scurried along the path, and suddenly to the left, instead of the high ridge of cinders, they could look down into a deep rocky ravine. From this hollow vapors were rising as from a witch's cauldron, but every now and then the wind dispersed them as if lifting a veil, revealing a glimpse of the crater. At the bottom of the ravine stood a great cone, from the mouth of which poured dense clouds of smoke, and between the smoke could be seen fire, as if the interior of the cone were a red-hot furnace. Sometimes the vapors were shadowy as gray phantoms, sometimes glowing red with the reflection of the fire within, and as they whirled round the dim ravine loud explosions broke the silence. The view was as fleeting and evanescent as a landscape in a dream; one minute there would be nothing but a bank of mist and deadly stillness, the next a vision of fire and sounds that rent the mountain air.

"It's like looking into the bottomless pit," shivered Delia.

"Oh, but it's magnificent!" gasped Peachy.

"I'd no idea it would be so grand as this," said Irene. "I wouldn't have missed it for worlds."

"Come along, girls. The guides can take us farther," said Miss Morley. "Don't be frightened, for it's perfectly safe, and they won't let us go into any danger."

So they went some way along the mountain and turned down a side path towards the crater. It was difficult walking, for they were all among lava and sliding cinders, but the guides kept close by them, and helped them over difficult places. When they had descended perhaps a hundred feet or so, the ground became percolated with steam, jets of it poured from holes among the rocks, and the cinders upon which they stood felt warm to their boots. The guides brought the party to a halt upon a ledge of volcanic rock, from below which ran a sheer slide of hot cinders into the ravine. From here there was a splendid near view of the cone, its top yellow with sulphur, and at its base a lake of molten lava. One of the guides, a venturesome fellow, climbed down by another path and fetched lumps of sulphur as souvenirs for the girls, and the other guide pressed upon them pieces of lava into which, while hot, he had inserted coins, so that they had set into the mass when cool. They were naturally immensely delighted with these mementoes, and put them in their pockets, quite unsuspecting of the sequel that was to ensue.

It was a fearful scramble back up the steep path over the sliding cinders. The guides held out a stick or a hand to help at awkward corners, and being young and active the party managed to scale the side of the ravine and regain the summit of the mountain without any accidents, though Delia confessed afterwards that she had fully expected to tumble backwards and roll into the lava, a fear which Miss Morley pooh-poohed entirely.

"There was no danger unless you fainted, and the guides were close at your elbow the whole time," she declared.

The smiling officials in the gray uniforms and red-banded caps had indeed seemed the good geniuses of the excursion, but alack! they exhibited a different aspect when they had conducted their party back to the entrance of the funicular railway. Not satisfied with the payment which the government tariff allowed them to charge, they demanded from each of the visitors exorbitant tips in consideration of the little lumps of sulphur and lava which they had given them from the crater. The girls, who had supposed these to be presents, were most indignant.

"Five francs for a scrap of sulphur!"

"And we'd just called him such a kind man!"

"Let him keep his wretched souvenirs!"

"No, no! I want mine!"

"It's too bad!"

"I want my money to buy post-cards!"

"It's absolute blackmail!"

The guides, no longer smiling and obliging, but clamoring loudly for extra money, were finally settled with by Miss Morley, who knew the customs of the country, and was aware that they would be quite content with less than half of what they had asked.

"It's always the way in Naples," she said philosophically, as she thankfully bundled her flock into the funicular. "You can't get along anywhere without tipping. The government may try its best to arrange fixed prices, but every one who goes sightseeing must be prepared to part with a good deal in the way of small change. The guides are not such brigands as they used to be, thank goodness. Thirty or forty years ago I suppose it was hopeless to come unless you brought a courier with you from Naples to keep the others off. Well, you have your little souvenirs of Vesuvius at any rate, even if they've turned out rather expensive ones. They're something to keep, aren't they?"

"I wouldn't have given up mine if they'd asked me twenty dollars for it," declared Peachy, fondling the nickel coin set in the lump of lava.

"I don't understand the Neapolitans," frowned Irene. "One minute they're so charming and persuasive and winning and gay, and the next they're absolute bandits."

"They're a mixed race, with a good deal of the Spaniard in them," explained Miss Morley. "We must make certain allowances for their southern temperaments and customs. They're very poor, and they look upon American and British tourists as made of money, and therefore fair game to befleeced. The best plan is to take them quite calmly, and never lose your temper however excited they may get. When you've lived here for a time you learn how to treat them."

By this time they had reached the bottom of the funicular, and were back in the little station near the observatory. A picturesque woman, with a yellow shawl round her shoulders, and long gold earrings in her ears, came hurrying up to sell post-cards, and offered to show the party the quickest way into the hotel. As every one was very tired and hungry Miss Morley succumbed to the voice of this siren, and permitted her to escort them by what she assured them would be a short cut and would save many steps.

111

But alas for Italian veracity! Their suave and smiling guide led them down a path at the back of the hotel to a shabby and dirty little restaurant of her own, where she vehemently assured them she would provide them with a far cheaper meal, an offer which, at the sight of the crumby table-cloth, they resolutely refused.

"The old humbug! I'd no idea she was decoying us away from the hotel. Really nobody can be trusted up here," fumed Miss Morley. "Come along, girls. I told the conductor to reserve a table for us, and there won't be time to have lunch before the train starts unless we're quick."

So they all hurried back again up the path—much to the chagrin of the siren—and found their own way into the hotel, where seats had been kept for them in the restaurant, and dishes of macaroni and vegetables and cups of hot coffee were in readiness.

The great attraction to the girls was the fact that if they bought post-cards at the hotel these could be stamped by the conductor of the train with the Vesuvius postmark, and posted in a special pillar-box at the station. The idea of sending cards to their friends actually from the volcano itself was most fascinating, and they scribbled away till the last available moment.

"I guess some homes in America will be startled when they see these," purred Peachy, addressing flaming representations of an eruption. "It ought just to make Nell Condy's eyes pop out."

"I'm only afraid they won't believe we've really been," sighed Delia, skeptically.

"They'll have to, with the Vesuvius postmark. The post-office can't tell fibs at any rate. I call these cards a bit of luck. Be a sport, somebody, and lend me an extra stamp. I'm cleared out, and haven't so much as a nickel left."

"Hurry, girls, or we shan't get places in the train," urged Miss Morley, sweeping her party from the hotel into the station, where other tourists were beginning to crowd into the carriages.

The platform was a characteristic Italian scene; a blind man with a guitar was singing gay Neapolitan songs in a beautiful tenor voice, a woman with a lovely brown-eyed baby was calling oranges, an old man with a red cap and a faded blue umbrella under his arm offered specimens of hand-made lace, while a roguish-looking girl tried to sell cameos carved in lava, throwing them on to the laps of the passengers as they sat in the train. Irene, who was beginning to learn Italian methods of purchase, commenced to bargain with her for a quaintly cut mascot, reducing the price asked lira by lira till at length, when the conductor blew his brass horn, she finally got it for exactly half of what was at first demanded.

"And quite enough too," said Miss Morley, who had watched the business with amusement. "She's probably more than satisfied, and will go dancing home to her mother. Let me look, Irene? This funny little hunchback is always considered the 'luck' of Vesuvius. I believe he's copied from a model found in Pompeii. He's the true mascot of the mountain. Yes, he's quite a pretty little curio and well worth having."

"I wish I'd had any money left to buy one with," sighed Peachy.

The train was speeding downhill now, leaving ashes and lava behind, and heading for the bright bay where the sun was shining on the sea. Seen from above against a gray background of olives and other trees not yet in leaf, the blossoming peaches and apricots had a filmy fairy look most beautiful to behold. Behind frowned the great volcano still belching out clouds of smoke.

"I've a different impression of old Vesuvius now I've seen his heart," said Peachy, looking back for a last farewell view.

"He still seems full of mischief, but I'm glad he played no tricks while we were up there," commented Delia.

"It's certainly one of the sights of the world, and I'm glad I've seen it," said Lorna. "Yes, I don't mind telling you I was scared when these explosions kept popping off. I thought it was going to erupt and give us the benefit."

Irene, when they were back at the Villa Camellia, patched up her squabble with Peachy, whom she had offended over the rosemary incident, and pressed the Vesuvius mascot upon her as a peace offering.

"I didn't mean to grab your flowers," she assured her. "Really, honest Injun, I didn't."

"Why, I'd forgotten all about it," declared her light-hearted chum. "I didn't mind a bit after my 'first mad' cooled off. Sorry if I was a bear. No, I won't take your lucky hunchback. Must I? Well, you're a dear! I'd adore to have it. I felt absolutely green when I saw you buy it. I'll hang him on a chain and wear him round my neck, and I expect I'll just be a whiz at tennis to-morrow. Oh, isn't he funny? Thanks ever so! I shall keep him eternally as a memory of this ripping day up old Vesuvius."

CHAPTER XII

Tar and Feathers

After the decided triumph of their Anglo-American tableau at the carnival, the Camellia Buds held up their heads against their rivals, the Starry Circle. There was hot competition between the two sororities, each continually trying to "go one better" than the other. If the Stars held a surreptitious candy party, the Buds, at the risk of detection by Rachel or some other prefect, gave a dormitory stunt, throwing out hints afterwards of the fun they had enjoyed. Both societies produced manuscript magazines, which were read in strict privacy at their meetings, and contained pointed allusions to their enemies' failings. No old-fashioned Whigs and Tories could have preserved a keener feud, the division between them waxing so serious that sometimes they could hardly sit peaceably side by side in class.

"It's all Mabel," declared Jess. "Of course we had two sororities before she came, but we weren't at daggers drawn like this. Mabel has spoiled Bertha, and those two lead everything — the rest are simply sheep."

"Humph! Pretty black sheep I should call them," snorted Peachy. "They're siding with one another now to break rules. I don't mean candy parties or just fun of that kind, but sneaking things: they're cheating abominably over their exercises, and cribbing each other's translations wholesale. I found them at it yesterday and told them what I thought about them. Some of them ought to know better. Rosamonde and Monica aren't really that sort."

"They're bear-led by Bertha and Mabel. I lay all the blame on them. It would be a good thing for the Stars if that precious pair could be caught tripping and taught a lesson."

"I dare say it would but it's not an easy business," said Peachy gloomily. "Mabel Hughes is an extremely slippery young person, and she generally manages to keep out of open trouble. I don't suppose any of the teachers, or even the prefects, have the least idea what she's really like."

"And we can't go sneaking and tell them, so we must try and engineer the matter for ourselves."

It was undoubtedly true that with the advent of Mabel Hughes a new and unpleasant element had crept into the Transition. Such an influence is often very subtle. Girls who a term ago would not have condescended to any form of cheating, accepted a lower standard of honor, and tried to excuse themselves on the ground that they merely did the same as others. The fact that the Camellia Buds did not share in the dishonesty was set down to priggishness on their part, Bertha and Mabel often making jokes at their expense. One day an unpleasant matter happened in the school. It was the fortnightly examination, and when the Transition took their places at their desks, with sheets of foolscap and lists of questions, it was found that the inkwells of each member of the Camellia Buds had been stuffed up with blotting-paper, so that it was impossible for them to dip their pens.

Miss Bickford, who did not even know of the existence of the sororities, and therefore could not perceive the significance of the fact that certain girls were thus served while others went free, flew into a towering rage, and accused Peachy, whose reputation as a practical joker was not altogether undeserved, of having played the shameless "joke." Peachy, smarting with the injustice of the false charge, forgot herself and retorted hotly.

"Priscilla Proctor!" thundered Miss Bickford. "I have sometimes excused high spirits, but I never allow impertinence and insubordination. Leave the room instantly and go upstairs to the sanatorium. You'll remain there until you apologize."

A dead hush fell over the class as Peachy, with flaming eyes and chin in the air, flounced out and slammed the door after her. It was an extreme measure at the Villa Camellia to banish a girl to the sanatorium, a public disgrace generally administered only by one of the principals, and scarcely ever resorted to by a form mistress.

Miss Bickford, with a red spot on each cheek, glared at the row of faces in front of her.

"Can any one give any information about this business?" she asked, then as nobody replied she continued, "I'm disgusted with the whole set of you. I wish to say that I'm not as blind as you seem to think, and I've noticed many points about your work that are, to say the least, extremely suspicious. I tell you once and for all this must stop! I won't have cheating, practical jokes, or impertinence in this form. Do you all thoroughly understand me? Very well then, don't let this kind of thing ever happen again. Empty those ink-pots out on to that tray, and, Winnie, fetch the ink-bottle out of the cupboard and refill them. This senseless proceeding has wasted a large part of your examination time, but I shall make no excuse for it. Your papers will be marked as if you had begun at nine o'clock."

With Miss Bickford on the war-path no one dared to say a single word, but at mid-morning interval the injured Camellia Buds snatched their biscuits, and fled to their grotto in the garden to hold an indignation meeting. Here they talked fast and freely.

"It's a jolly shame!"

"Most unfair!"

"Poor old Peachy!"

"Who did it?"

"Why, Mabel, of course!"

"Or Bertha?"

"One or other of them!"

"Miss Bickford has noticed their cheating!"

"Yes, and puts it off on to us all!"

"I like that!"

"It's so gloriously fair, isn't it?"

"She may say she's not blind, but she's an absolute cat!"

"What's to be done about it?"

"Those Stars won't ever tell!"

"Trust them to screen themselves!"

"Oh, it's too bad!"

Letting off steam, though comforting to their feelings, did not bring them any nearer to a solution of their problem. The unpleasant fact remained that the rival sorority had played an abominable trick, and that the blame at present rested upon Peachy. To prove her innocence required the wisdom of Solomon.

If they could have explained the whole situation to Miss Bickford she would at once have seen for herself that the offender must be among the ranks of the Stars, but such a proceeding would mean not only an entire breach of schoolgirl etiquette, but a betrayal of their own secret society. It was not to be thought of for a moment.

"Peachy'll have to climb down and apologize," decided Jess.

"Peachy eat humble-pie? Oh, good-night!"

"Well, she certainly was cheeky."

"Small blame to her!"

"It was very silly of her, though, to flare out."

"She's in the fix of her life now, poor dear."

"Can't we do anything to help her?"

"I don't know. Let's think it over and hold another meeting this afternoon."

Peachy's place at the dinner-table was empty that day, and her meal was sent up to the sanatorium upon a tray. Miss Bickford had told her side of the story to Miss Rodgers, who agreed that discipline must be maintained, and ordered the detention of the prisoner until she showed symptoms of repentance. Meanwhile Peachy, still in an utterly rebellious frame of mind, stayed upstairs, determined not to give way. It was dull, undoubtedly, to be banished to solitary confinement, for there was not even a book in the room to amuse her. Her own thoughts were her sole occupation. She had a very fertile brain, however, and suddenly a most brilliant suggestion occurred to her. The sanatorium was on the top story of the Villa Camellia, and by peeping from its window she could command a view of the iron balcony that fronted the rooms below. She calculated that she was probably exactly above dormitory 10, occupied by Joan, Esther, Mary, and Agnes, and that these chums would later on be engaged there at their preparation. With a little ingenuity it should be possible to communicate with them. She unfortunately had neither pencil nor paper with her, so could not write a note, but she took off her brooch and fastened it to the end of a long piece of string, which by extra good luck happened to be in her pocket. When she judged that the right moment had arrived she lowered her signal so that it would tap on the balcony. There was, of course, a certain amount of risk about the venture, for she might have miscalculated, and be dropping her token into the midst of enemies instead of friends. Greatly to her relief, however, Agnes appeared through the French window, and, after examining the brooch with apparent surprise, glanced upwards and saw Peachy's face. She gave a comprehensive smile, put her fingers on her lips for silence, bolted into her dormitory, and returned with a package of chocolate which she tied firmly to the end of the string, then waved her hand and darted back to her preparation.

Peachy drew up her present, chuckling with delight. She felt almost like a captive of the Middle Ages, and was beginning to plan a romantic escape down an improvised rope ladder, when it occurred to her that she would scarcely know what to do with her liberty if she regained it.

"Botheration!" she mused. "Unless I square things up I can't walk in to tea, and I can't haunt the garden like a wandering ghost, and I've no money to pay my passage on the steamer, so I can't go home to Naples. Nothing for it but to stay here, I suppose, and see who gets tired out first."

When the Camellia Buds were able to meet together again at a secret conclave in the garden, Agnes announced the important fact of having established communication with the prisoner. After an animated discussion they decided to write her a round-robin letter and set forth their idea of the situation. Each composed a sentence in turn, and Lorna acted as scribe. It ran thus:

The Grotto.

To our noble friend and Camellia Bud—

Greeting!

The Sorority desires to express a vote of sympathy for the very unpleasant occurrence that happened this morning.

A. DALTON.

Those Stars are the meanest things on earth and want spifflicating.

J. LUCAS.

We admire you for the magnificent stand you are making, but we don't see how you are going to keep it up.

M. FERGUSSON.

It's frightfully slow without you.

I. BEVERLEY.

We think you'll have to cave in and apologize.

S. YONGE.

But, of course, not own up to something you never did.

J. CAMERON.

We'll get even with those Stars to make up for this.

L. CARSON.

Don't stick in the Sanatorium all night.

E. CARTMELL.

It's no use getting too mad, old sport! Come right down and talk sense.

D. WATTS.

This united effusion was placed in an envelope, and carried by Agnes to her dormitory, where, after scouts in the garden had assured her that the coast was clear, she ventured on to the veranda, and gave a cooee which brought Peachy to the window above. The latter let down her string and drew up the letter, which she pondered upon in private. She was wise enough to accept the good advice, and when Miss Bickford appeared later on she tendered her apologies. The teacher had possibly repented of her hasty accusation, for she did not refer to the matter of the inkwells, but merely required satisfaction for "insubordination." That being given Peachy was once more free, though she could hardly consider herself restored to full favor.

"I used to like Miss Bickford," she grumped, "but I really don't think she's been fair over this. Why couldn't she ask each girl separately what she knew about it?"

"Much good that would have done. Bertha and Mabel wouldn't have told the truth, and things would only have been in a worse muddle. We'll catch those two sometime if we can only think of how to do it."

"Ah! That's just the question."

Even the Stars had been rather alarmed by Miss Bickford's firm attitude, and for the present they did not dare to cheat openly or to play any more tricks upon the form. Stopped in this direction their ringleaders turned their attention to other matters. What was the nature of these it was Irene's lot one day to discover. She happened to be walking in a rather quiet part of the garden, a portion reserved mostly for vegetables, which adjoined the great wall that separated the estate from the highroad. As she sauntered along, doing nothing in particular, she noticed Mabel, who was standing under an orange tree close to the wall. At the same moment, advancing towards them came the sound of Rachel's voice caroling an old English song. Now there is nothing in the least wrong or unorthodox in standing under an orange tree, yet the instant Irene glimpsed Mabel's face she was certain her schoolmate was in that particular spot for some reason the reverse of good. She looked uneasily at Irene, glanced in Rachel's direction, seemed to hesitate, and finally took to her heels and bolted away through the bushes. Next minute, over the top of the high wall descended a little parcel. It caught in the branches of the orange tree, fell to the ground, and rolled under a clump of cabbages. Irene took no notice, and sauntered on in the direction of Rachel, but when the prefect had passed out of sight she returned, groped among the vegetables, found the parcel, and slipped it into her packet.

"Miss Mabel Hughes, I believe I've caught you tripping this time," she chuckled. "I must send out the fiery cross and call an immediate meeting of the Camellia Buds."

Among the secret practices of the sorority was a private signal only to be used in times of urgent necessity. It had been suggested by Jess Cameron, who took the idea from The Lady of the Lake, in which poem a gathering of the clan is proclaimed by a runner bearing a cross of wood charred in the fire. Two burnt matches fastened together with thread served the Camellia Buds for their token, and it was the strictest rite of their order that any one receiving this cryptic symbol must immediately leave whatever she happened to be doing and proceed post-haste to the rendezvous.

So promptly did the members of the society respond to the summons that within ten minutes of the issue of the fiery cross they were assembled in the summer-house in a state of much expectancy. Irene explained how a parcel had been thrown over the wall, evidently for Mabel, who undoubtedly had been standing waiting for it. It was not addressed to Mabel, however, and as it bore no direction at all on the outside the Camellia Buds considered themselves justified in opening it. It contained a package of cheap chocolate, and a letter written in a foreign hand in rather bad English.

Beautiful Signorina,

Make me the compliment to accept of me this few chocolate. I like the letter you gave to me on Sunday. I will again present myself near to the hotel to wait upon you as you pass. Accept I pray you the assurance of my profoundest respects.

EMANUELE SUTONI.

"Who is Emanuele Sutoni?" gasped Delia. "And what's he got to do with us?"

"Nothing to do with us," frowned Jess. "But I'm afraid Mabel has been trying to get up some silly love affair. If Miss Morley or Miss Rodgers found this out she'd be expelled."

"What are we going to do about it? Tell Rachel?"

"I don't think so," pondered Jess. "You see, of course, we're perfectly certain among ourselves that the letter was meant for Mabel, but it isn't addressed to her so there's no real evidence. Not enough to convince Rachel. It would be better really to tell her we've found out and that she's got to stop it."

"I know! Let's tar and feather her!" squealed Peachy excitedly. "That's the best way to frighten her. Of course, I don't mean real tar, but soap does just as well. She thoroughly deserves it. I vote we do it to-night. We'll hold an inquisition in her dormitory. It will be easy enough to square Elsie."

Peachy's grim idea appealed to the Camellia Buds. They considered it was time that a public demonstration was made against Mabel, whose general behavior was very unworthy of the traditions of the Villa Camellia. They decided to have their tribunal immediately after the lights were turned out, while the prefects, who sat up later than the Transition, were still downstairs, and the mistresses were having cocoa in Miss Rodgers' study. The affair was to be a surprise for Mabel, but as Elsie also slept in the same dormitory it was necessary to secure her coöperation, in case she might give the alarm and summon a prefect. Elsie, however, proved an easily won ally.

"I can't bear Mabel," she assured Irene. "You may do anything you like to her as far as I'm concerned. I shall pretend to be asleep. Monica and Rosamonde and Winnie can't stand her either. I don't mind telling you that we're going to resign from the Starry Circle and found a new sorority of our own. It isn't good enough to be mixed up with such girls as Mabel and Bertha."

"I'm glad you've found them out," said Irene. "It was high time somebody made a protest."

The four occupants of dormitory 3 went to bed as usual that night, but as soon as the lights were out Lorna and Irene put on their dressing-gowns and stockings, and slipped into the bathroom. Here they hastily completed the details of their costumes in company with the rest of the Camellia Buds, who had rallied for the occasion. Three minutes afterwards a strange procession entered dormitory 3. Ten dressing-gowned figures, each wearing a black mask and holding a piece of lighted candle in her hand, startled the astonished eyes of Mabel Hughes, who sat up in bed to stare at them.

"What's all this about?" she asked.

"We've come here to hold an inquisition on your conduct," replied a solemn voice from behind one of the black masks. "Will you kindly get out of bed and seat yourself upon this chair. We should be sorry to use force, but I warn you you'll have to obey us."

Looking a little scared Mabel apparently thought discretion the better part of valor. She rose, put on her dressing-gown, and took the seat indicated. Her inquisitors grouped themselves opposite, placing their candles in a row upon the mantelpiece. Their spokeswoman, unfolding a large sheet of paper, proceeded to read the indictment.

This is to tell all whom it may concern that Mabel Hughes, having broken every rule of decent and orderly behavior, and being no longer worthy of the name of gentlewoman, is here arraigned on the following charges:

1. That she habitually takes advantage of and ill-treats the juniors when opportunity occurs.

2. That she cheats abominably at her work.

3. That she endeavors to persuade others to cheat.

4. That she degrades the name of the Villa Camellia by receiving letters which are thrown to her over the wall, and by handing answers to them on her way to church.

Mabel, who had smiled scornfully at the first three charges, changed color at the fourth.

"What do you know about letters?" she challenged sharply.

"We know all," ventured the solemn voice. "You had better confess at once, or the affair with Emanuele will be exposed to the prefects."

"It's my own business," said Mabel sulkily.

"No, it isn't. It's ours as well, and the whole school's. We don't want the Villa Camellia to be disgraced in the eyes of the town. You ought to be ashamed of yourself. It's so vulgar. Now, will you promise to give up all your bad habits and behave like a lady."

"I'll promise nothing," snapped Mabel.

"Then we shall be obliged to tar and feather you."

Mabel laughed, imagining it was an empty threat, but she was rapidly undeceived. Two inquisitors, seizing her by the arms, held her tightly in her chair, while several others smeared soap over her face and stuck on feathers which they took out of a cushion. She would have screamed, but every time she opened her mouth to do so she received a dab of soap upon her tongue. When they considered her countenance was sufficiently ornamented, they presented her with a looking-glass to view the effect.

"That's how we feel about it," the spokeswoman assured her. "This is just to show you we won't stand your horrid ways. Will you promise now to behave yourself, or do you want any more?"

Apparently Mabel had had enough. She seemed rather frightened. She grumbled that she would agree to what they wished.

"Just jolly well take care that you keep your promise then," warned her inquisitor. "If you begin any of your old tricks again we have evidence against you, and we shall take it straight to Rachel. If I know anything of Rachel she'll go to Miss Rodgers, and that means you're expelled. So now you know! You'd better be careful, Mabel Hughes. That's all we came to say. You may wash your face if you like before you get into bed again."

The ten members of the inquisition, knowing that time was passing, and that the prefects would soon be coming upstairs, judged it wise to break up the meeting, and taking their candles beat a stately retreat to their respective dormitories. Lorna and Irene, returning to their cubicles, heard Elsie chuckling. She had not interfered in any way with the performance, but it had evidently entertained her. She told the tale next day to her friends, with the result that Ruth, Rosamonde, Winnie, Monica, and Callie joined her in seceding from the Starry Circle, leaving Mabel and Bertha as sole remaining representatives of that sorority.

"We're fed up with you," Winnie assured the pair when they remonstrated. "We're tired of your sneaking ways, and you may just keep them to yourselves. We're not going to let you copy our exercises any more. And if we see you taking those kids' biscuits again there'll be squalls. No, we shan't tell you the name of our new sorority. We're not going to have anything to do with you ever again. So there!"

Public opinion had for once triumphed on the right side, and Mabel and Bertha, greatly discomfited, found their influence over the late Stars was at an end. The threat of telling Rachel had frightened Mabel; she was uncertain how much the Camellia Buds really knew, and judged it discreet to drop her clandestine correspondence. She had no wish for the matter to meet the ears of Miss Rodgers, who, she was well aware, would take the most serious view of it. Though she cherished a grudge against her late inquisitors, she submitted to their demands, and for the time at any rate gave no outward cause for complaint.

CHAPTER XIII

Peachy's Pranks

"I'm sorry to have to announce it," said Peachy, "but my spirits are fizzing over, and I guess if I don't go just the teeniest weeniest bit on the rampage I'll fly all to pieces and make a scene. Sometimes I'm tingling down to my toes and I've just got to explode. Being good is a lonesome job."

Peachy was sitting with Irene and Delia on one of the marble seats at the bottom of the lemon pergola. It was a favorite spot with the girls, for it was sheltered from the prevailing wind and the flowers grew particularly luxuriantly. Lovely irises were blooming, white narcissus, wallflowers, and beds of Parma violets, and the beautiful delicate blossom of the arbutula drooped from an archway that spanned the path. Irene, who was used by this time to Peachy's whimsical moods, laid aside the book she was reading and laughed.

"Poor old sport! You've evidently got it badly to-day. What can we do for you? How, where, and when do you want to rampage?"

Peachy shook her head dolefully.

"I don't know. Only wish I did. I'm tired of doing the same things over and over again every day. Getting up in the morning and dressing myself, having breakfast, going to classes, having dinner, grinding at prep, playing tennis, having tea and supper, and undressing and going to bed. I want to sleep in my clothes or go to class in my wrapper just for a change, and I'd like tennis in the morning and tea instead of dinner. I'm tired of the house and the garden. I want to dodge Antonio and go through the big gate and run down the road. I tell you I want to do absolutely anything that's weird and impossible and out of the ordinary. Yes, I know I'm wrought up. I'm just crazy for a real frolic. Who'll play 'Follow my Leader'?"

"If you won't do anything too outrageous," ventured Delia, replacing a dainty piece of sewing inside her workbag, and preparing to fall in with her friend's mood. "I've had one little difference with Miss Bickford this week, and if I have another Miss Rodgers may cut up rough and stop my next exeat."

"Honest Injun, I'll take all the blame if blame there is. Renie, dearie, you're coming too?"

"Got to, I suppose," chuckled Irene. "When the Queen of the South arises and gives her orders her slaves must 'tremble and obey.'"

"Not much trembling about you. Come on and be sports, both of you. Are you ready? Do as your Granny tells you then, and off we go."

The game of "Follow my Leader," as every schoolgirl knows, consists in exactly imitating everything which is done by your chief, no matter what extraordinary and peculiar antics she may perform. To submit to Peachy's guidance in the present exalted state of her spirits was a decided leap in the dark, but Irene and Delia were ready for fun, and prepared to take a few risks. At first their light-hearted companion contented herself with running in and out among the lemon trees, walking along the low wall of the terrace, jumping the culvert, or easy physical feats, then, having slightly worked off steam, she stood for a moment and paused to reflect.

"Christopher Columbus! I guess I know what I'll do. I've an exploring fit on me, and if I can't find America I'll find something else new and undiscovered. Here goes."

Peachy, with her satellites in her train, plunged her way across the garden in the direction of the kitchen. She had suddenly remembered an object which had more than once set her curiosity a-galloping. In the yard outside the scullery there was an iron staircase intended for use as a fire-escape from the servants' bedrooms, and also as a means of mounting the roof when workmen wished to attend to the chimney-pots. Up here she was determined to go. Fortunately the maids were safely inside the kitchen, and the defenses were left unguarded.

"This is my Jacob's ladder," she proclaimed. "Who'll follow me to the sky?"

"Go on, you lunatic," giggled Irene.

"And be quick about it if you don't want Dominica clattering at your heels," added Delia.

So they clambered up the steep iron stairway, and, passing by the door that led to the servants' apartments, they climbed on till they reached the roof. This part of the Villa Camellia was terra incognita to the school. They decided hastily, however, that it would be a very desirable acquisition. It was a large flat expanse covered with lead, and edged with a low battlement. It was evidently used by the maids, for a clothes-line was stretched between two chimneys, and a row of towels hung out to dry. The view was adorable. It was like being on the top of a mountain. They could see the town of Fossato, and a wide expanse of water, and Vesuvius, and the distant outline of Naples all spread in a panorama before them, besides having an excellent bird's-eye prospect of the garden below. Peachy, who was ready to do anything wild, went dancing about like a will-o'-the-wisp.

she extemporized. "Renie Beverley, you're not mad enough! Give me your hand. I tell you you've got to dance. We're witches who've flown over on our broomsticks and alighted here, and we'll have a frolic before we go back to — wherever we came from. Hello, what's this business? It looks like a water-tank. Give me a boost, somebody, for I'm going up to see."

It was rather a scramble even for Peachy's agile limbs, but she was resolved thoroughly to explore the capacities of the roof, and the cistern must not be left unvisited. She clung on to its slippery side and peered down at her own reflection in the water below.

"No idea I looked so nice," she perked. "The blue sky makes a charming background. Really, a pool is quite a becoming mirror. Does anybody else want to come up and peep? It's like looking at the view-finder of a camera. Rather painful hanging on, though. I think I'll drop if you're neither of you coming. Oh, botheration! I've lost my hair ribbon. It's gone right down inside the cistern. Well! It's done for now. I can't possibly fish it out."

"It wasn't your best!" consoled Delia.

"No, but the only scarlet one I possess, and just at present I've a wild fad for scarlet. I get crazes for various colors. Last term I'd look at nothing but pale blue, till Bertha Ford got that new blue chiffon dress, and that, of course, set me against it forevermore. I'd a rage for tartan once, only Jess was rather nasty about it; she thinks no one in the school has a right to wear Scotch plaids except herself. I've spent all my pocket money for this week, so I can't buy another ribbon till next Saturday. I shall have to go about in pink. Miau! I'll be such a good little pussy-cat. I'm sure different colors make me good or bad. Don't laugh at me! I mean it! I'm a different person according to what I wear."

For a short time the girls loitered about on the roof, enjoying the novelty of their position, and particularly the fact that they were on unlicensed ground, and would undoubtedly get into trouble if they were caught by Dominica or Anastasia. Naughty Peachy, to play the maids a trick, took down the row of towels, folded them neatly, and placed them in a pile behind the cistern, chuckling over the prospect of Anastasia's consternation when she came up to fetch them and found them missing.

"I owe her something for breaking my pink alabaster vase," she announced. "She's an awful smasher with her duster—just goes surging ahead over our mantelpiece and sends our ornaments flying. Mary's Pompeii pots went to smithereens yesterday. Now, Signorina Anastasia, you won't find your towels in too big a hurry. I guess I've paid you out."

"She'll pay you out if she catches us up here," suggested Delia, who was anxious not to forfeit her exeat. "Hadn't we better be getting a move on?"

"Words of wisdom, my child, fall from your lips like pearls and diamonds. The same sage thought was occurring to your humble servant. Anastasia has what is commonly called a tart tongue, and an inconvenient and inconsiderate habit of reporting trifles at headquarters. It would be quite unnecessary of her to mention to Miss Rodgers that she had seen us here, but I believe she'd go out of her way to do it."

131

"I'm sure she would, bad luck to her. Lead on, MacDuff! Let's descend from the Highlands to the Lowlands."

"We may find further sport farther afield. I'm not at the end of my resources yet. I've an idea or two more in my head," nodded Peachy, escorting her friends down the staircase to the comparative safety of the back yard.

There was no doubt that Peachy was in an exceedingly mischievous mood and ready for any prank which came to hand. She dodged with her followers successfully past the kitchen door, without attracting the hostile attention of Anastasia or any other of the servants. She was bent on exploring a patch of the garden which was only accessible from the rear of the scullery. She had observed it from the vantage-ground of the roof, and had decided that, by climbing on to a low shed, it would be quite possible to scale the wall which divided the grounds of the Villa Camellia from those of its next door neighbor. The girls had always been extremely curious about the Villa Sutri. From their dormitory windows they could catch a glimpse of its green shutters and creeper-covered walls, set away among a thick grove of trees, and they had decided that its garden looked immensely superior to their own. The estate belonged to Count Sutri, who often spent part of the winter and spring among his orange groves and his flowery pergolas. He was supposed to have a reputation for gardening, and rumors of his wonderful exotics had circulated round the school. None of the girls, however, had ever actually been inside the grounds.

Peachy's project was, of course, extremely audacious, and had the Count been at home she would hardly have dared to let it materialize. She had heard Mrs. Clark mention on Sunday that their neighbor had started for a cruise in his yacht, and that he would probably be away for a considerable time.

"The Villa will be shut up, and only a few gardeners left about the place," declared Peachy, "and if I know anything of Italian gardeners, they'll all be sitting smoking inside the summer-house, so we needn't trouble ourselves to worry about them. It's the opportunity of a lifetime. I saw the whole thing in a flash from the roof. There's a shed on our side of the wall and a shed on his. All you have to do is to step over and get down. Nothing could be simpler. I'm just aching to explore that garden."

Delia, still thinking of her exeat, demurred, and even Irene's valor slightly quailed.

"Oh, come on! Be sports!" tempted Peachy. "You'll never get such a chance in your lives again — never."

So they hesitated, and were lost, and finally followed their leader up the low, sloping roof of the shed.

As Peachy had prophesied, it was really remarkably easy. They had only to scale quite a low piece of wall, and drop on to the roof of the shed on the other side, then scramble down into Count Sutri's garden. In less than five minutes the feat was accomplished, and three rather awed but delighted girls were speeding along a green alley in quest of adventure.

There was no doubt about it being a beautiful garden. It was more carefully kept than that of the Villa Camellia, and contained choicer and rarer flowers. There were glorious tanks of water-lilies, and there were pergolas of sweet-scented creepers, and the statues and arbors utterly eclipsed even those of a public park. It was evidently the Count's favorite hobby, and he had spared no expense in laying out the grounds. Rather fearful of being caught by some chance gardener the girls walked on, holding themselves in readiness to dive away if necessary and make a quick escape.

"Do you feel like Adam and Eve in Paradise?" queried Delia tremulously.

"Not a bit, because they never got back after they were once turned out. I wish we could annex this place and add it on to the Villa Camellia. The Count can't want it while he's away."

The girls wandered about in breathless enjoyment. Stolen waters are sweet, and somebody else's garden seemed much more attractive than their own. They did not dare to venture too near the Villa, and kept carefully away from anything that looked like a grotto or a summer-house, in which they might find a gardener seated, enjoying his cigarette. At the end of a rose pergola, however, Peachy made a discovery. It was neither more nor less than a flight of steps leading down to a door in the ground. She stood gazing at it with curiosity.

"Now I wonder what that is?" she exclaimed.

"Looks like the entrance to a mausoleum," shuddered Delia.

"Or the strong room where the Count keeps his money," laughed Irene.

"I don't believe it's either. I shouldn't be surprised if it's the passage leading to the sea. I know there is one in the Sutri garden, to get down to the bathing cove. How priceless if we've happened to light upon it. Is that door open? I'm going to see."

Peachy ran down the steps, turned the handle, and somewhat to her own astonishment found the door unlocked. She was peering into a long dark tunnel, at the end of which could be distinguished a faint glint of light. This was indeed an adventure. It seemed a deed of daring to explore such hidden depths, but she was out to take risks that afternoon.

"Come along!" she commanded, bracing up the spirits of her more timorous comrades.

Holding one another's arms particularly tightly, the three entered the doorway and began to walk along the underground passage. It sloped sharply downwards, and was rough under foot, but the farther they descended the brighter grew the light in front of them. Presently they had stumbled out of the darkness, and were emerging from a tunnel at the foot of the cliffs, and stepping out on to the sandy shore of a little cove.

It had always been a great grievance at the Villa Camellia that the school had no bathing place, and the girls had greatly coveted the creek which was the exclusive property of their neighbor, Count Sutri. To find themselves on a level with the sea, facing the lapping waves, was exactly what they had hoped. They ran along the sand in huge delight, to the very edge of the water. It was really a beautiful cove. There were groups of rocks with smooth pools amongst them, and in the silvery sand were numbers of tiny fragile shells, very pretty and delicate, and just the thing for a collection.

"It's a shame it should all belong to one man who probably hardly ever uses it," flamed Peachy. "Now, if only we could all come down here to bathe, wouldn't it be a stunt? The cove is really mostly under the garden of the Villa Camellia. I say it ought to belong to us."

"It's ours for the moment at any rate," said Irene.

"Yes, isn't it great? We've got it all to ourselves," rejoiced Delia, dancing along the beach with outstretched arms, like an incarnation of Zephyr or a spring vision of a sea-nymph. She skimmed over the sand almost as if she were flying, but, as she reached the largest group of rocks, her exalted mood suddenly dissipated and her high spirits came down to earth with a thud. Sitting on the other side of the rock, calmly smoking a cigar, was a middle-aged individual in a tweed coat and a soft hat. The creek, which they had imagined was their private paradise, was occupied after all.

Delia fled back to her friends, this time on wings of fright, and communicated her awful discovery.

"It must be Count Sutri," gasped Peachy.

"He can't have started off in his yacht after all," agreed Irene.

"I don't think he saw me, but I'm not sure about it," panted Delia breathlessly.

"Whether he did or he didn't we'd better scoot quick," opined Peachy.

So three agitated girls dashed back over the sands and into the dark tunnel, and hurried as fast as they could up the underground passage, expecting every moment to hear a footstep behind them and a voice demanding to know what they were doing trespassing upon the premises. At the top of the tunnel a horrible surprise awaited them. The door through which they had entered was shut and bolted. At first they could hardly believe their ill luck. They groped for the handle in the darkness, and pushed and pulled and turned and tugged, but all in vain. They even thumped on the door and called, hoping to attract the attention of a gardener, but there was no reply. They were hopelessly locked inside the underground passage.

Now thoroughly frightened they were almost in tears.

"We shall have to go back to the cove," faltered Irene.

"And show ourselves to Count Sutri, and ask him to take us back somehow," gulped Peachy.

"We're in for the biggest row of our lives with Miss Rodgers," choked Delia.

There was certainly nothing else to be done. Time was passing quickly, and unless they could return at once to the Villa Camellia they would be late for preparation. Very sadly and soberly they walked back along the seashore to the rocks.

"You explain, Peachy," urged the others, and Peachy, though she did not relish the task thus thrust upon her, acknowledged that she was the instigator of the whole affair and therefore responsible for helping her companions out of a decidedly awkward situation.

The gentleman in the soft hat was still sitting under the shadow of the rock smoking, but he rose and threw away his cigar as the deputation of three advanced to address him. Peachy, in her very best Italian, began to stammer out an explanation and excuses. He listened for a moment or two, then shook his head and interrupted.

"Sorry I don't speak much Italian. I'm afraid I don't quite understand."

"O-o-h! You're American!" gasped Peachy, her face one broad smile of relief. "We—we thought you were Count Sutri."

"I haven't that honor! I'm only plain Mr. Bond. I've taken the Count's villa, though, for two months. Can I be of any service to you?"

"We're Americans too," sparkled Peachy; "at least Delia and I are. We're at school at the Villa Camellia up there. I—I'm sorry to say we're trespassing here. We climbed over the wall into your garden and came down the passage to the shore, and now the door's locked and we can't get back again."

"And it's nearly preparation time," added Delia desperately.

Mr. Bond's eyes twinkled with amusement.

"I'll take you back," he offered. "It was hard luck to find the door locked. I've hardly explored the place properly myself yet. I came down in the lift."

"The lift!" exclaimed Irene in surprise.

"Yes, here it is, and a very convenient arrangement too," said Mr. Bond, leading the way into an artificial cave close at hand.

Here to the girls' amazement was a perfectly modern and up-to-date "ascenseur," nicely upholstered and lighted by electricity. Mr. Bond ushered his visitors inside, closed the door, pressed a button, and immediately they shot aloft, landing ultimately in a kiosk in Count Sutri's garden at the top of the cliff. Feeling as if a magician had used occult means to transport them back to safety, the girls gazed round highly delighted to find themselves out of the cove. Their host, to whom they hastily confided some details of how they had penetrated into his premises, fetched a ladder, and by its aid they mounted to the roof of the shed, and skipped over the wall on to the top of their own wood-hut.

"You won't tell Miss Rodgers?" begged Peachy, waving a good-by to their rescuer after they had all protested their gratitude.

"I guess I know how to keep a secret," he laughed. "I won't betray you. Hope you'll be in time. There goes your school bell. You've run it fine but I believe you'll just do it if you hustle up."

Three breathless girls, with minds much too agitated to apply themselves properly to French translation, slipped into the Villa Camellia at the eleventh hour, and answered "present" as their names were read on the roll-call. Peachy's disheveled hair drew down a rebuke from Miss Bickford, but this was such a very minor evil that she took it meekly, smoothed the offending elf-locks with her fingers, and composed her dimples to an expression of docile humility.

"We got out of that very well," she purred in private afterwards.

"Thanks to Mr. Bond and the lift," agreed Irene.

"I guess I'm not going to try anything so risky again," declared Delia. "It was the fix of my life. I'll be down with nervous prostration to-morrow. Shouldn't wonder if I raise a temperature to-night. Peachy Proctor, you may coax and tease as you like, but nothing you say will ever induce me to climb that wall and go into Count Sutri's garden again. It's not worth the thrills. Sorry to be a crab, but I mean it."

CHAPTER XIV

The Villa Bleue

Delia's good resolution remained only half fulfilled, for after all she visited Count Sutri's cove again. This time, however, it was in a perfectly orthodox fashion. Mr. and Mrs. Bond, meeting Miss Morley at the house of an American resident in Fossato, invited the whole school to come and view the garden on Sunday afternoon, and clad in their best dresses the girls paraded in through the gate, and were shown the beauties of the lovely grounds. They were taken in relays down in the lift to the creek by the sea, and afterwards entertained with ice-cream and biscuits on the terrace in front of the villa, which was all very interesting and delightful, though not nearly so exciting as the surreptitious peep which the naughty trio had previously obtained on their own account. Mr. Bond might indeed be silent on the subject of that afternoon's adventure, but the expedition into his grounds had been only a part of Peachy's pranks in her game of "Follow the Leader," and for one of her sins at any rate she was to be called to account. The cistern on the top of the roof supplied a tap on the upper landing from which Anastasia, one of the chambermaids, was accustomed to draw water with which to fill the bedroom jugs.

On the morning after the events just narrated she took her can as usual, but was utterly horrified, when she turned the tap, to find the water running red. She was intensely superstitious, and immediately jumped to the conclusion that she was the victim of witchcraft, so she flung her apron over her head, commenced to sob, and deplored the early death which would probably overtake her. She sat on the landing making quite a scene, prophesying evil to the other servants who crowded round to condole and marvel, and showing the bewitched water in her jug with a mixture of importance and horror. The girls who occupied rooms on the upper landing were duly thrilled, and, after debating every possible or impossible solution of the mystery, were on the point of carrying the tale to Miss Rodgers when Peachy came hurrying along.

"I've only just heard. Don't, don't go to the 'Ogre's Den' about it. If you love me don't. I guess I know what's happened. The water's notbewitched. If you've any sense left in your silly head come with me on to the roof and we'll look at the cistern. We'll soon find out what's the matter. Callie, lend me your butterfly-net, that's a saintly girl!"

Anastasia, though somewhat protesting, allowed herself to be persuaded, and went with Peachy first to the kitchen floor and then up the iron staircase to the roof. Approaching the cistern Peachy climbed on to its edge, lowered her butterfly-net, and presently fished up a wet and draggled scarlet ribbon which stained her fingers red as she held it out to Anastasia's astonished gaze.

"I guess it's this that has been bleeding inside the tank and has stained the water," she explained.

"But, Signorina, I ask how it place itself there?" demanded the still puzzled chambermaid in her halting English, then mother-wit overmastering native superstition, she burst into laughter. "Oh! Oh! Oh! It is no magic but you, Signorina. Who hid my towels? I go to tell Mees Rodgers. Yes! You shall get into very big scrape!"

"No, Anastasia, don't tell," implored Peachy. "It was only a joke. Look here! Are you fond of chocolates? I had a box sent me yesterday, and you shall have them all. It won't do any good to tell Miss Rodgers, will it?"

"You not come on to this roof again and touch my towels?" conceded Anastasia doubtfully.

"Never! I promise faithfully."

"Then I not tell."

"Good! You're a white angel. I'll square the girls and get them not to mind washing in pink water for a day or two. It ought to improve their complexions. So we'll just say nothing at all about it at headquarters. That's settled. Anastasia, your English is improving wonderfully; I guess I'll teach you some American next—it's the finest language in the world.

Botheration, I've soused Callie's butterfly-net. I don't know what she'll say about it. I'm out of one scrape into another the whole time. Well, I'd rather face Callie than Miss Rodgers anyhow. She may storm, but she can't give me bad marks or stop my next exeat. Come along, Anastasia. We'll take the ribbon with us to show as a trophy. It will give them a little bit of a surprise downstairs if I'm not mistaken."

Owing to luck, and to the kindness of Anastasia, Peachy's pranks did not on this occasion meet with any punishment. Irene, who had been greatly fearing an exposure of the whole escapade, once more breathed freely. If the matter had come to the ears of Miss Rodgers the three girls would certainly have been "gated," and Irene was particularly anxious not to lose her approaching exeat. It was her turn to go to tea at the Villa Bleue, and she was looking forward greatly to the occasion. It would be her first visit, for she had forfeited her privilege earlier in the term, when she and Lorna lost themselves among the olive groves. Much to their satisfaction the buddies were invited together, in company with Mary, Sheila, Monica, and Winnie, who were also on the good conduct list. Of course there was considerable prinking in front of the looking-glasses, careful adjusting of hair ribbons and other trifles of toilet, before the girls considered themselves in party trim and ready to do credit to the Villa Camellia. Escorted by Miss Brewster, who acted chaperon, or "policewoman" as Sheila insisted on calling her, they walked in orderly file down the eucalyptus avenue to the town, past the hotel, along the esplanade, and up a steep incline to the Villa Bleue. The hospitable little parsonage seemed an exact materialization of the personality of its owners. Canon and Mrs. Clark were both small and smiling and charitable and particularly kind, and their tiny unpretentious dwelling, with its sunny aspect and its flowers and its pet birds, was absolutely in keeping with their tone of mind. From some houses seem to emanate certain mental atmospheres, as if they reflected the sum total of the thoughts that have collected there, and sensitive visitors receive subconscious impressions of chilly magnificence, intellectual activity or a spirit of general tolerance.

The Villa Bleue always felt radiant with kind and cheery impulses, and its flower-covered walls seemed almost to shine as the girls, secure of a welcome, parted from Miss Brewster, and ran up the steps to the pleasant veranda. Mrs. Clark made them at home at once. She had six cosy basket-chairs waiting for them, and a plateful of most delicious almond taffy, and she installed them to sit and admire the view, while she talked and put them at their ease. Schoolgirls are notoriously bashful visitors, and in certain circumstances all six would have been mum as mice and entirely devoid of conversation except a conventional yes or no, but with dear Mrs. Clark's beaming face and warm-hearted manner to disarm their shyness they were perfectly natural, and enjoyed themselves as entirely as if they were at a dormitory tea or a sorority supper. The best part about Mrs. Clark was that she had the happy knack of forgetting her age and throwing herself back into the mental environment of sixteen. She was certainly not a stiff hostess; indeed her treatment of her guests was less conventional than that adopted by Rachel Moseley at the prefects' parties; she laughed and chatted and asked questions about the school, till in a few minutes the girls were chattering like sparrows and behaving as if they had known her for years.

Tea was set out on little basket tables in the veranda, and there were all the delicious home-made things for which the Villa Bleue had gained a just reputation—brown scones and honey, potato cakes, Scotch shortbread, buttered oatmeal biscuits, iced lemon sandwich cake, and chocolate fingers.

When tea was taken away and the basket tables were once more free, Mrs. Clark produced dainty cards and scarlet pencils and organized a competition. It was entitled "Nursery Rhymes," and contained twenty questions to be answered by the competitors. These ran as follows:

NURSERY RHYMES COMPETITION

1. Who made Cock Robin's shroud?
2. Who was exhausted by family cares?

3. Who disliked insects?

4. Who showed an interest in horticulture?

5. Who summoned an orchestra?

6. Who pursued matrimonial intentions without the parental sanction?

7. Who showed religious intolerance?

8. Who took a joint that did not belong to him?

9. Who deplored the loss of hand gear?

10. Whose salary was restricted owing to slackness in work?

11. What animal pursued horological investigations?

12. Who made the record high jump?

13. Who wore a superfluity of jewelry?

14. Whose culinary efforts were temporarily confiscated?

15. Who pulled Pussy from the well?

16. Who slept instead of attending to business?

17. Who exhibited sanctimonious satisfaction over a meal?

18. Who lost a number of domestic animals?

19. Who had an accident during the performance of their duty?

20. Who was mutilated by a bird?

Some of the questions seemed easy and some were difficult. The girls sat puzzling over them, and writing the answers when they got inspiration. Irene scribbled away delightedly, but Lorna, who had almost forgotten the nursery rhymes of her childhood, was in much mystification, and only filled in a few of the vacant spaces. Numbers 6, 7, 13 and 14 proved the most baffling and no one was able to solve all twenty.

After allowing a considerable laxity in respect of time Mrs. Clark rang the bell and declared the competition closed. The girls changed cards, and waited with interest while their hostess read out the answers.

ANSWERS TO NURSERY RHYMES COMPETITION

ANSWERS TO NURSERY RHYMES COMPETITION

1.

I, said the beetle,

With my thread and needle.

2.

The old woman who lived in a shoe.

3.

Miss Muffet.

4.

Mary, Mary, quite contrary.

5.

Old King Cole, who called for his fiddlers three.

6.

Froggie would a-wooing go,

Whether his mother would let him or no.

7.

Goosey goosey gander,

Whither do you wander,

Upstairs, downstairs,

In my lady's chamber.

There I met an old man

Who wouldn't say his prayers,

So I took him by the left leg

And threw him down the stairs.

8.

Taffy was a Welshman,

Taffy was a thief,

Taffy came to my house

And stole a piece of beef.

9.

Three little kittens

Lost their mittens

And they began to cry.

10.

Johnny shall have a new master

And he shall have but a penny a day,

Because he won't work any faster.

11.

Dickery, dickery, dock!

The mouse ran up the clock!

12.

The cow jumped over the moon.

13.

The fair lady of Banbury Cross.

Rings on her fingers and bells on her toes

She shall have music wherever she goes.

14.

The Queen of Heart's tarts.

15.

Little Tommy Trout.

16.

Little Boy Blue.

17.

Little Jack Horner.

18.

Little Bo Peep.

19.

Jack and Jill.

20.

The maid was in the garden

Hanging out the clothes,

When by came a blackbird

And nipped off her nose.

There was a good deal of laughter over the competition and much counting up of marks. Irene, who had scored eighteen out of the possible twenty, came out top, and was accordingly handed the pretty little photograph frame which formed the prize.

"I only got six," mourned Lorna. "I was a perfect duffer at it."

"I had fifteen," purred Sheila, "but I couldn't for the life of me remember who made Cock Robin's shroud, or who pulled Pussy out of the well."

"It's such ages since I read any nursery rhymes," said Monica.

"That's just the fun of it, of course!" declared Mary. "Did you make up the questions, Mrs. Clark?"

"No, I got the Canon to compose them. He'll be glad you liked them. Oh, here he comes. He had to go to a committee meeting this afternoon. Did you get tea, dear, at Major Littleton's?" (to her husband). "That's right! Then sit down on this comfy chair and entertain us, please."

"Rather a big order," laughed Canon Clark, shaking hands with his young visitors, and taking the proffered seat. "How do you want to be entertained? No sermons to-day?" and his eyes twinkled. "Don't all speak at once. I'm beginning to get nervous!"

"You can tell the most beautiful stories," suggested Sheila, who had paid visits before to the Villa Bleue and knew the capabilities of her host.

"Oh, yes, please, do tell us a story!" agreed the others. "We'd like it better than anything."

"I have one inside my desk which is just ready to send off to a magazine. If it won't bore you to listen to it, I'll read it aloud and let you judge whether it has any interest in it or not. An audience of schoolgirls ought to be severe critics. As a rule they're omnivorous readers of fiction. If you turn it down I shall tear it up."

"Oh, but we shan't!"

"Please begin!"

Thus urged, Canon Clark fetched a manuscript from his study, and after passing round the plate of taffy, to "sweeten his narrative" as he put it, he sat down in his basket-chair on the veranda and began to read.

"THE LUCK OF DACREPOOL

"I had known Jack Musgrave out East; we had chummed at Mandalay, messed together at Singapore, hunted big game up in Kashmir, and shot tigers in Bengal, and, when we said good-by, as he boarded the homeward-bound steamer at Madras, it was with a cordial invitation on his part that I should look him up if ever I happened to penetrate into the remote corner of Cumberland where his family acres were situated.

"For a year or two my affairs kept me in India, and nothing seemed more unlikely than that—for the present, at any rate—Jack and I should cross paths again, but by one of those strange chances which sometimes occur in this world I found myself, on the Christmas Eve of 190-, standing on the platform of Holdergate Station, having missed the connection for Scotland, and with the pleasing prospect before me of spending the night, and possibly—if trains were not available—the ensuing Christmas Day at the one very second-rate inn in the village.

"It was then that I remembered that Holdergate was the nearest station to Dacrepool Grange, and that, if Jack's memory still held good, I might find a hearty welcome and spend a pleasant evening recalling old times and discussing past shots, instead of putting up with the inferior accommodation offered by the landlady of the King's Arms. As no one either at the station or in the village seemed willing to vouchsafe me definite information as to whether the owner of Dacrepool was at home or abroad, parrying my inquiries with such scant courtesy and in so uncouth and unintelligible a dialect as to be scarce understood, I resolved to chance it, and with some difficulty hiring a farmer's gig, I started out on a six-mile drive over the bleak moorlands, which seemed to stretch as far as the eye could reach in a dim vista of brown heath and distant snow-clad fell. It was a dreary and unseasonable evening, with a damp mist rising from the sodden ground, and occasional falls of sleet, mingled with rain that chilled one to the bone. I buttoned my coat closely round my throat, and braced my nerves to meet the elements, hoping I might find my reward at the end of my journey, and inwardly cursing every mile of the rough road.

"But even Cumberland miles cannot wind on forever, and my Jehu at length drew up at a massive stone gateway, which he assured me formed the entrance to Dacrepool Grange. There was neither light nor sound in the lodge, nor did any one come out in answer to our impatient calls, so we had perforce to open the gates for ourselves. They creaked on their rusty hinges, as if they had not been unclosed for many a day, and when I noted the neglected drive, where the overhanging trees swept our faces as we passed, I began to fear that I had come on a fool's errand, and that I should find the house shut up and my friend abroad.

"On this point, however, my driver reassured me. 'Nay, oo'be to home, theer's a light i' yon winder,' he said, pointing with his whip where a faint streak of yellow shone like a beacon into the surrounding gloom. The moon was struggling through the clouds, and I could dimly discern the outline of the quaint gabled front of the house, with its mullioned windows, and masses of clinging ivy. Dismounting at the old stone porch, I seized the knocker and beat a mighty tattoo. There was no reply. Even the light had disappeared from the window almost simultaneously with the approach of our carriage wheels, and though I hammered for fully five minutes I failed to obtain the slightest response to my knocks. I was on the point of turning away in despair and driving back in the gig to Holdergate, when a sound of footsteps was heard within, together with an unbolting and unbarring, the door was opened about six inches on the chain, and a hard-featured woman peeped cautiously out into the darkness.

"I at once proclaimed my identity and my errand, but, by the light of the candle which she held in her hand, she looked me up and down with a glance of keen distrust and evident disfavor. 'How am I to know it is as you say?' she replied guardedly, and without making any move to grant me admittance.

"'Then fetch your master,' I exclaimed with some heat, thrusting my card into her hand. 'He should know my name at any rate, though he seems to have trained you in strange notions of hospitality to keep a guest standing on the doorstep on a bitter evening in December.'

"Grumbling under her breath she went away, and I was half inclined to follow her example and quit this very unpromising spot, when a quick step resounded in the hall, the door was flung open wide, and I was dragged forcibly into the house by my friend Jack, who hailed me with such unfeigned delight and enthusiasm that there could be little doubt of the genuineness of his welcome.

"'You've sprung upon us at a queer time, as it happens, old man, but if you don't mind taking pot-luck we'll spend a ripping night together,' he cried, hauling me into the dining-room, where a pretty fairy of a girl sprang up to greet us. 'This is my sister Bessie, and I've talked about you so often that she'll give you as big a welcome as I do. It's only a poor best we can show you in the way of entertainment, but you'll make allowances when I tell you how I'm situated, and what we lack in kind we must make up in good will.'

"'What's good enough for you will be good enough for me,' I replied heartily, submitting to be relieved of my coat and installed in the best chair by the blazing fire—a pleasant change indeed from the cold and the sleet outside.

"'You must not think our guests usually receive such a churlish reception,' said Jack, laughing a little, 'but the fact is, we took you for the bailiffs. I'm sorry to say I've outrun the constable—it's really not my fault, for the old place was mortgaged to its last penny when it fell to me—but, as the case stands, I'm enduring a kind of siege; daren't put my nose out of my own door for fear I should be served with writs, and have to smuggle what supplies we can beg or borrow through the kitchen window. It's a queer kind of Christmas to spend, and a poor lookout for the New Year, for I'm afraid the old place is bound to go in the end, though I have vowed to stick to it as long as I can hold it, and Bessie has vowed to stick to me, though she might have a more cheerful home elsewhere if she liked. There's precious little to offer you in our larder, but perhaps we can furnish up something in the way of supper; can't we, Bessie?'

"Miss Musgrave laughed merrily.

"'Mr. Harper must imagine himself back in camp,' she replied; 'I hope he can manage to subsist on porridge and cheese and tinned provisions, for I don't think we have anything better to offer him.'

"I would have subsisted on a far poorer diet to remain within sight of those bright eyes, and I endeavored to convince my host and hostess that I desired nothing more than to be treated as one of themselves, with such success that I seemed to drop at once into the family circle, and never spent a pleasanter or more jovial evening in my life. Jack and I sat up late after Bessie had retired, chatting of bygone days and past adventures till the jungles and plains seemed almost more real than the cheery blaze of the fire before us; but the talk came round at last to the affairs of the moment.

"'Is not there any plan by which you could raise the wind, Jack?'" I inquired.

"'Never a one. I've tried every end up, but there seems no way out of the trouble unless, indeed, we could find Sir Godfrey's treasure.'

"'Who's he?'

"'An ancestor of mine, rather a back number, considering he died somewhere about two hundred and fifty years ago—but a restless old gentleman, for he is still said to have a trick of haunting the house, and, according to popular tradition, hoping to be able to point out the hiding-place of a treasure he stowed away.'

"'Was it genuine treasure?'

"'I believe so. He went off to fight in the Civil Wars, and hid the family plate and jewels in a secure place which nobody knew of but himself. He had not the sense to leave any record of the spot, and when he was killed at Naseby his secret died with him, and the valuables—unless, as I sometimes suspect, the old chap had previously pledged them—were not forthcoming, nor have they ever been heard of since.'

"'Has he ever appeared to you?'

"'Not he; I only wish he would. The hoard would be a jolly windfall to me if I could manage to light upon it. But I'm not the kind who goes about seeing ghosts. I'm too plain and matter-of-fact by half, and, though I often hear mysterious taps on the panels of my bedroom, I prosaically set it down to rats and mice. Now, you're a psychic sort of a fellow, the seventh son of a seventh son; if he wants to make himself visible, perhaps you may get a sight of him; I'm afraid it's more than ever I shall.'

"'Is there no clew at all left as to the hiding-place of the treasure?' I inquired.

"'Only an old rhyme so obscure as to be quite unintelligible:

Even you, with your fondness for antiquities and rummaging strange things out of old books, can scarcely make anything of that, I should say.'

"I shook my head, for the riddle seemed quite unreadable, and as we had already sat up until long past midnight I begged for my candle, and proposed to defer our conversation until the morning. Jack, declaring that none of the beds in the damp old house was fit to sleep in without a week of previous airing, insisted upon giving up his room to me, and passing the night himself on the dining-room sofa, and, in spite of my protestations, I was forced to acquiesce in his plans for my comfort.

"Left alone, I looked with some curiosity round the gloomy oak-paneled chamber, where the fire-light flashed on the carved four-poster, with its faded yellow damask curtains, and lit up the moth-eaten tapestry that adorned a portion of the upper part of the walls, but scarcely illumined the dark corners which lay beyond. There were quaint old presses and chests roomy enough to hide a dozen ghosts in, and a portrait of a gentleman in the elaborate costume of the Stuart period seemed to look down upon me with strangely haunting eyes.

"'A spooky enough place,' I murmured, 'hallowed by the spirits of numerous generations, no doubt. Well, I'll undertake they won't disturb me to-night, for I am dog-tired and mean to sleep like a log.'

"I am an old traveler, and was soon in bed and enjoying a well-earned slumber, but my dreams were wild, for I seemed now to be driving furiously over the moorland, pursuing ever the phantom of pretty Bessie, who, with her bewitching smile, was luring me into the fog and darkness, and now to be barring the front door to defend her from some unknown assailant, whose perpetual rapping rang like an echo through my brain. With the impotent strength of dreamland I struggled vainly to close the door, which was opening slowly to admit the nameless horror. I seemed to feel a hot breath on my cheek, and with a wild shriek I woke, to find the moonlight streaming in through the broad diamond-paned window, falling in a white shaft across the floor, while the last embers of the fire were smoldering to ashes upon the hearth.

"I sat up in bed with that feeling of broad awakeness and alertness which comes to us sometimes, and caught my breath as I listened, for through the stillness of the night came the unmistakable sound of a gentle tapping from behind the paneling of the wall. It was not continuous, but more as one might rap at the chamber door of a sleeping person, waiting every now and then to hear if one had obtained a response. An intense and vivid sensation came over me that I was not alone in the room; that there was some presence other than my own personality which was striving in some way to force itself upon my consciousness and arrest my attention. Was it only my fancy, or were the moonbeams actually shaping themselves into a human form, till against the dark background of the fireplace, I seemed to see the misty shadowy outline of a figure, so vague and ethereal that even as I looked it appeared to melt again into the moonlight and cease to exist?

"With every nerve on the stretch I strained my eyes to gain a clearer impression. A passing cloud left the room for a few moments in darkness, but, as the beams shone out full and clear once more, that shadowy figure seemed to gather substance, and I felt as if some unknown force were compelling my attention and chaining my every sense in a mute endeavor to establish some chord of connection between me and the dim spirit world which floats forever round us. Now waxing, now waning, the vision grew, till I fancied I caught a glint of armor. For an instant a wild imploring glance met my own, and a transparent finger pointed to the richly-carved paneling below the arras, but as I sprang from the bed the vision faded swiftly away, leaving me standing on the floor in the calm moonlight doubting the evidence of my senses, and half convinced that I must still have been in the continuance of my dream.

"Yet, as I looked, something in the carved paneling struck my notice, and, following the direction in which the spectral finger had pointed, I saw that the dragons and the twisted scrolls were united in the center by a Tudor rose. In an instant there flashed across my mind the old saying which Jack had quoted:

What impulse urged me I cannot say, but compelled by some seemingly irresistible suggestion I seized the sculptured rose and wrenched at it with all my strength. There was a dull thud, followed by a harsh grinding noise, and the whole of the paneling slid slowly back, revealing a cavity behind, where, half hidden by the accumulations of dust and cobwebs, I could catch a sight of silver tankards and masses of plate enough to make the mouth of a collector water with envy. Still scarcely certain whether I was sleeping or waking, I put in my hand and drew out a bag filled with something heavy, and even as I did so the rotten mildewed canvas broke with the strain, and a stream of golden coins descended with a clatter upon the floor.

"Like a maniac I rushed to my door and hallooed lustily for Jack, who, roused by my shouts, came hurrying up in scanty attire, with a revolver in one hand and a poker in the other.

"'What is it, old man, thieves or bailiffs? Just hold 'em till I come, can't you?'

"'It's neither,' I replied, as I hauled him in with triumph, 'but I believe I have had a visit from your esteemed ancestor, and, as a Christmas gift, allow me to introduce you to the long-lost family treasure.'

"There was no mistake about it—it was real enough, and, as the Christmas bells came chiming through the frosty air, we turned out bags of gold, piles of silver and priceless jewels warranted to redeem Dacrepool Grange twice over if necessary, and sending Jack into a very ecstasy of joy.

"'By Jove, old chap,' he exclaimed, 'I owe it all to you. Here I've slept in this room for years, and never paid any heed to the raps and taps, though I've heard them often enough, while the treasure was under my very nose, only waiting to be discovered. Then you come along with your ghost-seeing eyes, and the spirit, if spirit it was, is able to convey to you the secret it's been trying to get off its mind for hundreds of years. You've saved me from the bankruptcy court, and it's a debt of gratitude you'll find I shan't lightly forget.'

"It was a very jovial Christmas which we spent that day, for the news of the find got abroad at daylight, and we were promptly visited by the butcher and baker, bringing stores of good cheer and profuse apologies for past misunderstandings; even the severe old servant relapsed into smiles as she bore in a smoking sirloin of beef. Jack's spirits rose to the wildest pitch, and little Bessie, who persisted in calling me the savior of the family credit, could scarcely do enough to show her gratitude. Jack wanted me to share the best of the jewels with him, and was so annoyed at my refusal that I could only gain peace by a hint that I should sometime ask him for something more valuable still. And I got my way, for my unexpected visit lengthened out to a stay of some weeks, during which pretty Bessie's gratitude had time to ripen into a warmer feeling. So in the end it was quite a different treasure which I bore away from Dacrepool Grange, and I feel equally with Jack that I have cause to remember that strange Christmas Eve, and to render my thanks to old Sir Godfrey, who now sleeps soundly in his grave, secure in the accomplishment of his mission, having rid his soul of the burden of his secret and restored luck to Dacrepool."

"Is it true?" asked Sheila, as Canon Clark folded up his manuscript.

"Well, I can hardly call it a personal reminiscence, but you must allow for author's license. Old historic houses sometimes have secret hiding-places, and dreams are undoubtedly strange things. It's all founded upon legends which I have heard. Mrs. Clark and I first met in an ancient grange not at all unlike Dacrepool, didn't we, Bess? And if we didn't find treasure behind the paneling we certainly ought to have done so. Now I'm extremely sorry to have to hurry you, but I promised Miss Morley that you should be back at school by half past six, and I undertook to escort you through the town. I hope you'll all come and have tea with us some afternoon next term and we'll have another competition. Don't say good-by to Mrs. Clark. Give the Italian 'A rivederci' instead, because that means not a parting greeting but 'May we see one another again.'"

CHAPTER XV

Peachy's Birthday

Delia Watts, walking one afternoon along the lemon pergola, came across a small group of Camellia Buds ensconced in a cozy corner at the foot of the steps by the fountain.

"Hello! You've found a dandy place here. You look so comfy. May I join on?" she chirped.

"Surelee!" said Jess cordially, pushing Irene farther along to make room. "Come and squat down, dearie, and add your voice to the powwow. We're just discussing something fearfully urgent and important. Do you know it'll be Peachy's birthday next week?"

"Of course I know. Nobody could room with Peachy and not hear about that. She's the most excited girl on earth. She's been promised a gold wrist-watch and a morocco hand-bag, and I can't tell you what else, and she's just living till she gets them. I wish it was my birthday. I'm jealous!"

"Don't be such a pig," responded Jess. "You got your fun in the holidays. You can't have things twice over. What we were talking about was this — the sorority ought to rally somehow and give Peachy a surprise. Can't we get up a special stunt?"

"Rather! Put me on the committee, please! Couldn't we get leave for a dormitory tea? I know Miss Rodgers rather frowned on them last term, but perhaps if we wheedled Miss Morley she'd say 'yes.' We'd promise to clear up and not make any mess, and to finish promptly before prep time. That ought to content her. What votes?"

Every hand ascended with enthusiasm.

"Good for you, Delia!" complimented Jess. "We haven't had a dormitory tea for just ages; not, in fact, since Aggie upset the spirit-lamp. I think Miss Morley's forgotten that now, though. You must do the asking yourself. You're our champion wheedler. If anybody can soften Miss Morley's hard heart it will be you. Tell her Peachy will be homesick, and we feel it'll be our duty to cheer her up a little."

"I'll pitch it as strong as I can," said Delia, "but of course it's no use going too far. Peachy doesn't look a homesick subject in need of cheering. I'm afraid Miss Morley may snort if I put it on that score. I'd better just explain we want to have a stunt. I believe she'll catch on. Leave it to me and I'll try my best to manage her."

"Right-o! We give you carte blanche!"

"Then I'll waddle off now."

Delia's success mostly depended upon tact. She judged that if she asked Miss Morley, tired at the end of a busy morning, she would probably meet with a curt refusal, but that if she found her, seated in her own bed-sitting-room, soothed with afternoon tea and reading a delectable book, her sympathy would be much more readily aroused. On this occasion Delia's judgment was correct. After a perfectly harmonious interview with the Principal she scurried back to her fellow Camellia Buds, her face one satisfied grin.

"She said, 'Certainly, my dear!' We may ask Elvira for a special teapot and a plate of bread and butter, and we may give Antonio three lira apiece to buy us cakes. We may do what we like so long as the room is tidy again before prep. She'll send a prefect at 5.45 to inspect. If the place is in a muddle it'll be the last time, so we'd better be careful, for I could see she meant that."

"We're in luck!" cried Irene, giving a bounce of rapture.

"It's great!"

"Yummy!"

"I thought you'd congratulate me," smirked Delia. "Now let's get busy and decide what sort of a stunt we mean to have. Is Peachy to know, or is it to be a surprise?"

"That's the question! She'll have to be told and invited and all the rest of it, but she needn't hear any details beforehand. I vote we all arrange to come in fancy costume — that would really be a stunt."

"We shall have to tell Peachy that!"

"No, you mustn't. We'll have a costume all ready prepared for her, like the wedding garment in the parable. She'll have nothing to do but slip it on."

If Peachy was looking forward to her own birthday, her friends were anticipating the happy event with enthusiasm. They had decided to hold the festivities in her dormitory, but had required her to give a solemn pledge not to enter the room after 2 p.m. so as to give them a free hand. During the half-hour before drawing-class they met, and held a "Decoration Bee." Nine determined girls, who have prepared their materials, can work wonders in a short time, and in ten hurried minutes they accomplished a vast amount.

"Mary, lend a hand, and help me stand on the dressing table."

"She won't know the place when she sees it!"

"Aren't we all busy bees!"

"It begins to look rather nice, doesn't it?"

"Don't tug this chain! It's tearing! Now you've done it!"

"I flatter myself she'll get the surprise of her life!"

"Ra-ther!"

With flags, paper chains, and garlands of flowers, the decorators contrived to make dormitory 13 look absolutely en fête. They borrowed a table from another bedroom, placed the two together, covered them with a cloth, and spread forth the cakes which Antonio had been commissioned to buy.

"Elvira will fetch us the teapot and the bread and butter at four. We can yank into our costumes in a few seconds, so we needn't waste much time. Don't let Miss Darrer keep you dawdling about the studio," urged Agnes.

159

"No fear of that. The moment the bell goes it will be 'down pencils.' She can hold forth to the others to-day if she wants to talk after school. By the by, everybody's so jealous of us!"

"I know! The seniors are grumbling like anything because they didn't think of having a bedroom tea for Phyllis. It's their own fault. They haven't another birthday amongst them this term. That's the grievance. And Miss Morley won't give leave for a dormitory stunt unless it's somebody's birthday. She's firm on that point. We've certainly all the luck."

The Camellia Buds pursued their art studies that afternoon with a certain abstraction. Peachy worked with her left wrist poised, so that she could obtain a perpetual view of the new gold watch that had arrived by post that morning; Delia frittered her time shamelessly; Esther was guilty of writing surreptitious messages to Joan upon the edges of her chalk copy of "Apollo"; and Irene, usually interested in her work, had a fit of the fidgets. The moment the bell sounded and the class was dismissed they bundled their pencils into their boxes, and left the studio with almost indecent haste.

"Only an hour and a half altogether for our stunt doesn't leave us much time to be polite," remarked Aggie, smarting under a rebuke administered by Miss Darrer, who had restrained their stampede and insisted upon an orderly retreat. "It's all very well for people to saunter elegantly when they've nothing particular to do. I dare say the Italians may look dignified, but we can't stalk about as if we were perpetually carrying water-pots on our heads."

"American girls have more energy than that. I'm just ready to fly to bits," declared Delia, prancing down the passage like a playful kitten.

"I give everybody five minutes to get on their costumes," decreed Jess. "Peachy must stay outside in the passage and wait. I'll tinkle my Swiss goat-bell when you're all to come in."

Peachy, pulling a long face of protest, took her stand obediently in the corridor, while her three roommates entered dormitory 13. Their fancy dresses were lying ready on their beds, and they whisked into them with the utmost haste.

"There! Is my cap on straight? Jess, you look fine! I guess we shan't keep the crowd waiting. We'd earn our livings as quick-change artistes any day. Is that Elvira? Oh, thanks! Put the teapot down there, please. What a huge plate of bread and butter. We'll never eat it! Mary, if you're ready you might be uncovering the grub."

The girls had laid everything in preparation for their feast, and, to protect their dainties from flies, had put sheets of tissue paper over the table. Mary lifted these deftly, but as she removed them her smug satisfaction changed to a howl of dismay. Instead of the tempting dainties which they had placed there with their own hands stood a circle of bricks and stones.

For a moment all three gazed blankly at the awful sight. Then they found speech.

"Our beautiful cakes!"

"Where are they?"

"Who's done this?"

"Oh! the brutes!"

"Who's been in?"

"How dare they?"

"Wherever have they put them?"

"Have they eaten them?"

"Oh! What a shame!"

"What are we to do?"

It was indeed a desperate situation, for loud thumps at the door proclaimed the advent of the visitors, who seemed likely to be provided with a decidedly Barmecide feast. Delia, however, had an inspiration. She stooped on hands and knees and foraged under the beds, announcing by a jubilant screech that she had discovered the lost property. It did not take long to move away the stones and to transfer the plates from the floor to the table, after which three much flustered hostesses opened the door and gushed a welcome to their guests. It was rather a motley group who entered: Irene as a nun in waterproof and hood; Agnes as a Red Cross Nurse; Esther a Turk, with a towel for a turban; Joan a sportsman in her gymnasium knickers; Sheila, in a tricolor cap, represented France; and Lorna was draped with the Union Jack; Jess with a plaid arranged as a kilt made a sturdy Highlander; Mary was an Irish colleen; while Delia, in a wrapper ornamental with fringes of tissue paper, stood for "Carnival." A white dressing jacket trimmed with green leaves, and a garland of flowers were waiting for Peachy, and when the latter was popped on her head she was promptly proclaimed "Queen o' the May." Very much flattered by these preparations in her honor, the guest of the occasion took her place at the table.

"I'm absolutely astounded," she announced. "Where did you get all this spread? You don't mean to tell me Antonio was allowed to go and buy it! It's too topping for words!"

"We thought it had gone out of the window, a moment ago," said Jess, explaining their horrible predicament as she wielded the teapot.

The Camellia Buds listened aghast. Somebody had evidently been playing a shameful trick upon them.

"It's Mabel!"

"Or Bertha!"

"No, no! They'd have taken the cakes quite away instead of only hiding them!"

"Then it must be Winnie or Ruth!"

"Quite likely. They knew we were having the party."

"The wretches!"

"We'll pay them out afterwards!"

"What a mean thing to do!"

"They were honest, at any rate, and didn't take so much as a biscuit."

"They'd have heard about it if they had!"

"'All's well that ends well!'"

"And we'd better clear the dishes while we can. Have another piece of iced sandwich, Mary!"

"No, thanks! I really don't want any more."

The Camellia Buds, having disposed of the feast, and having yet half an hour of the birthday party left on their hands, decided to hold what they called a "Mixed Recitation Stunt." They sat in a circle on the floor and counted out till the lot fell upon one of them, whose pleasing duty it became to act entertainer for the next five minutes, when she was entitled to hand the part on to somebody else. Fate, aided perhaps by a little gentle maneuvering, gave the first turn to Jess.

"I adore poetry, but I never can remember it by heart," she protested, "so don't expect me to 'speak a piece,' please. No, I'm not trying to get out of it. I'll do my bit the same as everybody else. Stop giggling and listen, because I'm going to tell you something spooky. It's a real Highland story. It happened to an aunt of mine. Are you ready? Well then be quiet, because I'm going to begin:

"I have an aunt who lives in the Highlands. Her name is Jessie M'Gregor. Yes, I'm named after her! Some of her family had had the gift of second sight, but not all of them. Her grandmother had it very strongly, and used to foretell the strangest things, and they always came true. Aunt Jessie was a seventh child. That's always supposed to give people the power of seeing visions. If she'd been the seventh child of a seventh child then she'd have been a 'spey wife' and foreseen the future, but she wasn't that exactly. She came very near to it once, though, and that's what I want to tell you about. Uncle Gordon was going to London, and, the day before he started, Auntie was sitting alone in the garden. She hadn't been very well, so she was just leaning back in a deck-chair resting. She wasn't asleep; she was looking at the view and thinking how lovely it all was. She could see right across the moor and down the valley where the river ran; the heather was in blossom and it was a glorious sight. Suddenly it seemed as if everything became blurred and dark, as if a mist were before her eyes. A patch cleared through the midst of this and she could see the valley below as if she were looking through an enormous telescope. The river had burst its banks, and was flowing all over the line, and through the flood came the train, and dashed into the water. She saw this vision only for a moment, then it passed. She rubbed her eyes and wondered if it was a dream. She decided it was a warning. She's very superstitious. Most Highland people are. She didn't want Uncle Gordon to go next day by the little train that ran down the valley, but she knew if she told him her 'vision' he would only laugh at her. So she pretended she wanted to do some shopping at Aberfylde, a town fifteen miles away, where the local railway joins the main line. She told Uncle Gordon that if they motored there together she could see him off on the London express, and then have a day's shopping. So he agreed, and they went in the car. There was a tremendous storm in the night, and it was still raining when they started. Auntie spent the day in Aberfylde and motored back, and when she reached home she noticed the valley had turned into a lake. The terrific rain had swollen all the streams and made the river burst its banks, and the line was flooded, and it was impossible for the train to run. So her 'vision' really did come true after all. She's ever so proud of it, and wrote it all down so that she shouldn't forget it. That's my story. Now it's somebody else's stunt. Let's count out again."

Fortune cast the lot this time on Agnes, who wrinkled up her forehead and protested she didn't know anything to tell, but, when urged, remembered something she had heard during the summer holidays.

"It's true too!" she assured them. "We were staying at Tarana. We had a villa there. Water was very scarce, and we used to have two barrels of it brought every day on donkeyback by a woman whose business it was to act as carrier. Her name was Luigia, and she was very picturesque looking,and had the most beautiful dark eyes, though she always looked fearfully sad. Daddy is fond of sketching, and he painted a picture of her standing with her donkey under the vines. We guessed somehow that she had a history, and we asked Sareda, our cook, about her. Sareda knew everybody in the place. She was a dear old gossip. She got quite excited over Luigia's story. She said it had been the talk of Tarana at the time. Luigia used to be a lovely girl when she was young, and she was quite wealthy for a peasant, because she owned a little lemon grove on the hillside. She inherited it from her father, who was dead. Of course, because she was beautiful and a village heiress, she soon found a sweetheart, and became engaged to Francesco, a fisherman who lived down on the Marina. Everything was going on very happily, and the wedding was fixed, when suddenly it was found there was something wrong with Luigia's glorious eyes. She went to a doctor in Naples, and he told her that unless a certain operation were performed she would go blind. If she went to Paris, to a specialist whom he named, her sight might be saved. Poor Luigia sold her lemon grove in a hurry, to get the necessary money, and packed up and started for Paris immediately. She was away six months, and she came back penniless, but seeing as well as ever. She trudged all the way from Liparo to Tarana, along the coast road, because she could not afford to take the train. When she walked into her own village, the first thing she saw was a wedding party leaving the church. She stopped to watch, and as the procession passed her who should the gayly-dressed bridegroom prove to be but her own faithless sweetheart Francesco. She screamed and fainted, and some kindly neighbors took her in and cared for her. She got work afterwards in the village, but she did not find a husband, because her lemon grove was sold, and these peasants will not marry a wife without a dowry. No wonder she looked so sad. We were always frightfully sorry for her."

Sheila, who was the next entertainer, recited a ballad; and Delia also "spoke a piece," an amusing episode of child life, which she rendered with much humor. The next turn was Irene's, and the girls, who were in a mood for listening, clamored for a story.

"I haven't any first-hand or original adventures," she declared. "My aunts never have psychic experiences, and the people who brought us things to the door in London weren't interesting in the least. If you like romance, though, I remember a tale in a little old, old book that belonged to my great grandmother. It was supposed to be true, and I dare say it may have really happened, more than a hundred years ago, just as 'The Babes in the Wood' really happened in Norfolk in Elizabethan times. It's about a girl named Mary Howard. Her father and mother died when she was only four years old, and she was left an orphan. She was heiress to a very great property, and her uncle, Mr. John Howard, was made her guardian. She also had another uncle, Mr. Dallas, her mother's brother, but he lived in Calcutta and she had never seen him. Mr. John Howard wished to get hold of Mary's estates for himself, so he laid a careful plot. First, he sent all the servants away, including her nurse, Betty Morris, who was devoted to her. Betty offered to stay on without wages, but when this was refused she became suspicious, and wrote a letter to Mr. Dallas warning him to look after his sister's child. But it took many months in those days for a letter to get to Calcutta, and meantime Mr. Howard was pursuing a wicked scheme. Soon afterwards Betty heard that her charge had been stolen by gypsies for the sake of her amber beads, and could not be found anywhere. What had really happened was worse even than Betty had feared. Mr. Howard had hired a sailor, who was in desperate need of money, and bribed him to decoy the child away, take her to the seaside and there drown her. Robert, the sailor, fulfilled the first part of his bargain but not the second. He carried little Mary into a remote part of Wales, but he did not do her any harm. Instead, he became extremely fond of her and determined to save her from her uncle. So he bought a passage in a vessel bound for New Zealand and took her to sea with him, pretending she was his daughter. She was a sweet, gentle little creature, and soon became a favorite on board.

"Among the crew was a Maori boy named Duaterra, whose father was a great chief in New Zealand. The Captain, for some offense, ordered this boy to be flogged, and Duaterra could not forgive the indignity. He planned a terrible revenge. When they reached New Zealand he persuaded the Captain and crew to land in his father's territory; then, summoning his savage friends he ordered a general massacre and killed them all, saving only Robert and little Mary. Robert had been good to him and had given him tobacco, and Duaterra adored Mary, and called her his Mocking Bird. The Maoris plundered and burnt the ship after they had murdered the crew, but they were kind to Robert and Mary, and built a native house for them. Here they lived for four years, for they had no opportunity to escape. Robert married the chief's daughter and settled down as a member of the tribe, but he became very anxious about little Mary. He knew that Duaterra looked upon her as his prospective bride, and he could not bear to think of the lovely child ever becoming the wife of a savage.

"One day a marvelous opportunity occurred for sending Mary home. A ship put in to obtain fresh water, and on the vessel happened to be an old friend of Robert's, named John Morris, actually the brother of Betty Morris, Mary's former nurse. Robert told John the whole story and begged him to take the little girl to England, and deliver her into Betty's hands. He paid for her passage with the money which Mr. Howard had given him as a bribe, and which, as he could not use money in New Zealand, he had kept buried in the ground. Mary was carried on board ship when she was fast asleep at night, and poor Robert cried like a child at parting from her. John Morris proved a faithful friend. He took Mary to London, and sent a message to his sister Betty who was then living in Devonshire. When she arrived she was able to identify her nursling, and to tell John that Mr. Dallas had arrived from Calcutta and had offered a large reward for the recovery of his niece. So Mary was placed under the guardianship of her mother's brother, who took good care both of her and her estates, and the wicked uncle was so overcome with shame, when the story of his crime got about, that he went crazy and ended his days in a lunatic asylum."

"And the best place for him, too!" commented Jess. "He must have been a brute. I dare say things like that really did happen before there were daily papers to publish photos of lost children, and when the Maoris in New . Zealand were still savages. Look here, my hearties! Do you realize it's 5.35? We've got exactly ten minutes to clear up before Rachel arrives on the rampage."

"Gracious! Help me out of these duds! Rachel would never let me hear the end of it if she caught me as a May Queen. I know her sarcastic tongue," squealed Peachy. "Thanks just fifty thousand times for my birthday party. It's been absolutely prime, and I've never enjoyed anything as much for years. Sorry to send you others into the cold, cold world, but I'm afraid you'll have to scoot and change."

CHAPTER XVI

Concerning Juniors

Though all the Camellia Buds had keenly enjoyed Peachy's birthday festivities they were none of them satisfied to allow the mystery of the hiding of their cakes to remain unsolved. They questioned Elsie, who was often an envoy between themselves and the rest of the Transition, but Elsie professed utter ignorance, and assured them that the particular girls whom they suspected had been playing tennis during the whole of their recreation, and could not possibly have had time or opportunity to enter dormitory 13 unnoticed by some of their companions.

"We'd have seen them," declared Elsie. "Besides, they'd have boasted about it. Whoever's the trick was, it wasn't ours. If you want my opinion I should say ask some of those juniors. They're absolute imps and ready for anything."

This was quite a new view of the case. The Camellia Buds had fixed the mischief so certainly on the rival sorority that they had never thought of the younger girls. Peachy, catching Olive, Doris, and Natalie, the trio whom she had named her "triplets," taxed them solemnly with the crime. They burst out laughing.

"We 'did' you neatly!"

"Were you all this time guessing it was us?"

"I expect you had a hunt for those cakes!"

Peachy focussed a stern eye upon their giggling faces, and hypnotized them into attention.

"Now, what d'you mean by such impudence? How dare you go into our dormitory? Juniors aren't to play tricks on their seniors! That was bumped into my head when I was a kid, and I'll bump it jolly well into yours!"

The trio pouted.

"We thought you called yourself our Fairy Godmother," said Olive sulkily.

"Well! So I do!"

"Not much fairy about it, or godmother either. You do nothing for us now."

"You ungrateful little wretches! Haven't we settled Bertha and Mabel for you? Don't you get your biscuits all right at lunch now?"

"Oh, yes. But— —"

"But what?"

"You haven't given us a candy party for ages," broke out Natalie. "You keep all your cakes and fun to yourselves."

"You promised us all sorts of things. We don't think Fairy Godmothers are any use," snorted Olive. "Ta—ta! We're off to a basket-ball."

"Some people make a mighty palaver over next to nothing," sneered Doris, as the trio linked arms and tore away.

Peachy stood looking after them with wrinkled brows. She was a peppery little person, and her temper was up for the moment. All the same, Doris's parting shot struck home. Unfortunately it was true. The Camellia Buds had proclaimed themselves as "Fairy Godmothers, Limited," had adopted juniors with much flourish of trumpets, had certainly fought a crusade and defended them against injustice and infringement of their rights, and then—and then—alack!—in the excitement of other matters had almost forgotten all about them.

Peachy remembered clearly that for the first week of her championship she had made a point of speaking daily to Olive, Doris, and Natalie. Now, for a full fortnight she had scarcely nodded to them at the breakfast table. They had certainly had no opportunity of pouring their childish woes into the sympathetic and motherly ear which she had quite intended should be always open to them.

"I've a wretched memory," she ruminated remorsefully. "Poor kiddies. They've really got rather a grievance, though they needn't have been so cheeky—the young imps! I guess I'd better call a meeting of the Camellia

Buds and see what's to be done. I don't believe any of us have taken any notice of them just lately."

Nine would-have-been philanthropists, reminded of past schemes of benevolence, blushed uneasily, and tried to revive interest in their protégées.

"They always seemed very busy with basket-ball and other things, and not exactly hankering after us," urged Agnes in excuse.

"They could have come to us if they'd wanted, of course," added Mary.

"That wasn't entirely the pact," said Peachy, driving in her tacks with firm hammer. "We offered to 'mother' them, and then forgot all about them. No wonder they think us frauds. What's to be done about it?"

"Get some more cakes somehow and ask them all to a party," suggested Irene enthusiastically. "We have been pigs! I promised Désirée to paint something in her album, and the book's been in my drawer for weeks, and I've never touched it."

"How are we going to get the cakes?"

"Wheedle Antonio again, I suppose. We needn't have any ourselves. If there are two slices apiece for the kids, it will do. We must keep some of our biscuits from lunch so that we can seem to be eating something ourselves. Peachy, you can coax him."

"You always leave it to me. Antonio isn't so easy to manage. Sometimes he's an absolute Pharisee, and won't buy me so much as a single bit of candy. I'll do what I can. Those poor kids shall have a treat if it costs me my last dollar. We owe them something decent."

Antonio, whose lapses from duty were only occasional, and who had been reprimanded lately by Miss Rodgers, who suspected his delinquencies,proved deaf on this occasion to Peachy's blandishments. He protested, with quite aggravating virtue, that it was as much as his place

171

was worth to smuggle even a solitary cream-cake, and that for the future he must no more be the conveyor of contraband sweet stuff.

"Stumped in that quarter," mourned Peachy. "But I'm not going to let this beat me. I've been cultivating a friendship with the cook! Don't laugh! I thought it might come in useful some day. I gave her my blue butterfly brooch (I had two of them!), and I took a snap-shot of her in her Sunday clothes, and she was immensely pleased and flattered. I haven't developed it yet, by the by, but I will, and print her two copies and mount them. If that doesn't melt her heart into sparing me a little butter and sugar it ought to. We can square it this way: none of us ten must eat any butter or sugar at breakfast or tea to-morrow, then we'll have a real right to have it given us afterwards. Don't pull faces! You can have marmalade or jam. What sybarites you are!"

"Right-o," agreed the Camellia Buds, sorrowfully accepting the sacrifice.

"But couldn't the juniors contribute some butter, too?" added Sheila.

"It might be noticed if too many went without. Besides, it's the hostesses who ought to provide the party, not the guests."

Benedicta, the cook, was vulnerable, especially in view of the self-restraint exercised by the heroic ten. She made a hasty calculation of the amount of butter they would normally have consumed, added a package of sugar, and lent them a pan and a spoon. Peachy carried away these spoils chuckling, and hid them carefully behind the summer-house. Then she racked her brains and composed what she considered a suitable and telling invitation:

Peachy wrote her effusion upon a sheet torn from her best pad, folded it, sought out Olive and handed it to her, telling her to pass it round the form. The juniors grinned at its contents. They had felt themselves neglected, but were quite ready to forgive past omissions on the strength of a present invitation.

"Better late than never," decreed Doris. "I suppose we'll go?"

172

"It sounds as if it might be rather nice," agreed the others.

So once more the Camellia Buds were placed in the position of hostesses. Owing to the difficulty of the catering they judged it best to make the candy before the very eyes of their guests, so that they might see for themselves how little there was of it and not grouse if the supply only ran to one bit apiece.

"Otherwise they might think we'd had first go and only given them the leavings," remarked Peachy, who was a born diplomat.

They had counted on borrowing the spirit-lamp which the seniors used for brewing their after-dinner coffee, but at the last moment they found the bottle of methylated spirit was empty.

"What a nuisance! There's no time to send for more. Never mind! We won't be 'done.' Let's light a camp-fire and cook on that. We must manage somehow."

"We certainly can't disappoint them!"

"Not after all this fuss."

The back of the summer-house, as being a particularly retired and secluded spot, was chosen as the rendezvous, and when the nineteen juniors, interested and appreciative, came fluttering up the garden, they were met by scouts, conducted round, commanded to squat in a circle on the ground, and requested to make less noise.

"D'you want the whole of the school to butt in?" warned Jess. "Then keep quiet, can't you? Much taffy you'll get if Rachel catches us. Your only chance is to lie low, you little sillies."

"Rachel's playing tennis!" giggled Evelyn Carr.

"There are other prefects as well as Rachel. Pull yourselves together and don't get so excited."

The juniors, who had been talking at the top of their voices, squealing, and otherwise raising the echoes, restrained their transports and contented themselves with whispers and giggles. The Camellia Buds were fetching fuel, which they had purloined from the gardener's wood-shed. They commenced to build a camp-fire.

Before very long the flames were dancing up. Now, the hostesses in their enthusiasm to be hospitable had foolishly forgotten that it is one thing to stir a pan over a methylated spirit lamp, and quite another to hold it over a camp-fire. Peachy, Agnes, and Mary tried in turns and scorched their hands, egged on by the interested circle watching their performance.

"Make a big bonfire, and let it die down, and put the pan in the hot ashes, just as we cook chestnuts," proposed Irene.

It was, at least, a feasible suggestion. Anything seemed better than open failure before those nineteen pairs of expectant eyes. Volunteers went off for fresh supplies of wood, which was soon crackling merrily. But alas! the Camellia Buds, being rather overwrought and flustered with their experiments, did not calculate on the fact that the smoke of their bonfire would give away their secret. Rachel had handed her tennis racket to Phyllis, and was taking a turn among the orange trees to try to memorize her recitation for the elocution class.

she repeated; then, catching sight of the gray cloud rising from the back of the summer-house, "Hello! What's Giovanni burning? He'll set those orange trees on fire if he doesn't mind."

Abandoning Shakespeare Rachel stalked away to investigate, and surprised the candy party by a sudden appearance in their midst.

"Good gracious, girls! Whatever are you doing here?" she demanded in idiomatic, if hardly strictly classical English.

At the unwelcome sight of the head prefect the juniors one and all simply stampeded, and I regret to say that the more timid of the Camellia Budsfollowed their example. Peachy, Irene, Lorna, Delia, and Jess stood their ground, however.

"We—we were only giving those kids a little fun," answered Peachy.

In dead silence Rachel reviewed the pan, its contents, and the blushing faces before her. Then she said:

"Rather dangerous fun. If that tree catches it will set the summer-house in a blaze next. You know your fire drill? Well, each fetch a bucket of water and put this out! Right turn! Quick march!"

At the words of command the luckless five fled to the house and into the back hall where the fire buckets were kept. They returned with what speed they could, and thoroughly soused their bonfire. Rachel assured herself that it was safely out, then commenced further inquiries.

"We didn't mean any harm," explained Peachy, much on the defensive. "We were only trying to amuse those juniors. They never have a chance to get hold of the tennis courts, and they're tired of eternal basket-ball, and they've rather a thin time of it. We started taking them up because they were so bullied. Bertha and Mabel used to snatch their biscuits away from them at lunch."

Rachel's face was a study.

"Bertha and Mabel snatched their biscuits?" she repeated.

"Yes; we stopped that though."

"I never saw it!"

"They took jolly good care you shouldn't."

"Why didn't you come and tell me?"

Peachy looked embarrassed.

"Well, if you really want to know," she blurted out, "you're so aloof and superior nobody cares to come and tell you anything. We managed it by ourselves."

Rachel winced as if Peachy had struck her a blow.

"I'm sorry if—if that's how I seem to you," she faltered. "I must have failed utterly as head girl if you can't confide in me. The prefects want to be the friends of all the school."

Peachy shrugged her shoulders eloquently.

"I don't quite see where the friendship comes in," she murmured. "You bag the best tennis courts and have the best dormitories, and give your own stunts there. You never ask any of us to them. Do you, now?"

"No, I'm afraid we don't," admitted Rachel, still in the same constrained, almost bewildered, manner. "We really never thought of it."

The four Camellia Buds, listening to their friend's outspoken comments, expected an explosion of wrath from the head prefect, but Rachel only told them to take the buckets back to the house.

"And that too," she added, pointing to the pan. Peachy stooped and picked it up, turned to go, then delivered herself of a last manifesto:

"It's our own butter and sugar that we saved from breakfast and tea, so please don't blame anybody else."

"I blame myself most," whispered Rachel, as she was left alone.

The immediate result of the incident was a prefects' meeting, at which the head girl, full of compunction, stated the facts of the case to her fellow officers.

"We thought we were doing our duty, but it isn't enough just to act as police," she urged. "Those girls in the Transition were on the right track in getting hold of the juniors, though perhaps they did it in the wrong way. This school isn't really united. We're all divided up into our own sororities, and we're not doing enough for one another. We've got to alter it somehow or confess ourselves failures. Do any of us seniors really know the little ones? I'm sure I don't! Yet we ought to be elder sisters to them! That's the real function of prefects—we're not just assistant-mistresses to help to keep order. Don't you agree?"

Sybil, Erica, Phyllis, and Stella were conscientious girls, and when the matter was thus stated they saw it from Rachel's new point of view. They were ready and willing to talk over plans. They decided, amongst other developments, that with Miss Morley's permission, they would invite the juniors in relays to dormitory teas, in order to win their confidence and establish more friendly relations with them. The Transition were also to be cultivated, and their opinion asked on the subject of term-end festivities and other school affairs about which the prefects had never before deigned to consult them. The altered attitude promised a far more healthy and satisfactory state, and Miss Morley, to whom Rachel hinted some of their reasons for offering hospitality, readily agreed, and allowed the juniors to be entertained with cakes and tea upon the veranda.

"The seniors gave us a simply top-hole time," confided Désirée to Irene afterwards. "We'd cream puffs and almond biscuits and preserved ginger, and we played games for prizes. But don't think we liked it any better than your candy parties. The prefects are awfully kind to us now, but it was you who took us up first! We can't forget that!"

CHAPTER XVII

The Anglo-Saxon League

There was an old established custom at the Villa Camellia that on the evening of the last day of March (unless that date happened to fall on a Sunday) the pupils were allowed special license after supper, and, regardless of ordinary rules, might disport themselves as they pleased until bedtime. Irene, who had not yet been present on one of these occasions, heard hints on all sides of coming fun, mingled with mystery. Peachy twice began to tell her something, but was stopped by Delia. Joan and Sheila seemed to be holding perpetual private committee meetings; Elsie spent much time in Jess Cameron's dormitory; and, wonder of wonders, Esther Cartmell was seen walking arm in arm with Mabel Hughes. Though Irene asked many questions from various friends as to the nature of the evening's amusement she could get no certain information. They laughed, evaded direct answers, made allusions to things she did not understand, and whisked away like will-o'-the-wisps. Very much puzzled, and not altogether pleased, she sought her buddy.

"They've all gone mad," she assured Lorna. "I can't get a word of sense out of Peachy; Esther was almost nasty, and Jess shut the door in my face. What's the matter with them? Have I developed spots or a squint? Why have I suddenly become a leper?"

Lorna, who was busy with French translation, shut her dictionary with a bang.

"I've no patience with them," she groused. "It's because you're English. I suppose we shall have to get up a stunt of our own, just out of retaliation, but I'm sick of the whole business."

"What do you mean?"

"Why, it's become a sort of custom to make this a nationality night. The American girls all band together, and so do the South Africans and the Australians; and the Scotch girls are a tremendous clique of their own.

They play jokes on every one else, and sometimes it almost gets to fighting."

"Between the sororities?"

"Sororities are forgotten for the time being. Your dearest chum in the Camellia Buds will turn against you if it's a question of Scotch or English, or American or British. I advise you to put away everything you value. The South Africans came into my cubicle last year and smeared my cold cream over my pillow. Of course your bed will be filled with brushes and boots, and any hard oddments they can find lying about. You won't be able to find anything in the morning. The place is an absolute muddle."

"How horrid!"

"Yes, it is horrid. I can't see the fun of it, myself. Practical jokes can go too far, in my opinion, and some of those juniors get so rough they hurt each other. I'd keep out of it only it's wise to stay and defend your own cubicle, or you'd find your blanket hidden and your soap gone."

"Do the seniors join in?"

"No. They barricade themselves in their bedrooms and have some private fun, but they leave us to do as we like. It's the Transition and juniors who play the tricks. Of course, the seniors must know what's going on, because they used to do the same themselves, but they just shut their eyes."

"Oh," said Irene thoughtfully. "And because a thing has always been must it always be? Can't it ever be altered? Are we bound to do nothing but play tricks on the last night of March?"

"It ought to be altered. I've a jolly good mind to go to Rachel and tell her my views about it. She's been much nicer lately than she used to be. Perhaps she'd listen. If she doesn't there'd be no harm done, at any rate. Will you come with me? I don't like going by my little lonesome."

The two girls tapped at the door of dormitory 9, and fortunately found the head prefect within and alone. She received them quite graciously and listened with interest to what Lorna had to say.

"I'm so thankful you've told me," she said in reply. "I agree with you absolutely. It's time this silly business was put a stop to. We prefects have held back because we didn't want to be spoil-sports, but I believe you really voice the opinion of a good many girls. I used to get very tired of it when I was in the Transition myself. If Miss Rodgers found out some of the tricks that are played she'd never let us have the holiday again."

"Can't we persuade them to do something else instead—something really jolly?"

"We must. I'll think about it. Leave it to me. I've been turning it over in my mind for some time, though my ideas never crystallized. I'll have some scheme ready. I can depend on you two to support me in the Transition?"

"Rather!"

Rachel, reporting the interview to her fellow prefects, found them entirely in agreement. They were dissatisfied with many things in the Transition and junior forms, and this Nationality evening was considered the limit. Something seemed to be needed at the present crisis to weld together the various factions of the Villa Camellia, and turn them into one harmonious whole. The prefects were aware that the various sororities were really rival societies, and that, though they might give great fun and enjoyment to their respective members, they were productive of jealousy rather than union.

"We want a common motive," said Rachel. "An inspiration, if possible. I believe some sort of a league would do it. Something outside ourselves, and bigger than just the little world of school. Something that even the smallest juniors could join, and in which girls who have left could still take an interest. It's dawning on me! I believe I've got it! I'm going to call it 'The Anglo-Saxon League.' We'll get everybody to join, and fix its first festival for the 31st of March. It should just take the wind out of those silly nationality tricks. I'll speak to Miss Rodgers and ask her to let us have a parade and dance, with prizes for the best costumes. They'd love that, anyhow. I'll call a meeting in the gym and put it to them. I believe it will catch on."

The pupils at the Villa Camellia were not overdone with public meetings. They responded therefore with alacrity to the notice which Rachel, after obtaining the necessary permission from the authorities, pinned upon the board in the hall. They were all a little curious to know what she wanted to talk to them about. A few anticipated a scolding, but the majority expected some more pleasant announcement.

"Rachel's wrought up, but she doesn't look like jawing us," was the verdict of Peachy, who had passed the head prefect in the corridor. Some of the seniors constituted themselves stewards and arranged the audience to their satisfaction, with juniors on the front benches and the Transition behind. When everybody was seated, Rachel stepped on to the platform and rang the bell for silence. Her cheeks were pink with excitement and there was a little thrill of nervousness in her voice, as if she were forcing herself to a supreme effort, but this passed as she warmed to her subject.

"Girls," she began, "I asked you to come here because I want to have a talk with you about our school life. You'll all agree with me that we love the Villa Camellia. It's a unique school. I don't suppose there's another exactly like it in the whole world. Why it's so peculiar is that we're a set of Anglo-Saxon girls in the midst of a foreign-speaking country. We ourselves are collected from different continents — some are Americans, some English, some from Australia, or New Zealand, or South Africa — but we all talk the same Anglo-Saxon tongue, and we're bound together by the same race traditions. Large schools in England or America take a great pride in their foundation, and they play other schools at games and record their victories. We can't do that here, because there are no foreign teams worth challenging, so we've always had to be our own rivals and have form matches. In a way, it hasn't been altogether good for us. We've got into the bad habit of thinking of the school in sections, instead of as one united whole. I've even heard squabbles among you as to whether California or Cape Colony or New South Wales are the most go-ahead places to live in. Now, instead of scrapping, we ought to be glad to join hands. If you think of it, it's a tremendous advantage to grow up among Anglo-Saxon girls from other countries and hear their views about things. It ought to keep you from being narrow, at any rate. You get fresh ideas and rub your corners off. What I want you particularly to think about, is this: it's the duty of all English-speaking people to cling together. If they've ever had any differences it's time they forgot them. The world seems to be in the melting-pot at present, and there are many strange prophecies about the future. Black and yellow races are increasing and growing so rapidly that they may be ready to brim over their boundaries some day and swamp the white civilizations. Anglo-Saxons ought to be prepared, and to stand hand in hand to help one another. I've been reading some queer things lately. One is that a new continent is slowly rising out of the Pacific Ocean — Lemuria they call it — and some day, hundreds of years hence, there may be land there instead of water, and people living on it. They say too that the center of gravity of both the British Empire and the United States is moving towards the Pacific. Sydney may grow more important than London, and San Francisco than New York when the trade routes make them fresh pivots of energy. Another funny thing I read is that as the world is changing a new race seems to be emerging. Travelers say that the modern children in Australia don't look in the least like English children or French children, or any European nation — they are a fresh type. America has been populated by people from practically all the older countries, but I read that children who are being born there now differ in their head measurements from babies of the older races. Perhaps some of you may be interested in this and some of you may only be bored, but what I want to rub in is that if a new, and perhaps superior, race is evolving it's surely part of our work to help it on. Here we all are, girls from England, America, and the British Colonies, of the same race and speaking the same language. Let us make an

Anglo-Saxon League, and pledge ourselves that wherever we go over the face of the world we will carry with us the best traditions. We're out for Peace, not War, and Peace comes through sympathy. The women of those great eastern nations, the Chinese, the Japanese, and the Hindoos, who are only just awakening to a sense of freedom, will look to us Westerners for their example. Can't we hold out the hand of sisterhood to them, and teach them our highest ideals, so that in the centuries to come they may be our friends instead of our enemies? It's a case of 'Take up the White Man's burden.' We stand together, not as Scotch, or Canadians, or New Zealanders or Americans, but as good Anglo-Saxons, the apostles of peace, not 'frightfulness.'

"I'm going to ask every girl in this room to join the League. There'll be various activities in connection with it. We haven't decided all yet, but we hope one of them will be to establish a correspondence between this school and other schools in England and the Colonies and in America. We'd like to write letters to their prefects and hear what they are doing, and have copies of their school magazines. It would be like shaking hands over the ocean. Then why shouldn't we correspond with girls in missionary schools in India or China or Japan? Think how exciting to have letters from them and read them aloud. We should hear all about their eastern lives, and all kinds of interesting things.

"Well, these are far-away schemes yet that need a little time to establish. I've something much nearer to put before you. Miss Rodgers has given us seniors leave to hold a fancy-dress dance on the 31st of March, from 7.30 to 9.30, here in the gym. We invite every girl who joins the League to come. Nationality costumes will be welcomed. There will be first, second, and third prizes for the best dresses. The judges will take into consideration the scantiness of the materials available, but they wish to announce that any girl found guilty of borrowing articles for her costume without the leave of their owners will be disqualified, and further, that any member of the League convicted of playing practical jokes will be expelled from the dance. The prefects think it wise and necessary to mention that, though the evening of March 31st has been set aside as a holiday and certain rules have been relaxed, the school is nevertheless bound to preserve its usual code of good manners, and every girl is put on her honor to behave herself. I'm sure I need not say more, for you surely understand me, and agree that when Miss Rodgers has allowed us to have this fun we ought not to abuse her kindness. Will every one who's ready to join the League and wants to come to the dance hold up her hand."

Almost every girl in the room responded to Rachel's invitation. Some—the higher-thinking ones—were attracted by the ideals of the League itself; others were merely anxious not to be left out of the festivities. It was a long time since the school had had a fancy ball. There had been private carnivals in the dormitories, but not a public official affair at which everybody could compete in the way of dresses. Rumor spread like wild-fire round the room. It was whispered that Miss Morley herself meant to come, disguised as Hiawatha, that Miss Rodgers had offered a gold wrist-watch as first prize, and that there were yards of gorgeous materials in the storeroom to be had for the asking. The thrill of these manifold possibilities was sufficient to eclipse the attractions of their former intentions for the evening's amusement. It was really more interesting to evolve costumes than plan tricks. Every true daughter of Eve loves to look her best, and womanhood, even in the bud, cannot withstand the supreme magnet of clothes. Little Doris Parker, South African hoyden as she was, voiced the general feeling when she confessed:

"I'd meant to give those Australians a hot time of it. They may thank their stars for the League. Though I'm rather glad I shan't have to tease Natalie, because she's my chum. We're both going together as southern hemispheres. It'll be ripping fun."

The Camellia Buds, who had been temporarily estranged by the impending national divisions, returned to the friendly atmosphere of their sorority, and lent one another garments for the fête.

"It's a good thing Rachel put a stopper on commandeering," commented Delia. "Mabel was simply shameless at the Carnival. Had anybody told?"

"Sybil and Erica knew; and Rachel isn't really as blind as we thought. At any rate, she's awake now, and a far nicer prefect than she used to be. By the by, we're to draw lots as to who may borrow out of the theatrical property box."

"Oh, goody. I hope I'll win. There's a little gray dress there I've set my heart on. I'll cry oceans if I don't get it," declared Peachy.

"Cheer up, poor old sport! If the luck comes my way I'll try and grab it for you. I don't need anything for myself, thank goodness."

"You white angel! That's what I call being a real mascot. I'll share my last dollar with you some day — honest Injun!"

The contents of Miss Morley's theatrical property box, apportioned strictly by lot, did not go far among fifty-six girls. Miss Rodgers allowed two ofthe prefects, with a teacher, to make an expedition into Fossato and rummage the shops for some yards of cheap, gay materials, imitation lace, and bright ribbons, which they were commissioned to buy on behalf of certain of their schoolfellows, but most of the dancers had to contrive their costumes out of just anything that came to hand, often exercising an ingenuity that was little short of marvelous. Acting upon Rachel's suggestion many of them personified various continents or countries. The Stars and Stripes of the American flag were conspicuous, and there were several Red Indians, with painted faces and feathers in their hair.

Sheila, Mary, Esther, and Lorna repeated the costumes they had worn at the tableau, and went as representatives of Canada, South Africa, India, and New Zealand, but Peachy lent her cowboy costume to Rosamonde, and turned up as Longfellow's "Evangeline," in gray Puritan robe and neat white cap, a part which, though very becoming, did not accord with her mischievous, twinkling eyes.

"Not much 'Mayflower Maiden' about you!" giggled Delia.

"Why not?" asked Peachy calmly. "I guess poor Evangeline wasn't always on the weep! No doubt she had her lively moments sometimes. I'm showing her at her brightest and best. You ought to give thanks for a new interpretation of her!"

Winnie Duke scored tremendously by robing in skin rugs as a Canadian bear, while Joan was able to carry out a long-wished-for project and turn herself into a very good imitation of a kangaroo.

Fifty-six girls, arrayed fantastically in all the colors of the rainbow, made a delectable sight as they paraded round the gymnasium. The prefects had shirked the difficult and delicate task of judging, and had called in Miss Rodgers and Miss Morley to decree who were to receive the prizes. Perhaps they also found the decision too hard, for they chose a dozen of the best, put them to the public vote and counted the shows of hands. Gwen Hesketh, a member of the Sixth, in a marvelously contrived Chinese costume, was first favorite; little Cyntha West, as a delightful goblin, secured second prize, while the kangaroo, to the satisfaction of the Transition, was awarded the third. The gold wristlet watch was of course a myth, and the rewards were mere trifles, but the principals had risen to the occasion sufficiently to contribute to the entertainment by providing lemonade between the dances, which in the opinion of the girls was a great addition to the festivities, and made the event seem more like "a real party."

Before they separated, the League formed an enormous circle round the room and each clasping her neighbor's hand, all joined in the singing of "Auld Lang Syne": cowboy and Indian princess, Redskin and Scotch lassie, Canadian and Jap roared the familiar chorus, and having thus worked off steam retired to their dormitories and went to bed without breaking their pledge of good behavior. Rachel, returning from her round of supervision, heaved a sigh of immense relief.

"I was dreading this evening," she confided to Sybil. "I was so afraid they'd forget their promises and begin that rowdy teasing. I believe we've broken the tradition of that, thank goodness. I hope it may never be revived again."

"Thanks to the Anglo-Saxon League!"

"And may that go on and flourish long after we have left the Villa Camellia," added Rachel.

CHAPTER XVIII

Greek Temples

The opening of the post-bag at the Villa Camellia, bearing as it did missives from most quarters of the globe, was naturally a great daily event. Some of the girls were lucky in the matter of correspondence — Peachy received numerous letters — and others were not so highly favored. Poor Lorna was generally left out altogether. Her father wrote to her occasionally, but she had no other friend or relation to send her even a post-card. She accepted the omission with the sad patience which was her marked characteristic. Her affection for Irene had been an immense factor in her school life this term, but she was still very different from other girls, and kept her old barrier of shy reserve. Irene, noticing Lorna's wistful look towards the post-bag, often tried to share her correspondence with her buddy; she would show her all her picture post-cards, briefly explaining who the writers were and to what their allusions referred. At first Lorna had only been languidly polite over them, but later she grew interested. Second-hand articles may not be as good as your own, but they are better than nothing at all, and the various items of news made topics for conversations and gave her a glimpse of other people's homes.

Irene, finishing her budget one morning, sorted out any which she might hand on to her chum.

"Not home letters — yours are sacred, Mummie darling! — and she wouldn't care to hear about Aunt Doreen's attack of rheumatism. There are two post-cards she may like, and this lovely long stave from Dona. Lorna, dear! I've told you about my cousin Dona Anderson? She's at Brackenfield College. She's older than I am, but somehow we've always been such friends. I like her far and away the best out of that family. She doesn't find time to write very often, because she's in the Sixth and a prefect, and it keeps her busy, and besides she never has been much of a scribbler. I haven't heard from her for months. This is ever such a jolly letter, though, if you care to look at it."

"Thanks," said Lorna, accepting the offer. "Yes, I remember you told me about her. She must be rather a sport. I wish she were at the Villa Camellia instead of in England."

"And Dona thinks there isn't any other school in the world except hers."

But Lorna had opened the closely-written sheets and was already reading as follows:

St. Githa's,

Brackenfield College,

March 30th.

Renie dear!

I've been meaning to write to you for ages! Mother told me the news of how you all packed off to Naples, and she sent me the address of your school. I do hope you like it and have settled down. I always wanted you to come to Brackenfield! You know Joan is here now? It's her first term and she's radiantly happy. She's a clever little person at her work, and we think she's going to be great at games. Of course she's only in New Girls' Junior Team, but she's done splendidly already. Ailsa was looking on yesterday and complimented her afterwards.

We've had quite a good hockey season. The Coll. played "Hawthornden" last week, and when the whistle went for "time" the score was 4-2 in our favor! An immense triumph for us, because we've never had the luck to beat them before, and we were feeling desperate about it. They were so cock-sure of winning too! Do you get any hockey at Fossato? Or is it all tennis?

We'd a rather decent gymnastic display a while ago. Mona and Beatrice are very keen on gym practice and they did some really neat balance-walking on the bars, also side vaulting. The juniors gave country dances in costume, and of course that sort of thing is always clapped by parents. We're working hard now for the concert. Ailsa and I have to sing a duet and we're both terrified. Hope we shan't break down and spoil the show!

I'm enjoying this year at Brackenfield most immensely. It's lovely being a prefect. I was fearfully scared when first the Empress sent for me and told me I was to be a school officer, but I've got on swimmingly, thanks largely to Ailsa, I think. Of course we're still inseparable. We always have been since our first term at St. Ethelberta's, when I smuggled the mice into No. 5 to scare Mona out of the dormitory and leave room for Ailsa.

I go nearly every week to The Tamarisks. It cheers Auntie up to see me. She's rather lonely since Elaine was married. By the by you asked me what had become of Miss Norton's little nephew Eric. You admired his photograph so much, with those lovely golden curls. Of course they're cut off now. He's ever so much stronger and has gone to a preparatory school. I still send him books and things and he writes me sweet letters. I'm planning to coax Mother to let me invite Nortie to bring him to us for part of the summer holidays. I don't want to lose sight of the dear little chap.

Now for home news. Leonard is in India, and likes the life there, and Larry is at Cambridge. Peter and Cyril are still at St. Bede's, and getting on well. Their letters are full of nothing but football though. Nora's baby girl is a darling, and Michael is still very sweet though he's growing rather an imp. You know we always describe ourselves as an old-fashioned rambling family. Well, one of us is rambling in your direction! Marjorie is making a tour in Italy with some friends of hers — the Prestons. Isn't she lucky? The last post-card she sent me was from Rome, and she said they were going on to Naples, so it's just within the bounds of possibility that you may see her. I wish I could have come out for Easter and had a peep at you. I'd like to see oranges really growing on orange trees! Perhaps Ailsa's going to ask me for the holidays though. They have a country cottage in Cornwall and it would be top-hole there.

Write and tell me about your southern school when you have time. I'd love to hear. Do you have to speak Italian there?

Well, I must stop now and do my prep. There's a junior tapping at the door too and wanting to see me. Prefects don't get much time to themselves!

With best love,

Your affectionate coz,

Dona Anderson.

"What a jolly letter," commented Lorna, as she handed it back.

"Yes, Dona is a dear. I used to want to go to Brackenfield, but I wasn't well last year, and Mother said it was too strenuous a school for me. Isn't it a joke that Marjorie is in Italy? What fun if she were to turn up some day. I have a kind of feeling that I'm going to see her. I'm getting quite excited."

Lorna did not reply. Irene's correspondence was after all only a matter of half importance to her. Indeed the thought of that lively family of cousins brought out so sharply the contrast of her own loneliness that she almost wished she had never heard of them. Why did other people get all the luck in life?

"What's the matter? You're very glum," said Irene.

"Nothing! I can't always be sparkling, can I?"

"I suppose not. But I thought you'd be interested in Marjorie coming."

"How can I be interested in some one I've never seen?" snapped Lorna, walking abruptly away.

Irene looked after her and shook her head.

"I've put my foot in it somehow," she ruminated. "You never know how to take Lorna. A thing that pleases her one day annoys her the next. She's certainly what you'd call 'katawampus' this morning."

It was getting very near the end of the term now, and all the girls were talking eagerly about going home. Before they separated for their vacation, however, there was to be one more of Miss Morley's delightful excursions. Next term would be too hot to do much sightseeing, so those of the pupils who had not yet been shown the wonders of the neighborhood were to have the chance of a visit to the Greek temples at Pæstum. It would be a longer expedition even than to Vesuvius, and as many were anxious to take part it was arranged to hire a motor char-à-banc to accommodate about twenty-four girls and several teachers. The lucky ones were of course well drilled beforehand in the history and architecture of the place, and knew how a Greek colony had settled there about the year 600 B.C. and had built the magnificent Doric temples, which, with the sole exception of those at Athens, are the finest existing ruins of the kind.

Miss Rodgers had limited the excursion to seniors and Transition, thinking it too long and fatiguing a day for the juniors. All the prefects were going, while the Camellia Buds, with the exception of Esther and Mary, who had been before, were also included in the party.

"This is one thing you wouldn't get at any rate in an ordinary English school," said Lorna. "I don't suppose the Brackenfield girls are taking excursions to Greek temples."

"There aren't any Greek temples in England for them to go and see, silly," laughed Irene.

"Well, Abbeys or Castles or anything ancient."

"From Dona's accounts that sort of thing is not in their line. They concentrate on games."

"Hockey is all very well, but give me our orange groves and the blue sea."

"Ye-es; but I sometimes hanker for a really A1 hockey match!"

"Don't you like the Villa Camellia?"

"Of course I do. What's the matter, Lorna? I believe you're jealous of Brackenfield!"

"No, I'm not, though I'm sure I'm right in fancying you'd rather be there than here."

"How absurd you are!"

"Am I? All right! Call it absurd if you want. Are you going to sit next to me in the char-à-banc?"

Irene looked conscious.

"I promised Peachy! But you can sit the other side, you know."

"Oh, no, thanks! If you've made arrangements already I'm sure I don't want to interfere with them. I wouldn't spoil sport for worlds."

"You are the limit!"

"Am I? Indeed! Perhaps you'd rather not have me for a buddy any more?"

"For gracious' sake stop talking nonsense! You're the weirdest girl I've ever met," snapped Irene. Then to avoid an open quarrel she walked away, leaving her chum in the depths of misery.

Lorna knew her own temper was at fault, but she was in a touchy mood and laid the blame on fate.

"If I had a nice home like other girls, and had been going there for ripping holidays, and had brothers and cousins to write to me I'd be different," she excused herself, quite forgetting that, however much we may be handicapped, the molding of our character is after all in our own hands.

As it was she sulked, and when the char-à-banc arrived, although Irene beckoned her to a place beside herself and Peachy, she took no notice and waited till everybody else had scrambled in. The result of this was that she finally found herself seated away from all her own friends and next to Mrs. Clark, the wife of the British chaplain, who by Miss Morley's invitation had joined the excursion. Perhaps on the whole it was just as well. Mrs. Clark was what the girls called "a perfect dear," and a few hours in her company was a restful mind tonic. She had a cheery manner and chatted upon all sorts of pleasant subjects, so that after a time Lorna began to forget her "jim-jams" and even to volunteer a remark or two, instead of confining her conversation to monosyllables.

Certainly any girl must have been hard to please who did not enjoy herself. The motor drive was one of the loveliest in Italy. They passed through glorious scenery, all the more beautiful as it was the blossoming time of the year and flowers were everywhere. On a marshy plain, as they reached Pæstum, the fields were spangled with the little white wild narcissus, growing in such tempting quantities that Miss Morley asked the driver to stop the char-à-banc, and allowed all to dismount and pick to their hearts' content.

"Isn't the scent of them heavenly!" said Lorna, burying her nose in a bunch of sweetness.

"Luscious!" agreed Mrs. Clark. "I think the old Greeks must have gathered these to weave garlands for their heads when they went to their festivals. I'm glad tourists are safe here now. This marsh, just where we're standing, used to be a tremendous haunt of brigands, and any travelers coming to see the ruins ran the chance of being robbed. My father had his purse taken years ago. Don't look frightened. The government have put all that down at last. The neighborhood of Naples has improved very much since I was a girl. I remember pickpockets used to be quite common on the quay at Santa Lucia, and nobody troubled to interfere. You can walk to the boat nowadays and carry a hand-bag without fearing every moment it will be snatched."

But the driver was urging the necessity of pushing on, so all took their seats again, and in due course reached Pæstum. The girls had, of course, seen photographs of the place beforehand, yet even these had hardly prepared them for the stately magnificence of the three great temples that suddenly broke upon their vision. Their immense size, their loneliness, far from town or city, and their glorious situation betwixt hill and blue sea, almost took the breath away, and filled the mind with glowing admiration for the genius of Greek architecture. The rows of fluted Doric columns, tapering symmetrically towards the roof, were like beautiful lily stems supporting flowers, the mellow yellow tone of the stone was varied by the ferns and acanthus which grew everywhere around, and the sunshine, falling on the rows of delicate shafts, seemed to linger lovingly, and invest them with a halo of golden light.

"What must these temples have been when the world was young!" said Miss Morley. "If we could only get a glimpse of them as they were more than two thousand years ago. Think what processions must have paced down those glorious aisles. Priests and singers and worshipers all crowned with flowers. The rose gardens of Pæstum used to be famous among the Roman poets. The marvel is that the stones have stood all these centuries of time. It seems as if Art and Beauty have triumphed over decay."

The party had brought lunch baskets, and they now sat down on the steps of the Temple of Neptune to enjoy their picnic. Fortunately the grounds of the ruins were enclosed by railings, so they were preserved from the attentions of a group of beggar children, who had greeted the arrival of the char-à-banc with outstretched palms and torrents of entreaties for "soldi," and who were hanging about the gate evidently waiting for any fresh opportunity that might occur of asking alms. Four lean and hungry dogs, however, had managed to slip into the enclosure, and made themselves a nuisance by sitting in front of the picnickers and keeping up an incessant chorus of loud barking. The girls tried to stop the noise by throwing them fragments of sandwiches, but their appetites were so insatiable that they would have consumed the whole luncheon and have barked for more, so Miss Morley, tired of the noise, finally chased them off the premises with her umbrella.

"They're as bad as wolves. And as for the children they're shameless. They've been taught to look upon tourists as their prey. If you go near the gate dozens of little hands are poked through the railings and an absolute shriek of 'soldi' arises. It spoils people's enjoyment to be so terribly pestered by beggars. And the more you give them the more they ask."

"They're having a try at somebody else now," remarked Rachel, watching the crowd of small heads leave their vantage ground of the railings and surge round a carriage which drove up. "Some other tourists are coming to see the sights—two gentlemen and three ladies, very glad I expect to show their tickets and get through the gate out of the reach of that rabble. They're walking this way. They must be rather annoyed to find a school in possession of the place."

The strangers also carried luncheon baskets, and seemed seeking a spot for a picnic. They were filing past the group on the steps when Irene suddenly sprang up.

"Why, Marjorie! Marjorie!" she exclaimed joyfully. "Don't you know me?"

The handsome, gray-eyed girl thus addressed looked puzzled for a moment, then her face cleared with recognition.

"Renie! You've grown out of all remembrance! To think of meeting you here of all places. I'm with some friends—the Prestons. We're on a six weeks' tour in Italy. I went to see your mother in Naples yesterday. What a jolly flat you have there! Isn't this absolutely glorious? I'm having the time of my life."

"I should think you are by the look of you," laughed Irene. "Dona wrote and told me you were coming to Italy, but I never expected to find you here to-day. If Miss Morley will let me, may I bring my lunch along and join your party for a little while? There are ten dozen things I want to ask you."

"Of course. Come and share our sandwiches. We've plenty to spare."

Having received the required permission, Irene went away to talk to her cousin, considerably to the admiration of most of her chums, and decidedly to the envy of one. Lorna, who had settled herself by her side on the steps, was not pleased to be deserted. She could never quite forgive Irene for having so many friends. The brooding cloud that had temporarily dispersed settled down again. When the girls got up to explore the temple she marched glumly away by herself. All the beauty and wonder and loveliness of the scene was lost upon her; for the sake of a foolish fit of jealousy she was spoiling her own afternoon.

She was sitting upon a fallen piece of masonry, very wretched, and indulging in a private little weep, when a footstep sounded on the stone pavement, and somebody came and sat down quietly beside her. It was Mrs. Clark, and she had the tact to take no notice as Lorna surreptitiously rubbed her eyes. She knew far more about the girls at the Villa Camellia than any of them suspected, and she had a very shrewd suspicion what lay at the bottom of Lorna's mind. A skillful remark or two turned the conversation on to the topic of the holidays.

"It's nice to go home, isn't it?"

Lorna gave a non-committal grunt.

"Even if you miss your friends!"

"I suppose so."

"And it's pleasant to think they may miss you?"

"I don't flatter myself they'll do that," burst out Lorna. "They're so happy they never think about me. Mrs. Clark, you don't know my home. I've nobody—nobody except my father. The others have brothers and sisters and friends, and all they want—and I have nothing."

"Except your father," added Mrs. Clark. "How about him? Sometimes when two people are left lonely they can make the world blossom again for one another. Isn't it time you began to take your mother's place? Can't you set yourself these holidays to give him such a bright, cheerful daughter that he'll hardly want to part with you when you go back to school? Wouldn't you rather he missed you than your chums? He's closer to you than they are. Ask yourself if you were to lose him is there one of your friends who could mean as much to you? I sometimes think that girls who are brought up at boarding-school are apt to lose the right sense of value of their own relations. Their companions and the games fill their lives, and they go back for the holidays almost like visitors in their own homes. When they leave school they're dissatisfied and restless, because they've never been accustomed to suit themselves to the ways of the household, and have no niche into which they can fit. The old round of 'camaraderie' is over, and they have been trained for nothing but community life. Take my advice and make your niche now while you have the opportunity. Show your father you want him, and that he's your best friend, and he'll begin to realize that he wants you. How old are you? Nearly sixteen! In another year or so you should be able to live with him altogether and be the companion to him that he needs. You say you envy girls with many brothers and sisters, but there's another side to that—if you're the only child you get the whole of the love. Remember you're all your father has, and let him see that you care. It's a greater thing to be a good daughter than to be the favorite of the school. If you keep that object in view you ought to have many years of happiness before you."

"I know. I was forgetting that side of it," said Lorna slowly.

"Think it over then, for its worth considering. A woman may have many brothers and sisters, she can have another husband or another child, but it's only one father or mother she'll get, and the bond is a close one. Is that Irene waving to us? What is she calling? We're to come on with the party! Yes indeed, we ought to be moving along. We shall only just have time to explore the other temples before we must start back in the char-à-banc."

CHAPTER XIX

In Capri

April, the beautiful April of Southern Italy, was half-way spent before the Villa Camellia broke up for the holidays. There were the usual term-end examinations, at which distressed damsels, with agitated minds and ink-stained fingers, sat at desks furnished with piles of foolscap, and cudgeled their brains to supply facts to fill the sheets of blank paper; there was the reading out of results, with congratulations to those who had succeeded, and glum looks from Miss Rodgers to those who had failed; then followed the bringing down of boxes, the joyful flutter of packing, the last breakfast, and the final universal exodus.

"Good-by, dear old thing!"

"Do miss me a little!"

"Hope you'll have a ripping time!"

"Be a sport and write to me, won't you?"

"Hold me down, somebody, I'm ready to fizz over!"

"You won't forget me, dearie? All right! Just so long as we know!"

Lorna, who had anticipated previous vacations as simply a relief from the toil of lessons, went home to Naples with quite altered feelings from those of former occasions. She was determined that, if it possibly lay in her power, she would make her father enjoy the time she spent with him. In spite of injustice and cruel wrong there might surely be some happy hours together, and she would win him to live in the present, instead of continually brooding over the past. The immense, terrible pathos of the situation appealed to the deepest chords in her nature. Her father was still in the prime of his years, a handsome, clever man, who might have done much in the world. Was it yet too late? Lorna sometimes had faint, budding hopes that in some fresh country his wrecked career might be righted, and that he might make a new start and rise triumphant over the ruin of other days. He was glad to see her. There was no doubt about that. The knowledge that she now shared his secret placed her on a different footing. It was a relief to him to have some one in whom he could confide, some one who knew the reason for his hermit mode of living, and above all who believed in his innocence. Insensibly Lorna's presence acted upon him for good. The nervous, hunted look began to fade out of his eyes, and sometimes he actually smiled as she recounted the doings of the Camellia Buds, or other happenings at school.

"Daddy!" she said once, "couldn't we go out to Australia or America, or somewhere where nobody would know us, and make a fresh life for ourselves?"

A gleam of hope flitted for a moment over the sad face.

"I've thought of that, Lorna. Perhaps I've been too morbid. It seemed to me that every Englishman must know of what I had been accused. And I had no credentials to offer. Now, with a five years' reference from the Ferroni Company in Naples I might have a chance of a job in Australia. It's worth considering—for your sake, child, if not for mine."

During the whole of the first week of the holidays Lorna amused herself as best she might in their little lodgings in Naples. While her father was at the office she read or sewed, or played on a wretched old piano, which had little tune in it but was better than nothing. The evenings were her golden times, for then they would go out together, sometimes into the Italian quarters of the city, or sometimes by tram into the suburbs, where there were beautiful promenades with views of the sea. In these walks she grew to be his companion, and instead of shrinking from him as in former days, she met him on a new footing and gave him of her best. Together they planned a home in a fresh hemisphere, and talked hopefully of better things that were perhaps in store for them over the ocean. And so life went on, and father and daughter might have realized their vision, and have emigrated to another continent where no one knew their name or their former history, and have made a fresh start and won comparative success, but Dame Fortune, who sometimes has a use for our past however bitterly she seems to have mismanaged it, interfered again, and with fateful fingers re-flung the dice.

It certainly did not seem a fortunate circumstance, but quite the reverse, when the grandchildren of their landlady, who occupied the étage above their rooms, sickened with measles. Lorna had never had the complaint, and it was, of course, most important that she should not convey germs back to the Villa Camellia, so it was a vital necessity to move her immediately out of the area of infection. Signora Fiorenza, harassed but sympathetic, suggested a visit to Capri, where her sister, Signora Verdi, who owned a little orange farm and had a couple of spare bedrooms, would probably take her in for the remainder of the holidays, which would give the necessary quarantine before returning to the school.

Mr. Carson jumped at the opportunity, and Lorna was told to pack her bag.

"But Daddy, Daddy!" she remonstrated. "I don't want to leave you. Just when we're happy together must I run away? Do measles matter? I'd rather have them and stay here. I would indeed."

"Don't be silly, Lorna. Miss Rodgers wouldn't thank you to start an epidemic. Of course you must go to Capri. It's a splendid opportunity. Signora Verdi has a nice little villa. Cheer up, child. I'll tell you what I'll do. I'll take you myself to-morrow, stay over Sunday, and come again and spend the next week-end with you. I can get an extra day or two of holiday if I want, and the Casa Verdi is a quiet spot, quite out of the way of tourists. We can have the orange groves to ourselves and see nobody. If I catch the early boat I'm not likely to be troubled with English trippers; that's one good business."

"Daddy! You darling! Oh, that would be glorious! I'd go to the North Pole if you'd come too. Two week-ends with you in Capri! What fun. We'll have the time of our lives!"

To poor Lorna, who so seldom had the opportunity of enjoying family outings, this visit indeed was an event. She packed her bag joyously, and was all excitement to start.

Following his usual custom of avoiding the vicinity of English people, Mr. Carson decided not to go to Capri by the ordinary steamer that conveyed pleasure-seekers, but to secure passages in a cargo vessel which was crossing with supplies. To Lorna the mode of conveyance was immaterial; she would have sailed cheerfully on a raft if necessary. She rather enjoyed the picturesque Neapolitan tramp steamer with its cargo of wine barrels and packing cases, and its crew of bare-footed, red-capped seamen, talking and gesticulating with all the excitability of their Southern temperament. The voyage across the blue bay was longer than that to Fossato, and she sat in a cozy nook among the casks, and watched first the white houses of Naples fading away, then the distant mountains of the coast, then the gay sails of the fishing craft that plied to and fro over the water.

It was sunset when they reached the beautiful island of Capri, a pink ethereal sunset that flooded headland and rock, orange orchard and vineyard, in a faint and luminous opal glow. Their vessel anchored outside the quay of the Marina Grande, and signaled for a boat to take them off. A little skiff put out from the beach, and into this they and their luggage were transferred. The transparent crystal water over which they rowed was clear as an aquarium, and alive with gorgeous medusæ whose pink tentacles seemed to flash with the colors of the sunset; to gaze down at them was like watching a flock of sea-butterflies flitting across a background of undulating green.

They landed at the jetty, walked to the shore, and after securing a carriage started on a long drive uphill to the terreno of Signora Verdi. Capri, betwixt the glow of the fading sunset and the light of the rising full moon, was a veritable land of romance, with its domed eastern-looking houses set in a mass of vines and lemon trees, and the luscious scent of its many flowers wafted on the evening air. It seemed no less attractive in the morning, when, after drinking their coffee in a rose-covered arbor that stood at the bottom of their landlady's orange grove, they wandered away through the bosco and up on to the open hillside. Here Flora had surely played a trick to plant golden genista against the intense sapphire blue of a Capri sea, and she must have emptied her apron all at once to have spangled the rough grass with cistus, anemone, and starry asphodel. Below them lay a stretch of rugged rocks and turquoise bay, with no sound to break the silence but the tinkling of goat-bells, or the piping of a little dark-eyed boy who practiced a rustic flute as he minded his flock. To poor Mr. Carson, wearied with the noise and clamor of Naples, it was a veritable Paradise, a haven of refuge, a breathing space in the dreary pilgrimage of his sad life. On the top of this sunlit, rock-crowned islet he gained a short period of peace and rest before he once more shouldered his heavy burden.

"If I could live all my days here, Lorna, who knows, I might learn to forget," he said wistfully.

"Oh, Dad! We must find a way out somehow. You can't go on like this! It's killing you. Why have we to suffer under this unjust accusation? Why should some one else do a shameful deed and shift the blame on to you? Is there no plan by which you could clear your name?"

"I've asked myself that question, Lorna, through many black hours, but I've never hit on an answer."

"I hate the man who's wronged you," she sobbed passionately. "Yes! I hate him — hate him — hate him — and all belonging to him. Is it wicked to hate? I can't help it when it's my own father's honor that's at stake. Oh, Daddy, Daddy, if I could only 'get even' I'd be content. It seems so hard to let the wicked prosper and just do nothing. Why should some people have all the laughter of life and others all the tears?"

Lorna parted reluctantly from her father on Monday morning. He sailed by a very early boat, so that the sun had not yet risen high, as, after watching his vessel leave the harbor, she turned from the Marina to walk back to the Casa Verdi. Half of the little town was still asleep. There were no signs of life in the hotel, where the wistaria was blooming in a purple shower over the veranda, and green shutters barred the lower windows of most of the villas. A few peasant people were stirring about; three dark-eyed girls, as straight as Greek goddesses, were coming down the steep path from Anacapri with orange baskets on their heads, and their hands full of posies of pink cyclamen; a mother with a child clinging to her yellow-bordered skirt was taking an earthenware pitcher to the well for water; a persistent bell in the little church of S. Costanzo was calling some to prayers, and others were starting the ordinary routine of the day, attending to animals, cutting salads in their gardens, spreading out fishing-nets, or getting ready the hand barrows on which they sold their wares. In the gleaming morning light the beautiful island seemed more than ever like a radiant jewel set in a sapphire sea. Lorna had left the winding highroad, and was taking a short cut up flights of steep steps between the flowery gardens of villas, where geraniums grew like weeds, and every bush seemed a mass of scented blossoms. She was passing a small flat-topped eastern house, whose gatepost bore the attractive title of "La Carina," when she suddenly heard her own name called, and turning round, startled and surprised, what should she see peeping over the cactus hedge but the smiling face and blonde bobbed locks of Irene. The amazement was mutual.

"Hello! What are you doing in Capri?"

"What are you doing here?"

"I'm staying up on the hill!"

"And we're staying at this villa!"

"To think of meeting you!"

"Sporting, isn't it? Come inside the garden! I can't talk to you down there in the road."

That her chum should actually also have come to Capri for the holidays seemed a marvelous piece of luck to Lorna.

"We decided quite in a hurry," explained Irene. "Dad heard this little place was to let furnished, and took it for three weeks. The Camerons have taken that big pink house over there, with the umbrella pine in the garden. Peachy is staying with them. Isn't it absolutely ripping? I was only saying yesterday I wished you were here too. And my cousin Marjorie Anderson and her friends are stopping at the hotel, just down below. We're having the most glorious times all together. Here's Vincent! Vin, you remember meeting Lorna at school? She's actually staying in Capri! No, don't go, Lorna! Sit down and talk! Now I've found you I mean to keep you. We're not generally up so early, but Dad wants to catch the first steamer. He has to get back to Naples this morning."

"My father has gone already by a sailing vessel."

"Then you are alone? Oh, I say! You must spend most of your time with us. It's a lucky chance that has blown you our way, isn't it? We seem quite a cluster of Camellia Buds in Capri."

So Lorna, who had expected a very quiet, not to say dull, visit at the Casa Verdi during her father's absence, found herself instead in the midst of hospitable friends who extended cordial invitations to her for every occasion.

"By all means let your friend join us," agreed Mrs. Beverley, in answer to her daughter's urgent request. "We've heard so much about Lorna in your letters. She seems a nice girl. I remember I was quite struck with her when I saw her at your school carnival. One more or less makes no difference for picnics. It must certainly be slow for her up there with only an Italian landlady to talk to, poor child."

Capri was an idyllic place for holiday-making. The beautiful climate, perfect at this season of the year, made living out of doors a delight. Every day the various friends met together, and either went for excursions or passed happy hours in each other's gardens. The Camerons had several young people staying with them as well as Peachy, and the party at the hotel proved a great acquisition. This consisted of Captain Hilton Preston and his sister Joyce, their married sister Kathleen and her husband, Mr. Frank Roper, and Marjorie Anderson, who was traveling under their chaperonage. They were fond of the sea, and had at once made arrangements to hire a boat and a boatman for their visit, so that they might have as much pleasure as possible on the water during their short stay.

"We shan't be able to paddle about on the Mediterranean when we get home," said Captain Preston with mock tragedy. "My leave will soon be up and I shall be off to India again. It's a case of 'Let's enjoy while the season invites us.' These rocks and bays and coves are simply magnificent. We've decided to go to the Blue Grotto to-day. Who cares to join us?"

This was an expedition which could only be undertaken when the sea was absolutely calm, so, as even the Mediterranean may be treacherous, and sudden squalls can lash its smooth surface into waves, it was wise to take advantage of a cloudless day.

"We'll start early, so as to arrive there before the steamer, and have the grotto to ourselves, instead of going in with a rabble of tourists," decreed Hilton Preston.

"Four boatfuls of us will be a big enough party," agreed Vincent. "They say the best light is at about eleven."

The group of friends therefore set off from the Marina in their various craft. The row along the base of the precipitous craggy shore was most beautiful, the water swarmed with gayly-colored sea-stars and jelly-fish, and on the rocks at the edge of the waves grew gorgeous madrepores, and other "frutti di mare." The Blue Grotto is one of the wonders of Italy, but to explore it is not a particularly easy matter, for its entrance is scarcely three feet in height.

"My! Have we got to squeeze under there!" exclaimed Peachy wonderingly, looking at the tiny space at the foot of the crag through which they would be obliged to pass.

"Not in these boats, of course," said Vincent. "The skiffs are waiting, and if we just leave it to the boatmen they'll show us how to manage."

The tiny craft that were in readiness for visitors now came forward, and the party was transferred to them. Three passengers were taken in each skiff, and were required to lie flat on their backs in the bottom of the boat. The boatman paddled to the entrance of the grotto, then also lying on his back he directed the skiff into a low passage, working his way along by pulling at a chain which was fastened to the roof of the rocky corridor. In a short space of time they shot into an enormous cavern, 175 feet in length, and over 40 feet in height. Here for a moment or two all seemed dazzled, but as their bewildered vision gradually grew accustomed to the light they saw that everything in the grotto, walls, sea, or any objects, appeared of a heavenly blue color. The faces of their friends, their own hands, the water when they scooped it up and dropped it again, all were turned to sapphire, while articles under the sea gleamed with a beautiful silver shade. The girls bared their arms and enjoyed dipping them to obtain this effect. The glorious blue of the cave was indescribable.

"I feel like a mermaid at the bottom of the ocean," exulted Peachy.

"Or a cherub in the sky!" said Jess.

"Why is it blue though?" asked Lorna.

"Because of the refraction of light," explained Mrs. Beverley from the next boat. "We see a kind of concentrated reflection of the sky sent to us under the sea. If it were a gray day outside it would be gray in here too. Some people think that the Mediterranean has risen, and that once the water in this grotto was much lower, so that boats could sail in and out of it quite easily. Do you see that landing-place over there? It leads to some broken steps and a blocked-up passage that tradition says wound up through the cliff right to the villa of Tiberius. Perhaps it was a secret way by which he thought he might escape if danger threatened him."

"How I'd love to explore it," sighed Irene.

"It only goes a little way before it is blocked. It's hardly worth landing to look at it. Be careful, Renie! If you lean over the edge of the boat so far you'll be upsetting us, and, although we might look very delightful and silvery objects under the water, I'm not at all anxious to offer myself for the experiment."

"Why don't they enlarge the entrance?" asked Vincent.

"Because nobody is sure whether by doing so they might or might not spoil the beautiful effect of blue light in the grotto. It's too risky a venture to try. Besides in present conditions the boatmen make a great deal of money by taking tourists into the grotto. If it were very easy to get in they could not charge so much. It's a little mine of wealth to the Capri fisherfolk now, though years ago they used to say the place was haunted, and tell terrible tales about it. They said fire and smoke had been seen issuing from the entrance, that creatures like crocodiles crept in and out, that every day the opening expanded and contracted seven times, that at night the Sirens sang sweetly there, that any young fishermen who ventured to sail near disappeared and were never seen again, and that the place was full of human bones."

"What a gruesome record," declared Vincent. "I agree with Renie though, I'd like to explore that passage with a strong bicycle lamp, or an electric torch. Who knows what we might find if we looked about—a coin that Tiberius had dropped out of his pocket, or one of the Sirens' hairpins, or a crocodile's tooth at least. Yes, I must positively come again, Mater. Just to prove the truth of your stories."

"Silly boy," laughed his mother. "I expect every stone of the place has been well turned over in search of treasure. Trust the fisher people not to lose a chance. Now our stay here's limited by the official tariff to a quarter of an hour, and if we stop any longer we shall have to pay our dues a second time. If you're ready so am I. Tell the first boat to go on. Don't forget we must lie on our backs again to scrape through the entrance."

CHAPTER XX

The Cameron Clan

Lorna had never realized before how much of life can be compressed into a few days. The interval between her father's departure for Naples and his return for the week-end was spent almost entirely with her friends. It marked for her an altogether new phase of existence. She had read in books about jolly families of brothers and sisters, and parties of young people, but her own experience was strictly limited to school. Here in Capri, for the first time she tasted the delights of which she had often dreamed, and found herself cordially included in a charmed circle. Though the Beverleys were mainly responsible for thus taking her up, the Camerons also offered much kindness. "The Cameron Clan" as they called themselves, consisted of father, mother, Jess, and two brothers, Angus and Stewart, and almost every evening the young folk would meet at their villa and gather round a wood fire in the salon. Though the days were so warm the nights were chilly, and it was cheerful to watch the blazing logs. What times they had together! It was an established rule that everybody contributed some item to the general entertainment, and in spite of fierce denials even the least accomplished were compelled to perform. It brought out quite unexpected talent. Peachy, who had always declared her music "wasn't up to anything," charmed the company by lilting darkie melodies or pathetic Indian songs, Captain Preston remembered conjuring tricks which he had learned in India, Mr. Roper proved a genius at relating short stories, and Mrs. Cameron could recite old ballads with the fervor of a medieval minstrel. The walls of the Italian salon seemed to melt away and change to a wild moorland or a northern castle as she declaimed "Fair Helen of Kirconnell," "The Lament of the Border Widow," "Bartrum's Dirge," or "The Braes o' Yarrow."

"Modern people want more poetry in their veins," she insisted. "I've no patience with the stuff most of them read. There's more romance in one of those stories of ancient times than you'd find in a whole boxful of the latest library books. People weren't ashamed of their feelings then, and they put them into beautiful words. Nowadays it seems to me they've neither the feelings nor the language to clothe them in. I'm a century or two too late. I ought to have lived when the world was younger."

If his wife adored her native ballads Mr. Cameron, on his part, had a good stock of Scottish songs, and would trill them out in a fine baritone voice, the audience joining with enthusiasm in the choruses of such favorites as "Bonny Dundee," "Charlie is my Darling," and "Over the Sea to Skye."

"There's a ring about Jacobite melodies that absolutely grips you," said Mrs. Beverley, begging for "Wha wad na fecht for Charlie," and "Farewell Manchester." "Perhaps it's in my blood, for my ancestors were Jacobites. One of them was a beautiful girl in 1745, and sat on a balcony to watch her prince ride into Faircaster. The cavalcade came to a halt under her window and 'Charlie' looked up and saw her, and asked her to dance at the ball that was being given that night in the town. She was greatly set up by the honor, and handed the tradition of it down the family as something that must never be forgotten. Oh! I'd have fought for the 'Hieland laddie' myself if I'd been a man in his days. Is the spirit of personal loyalty dead? We give patriotic devotion to our country, but love such as that of an ancient Highlander for his hereditary chief seems absolutely a thing of the past."

While their elders entertained the circle with northern legends or border ballads the young people also did their share, and contributed such choice morsels as ghost stories, adventures in foreign lands, or weird tales of the occult. Stewart, who was an omnivorous reader of magazines, tried to demonstrate the romance of modern literature, though he could never convince his mother of its equality with old-world favorites. Marjorie Anderson, who had a sweet voice, loved soldier ditties, and caroled them much to the admiration of Captain Preston, who always managed to contrive to get a seat near her particular corner of the fireside.

"I believe those two are 'a match,'" whispered Peachy to Irene one evening.

"So do I. They met first when Marjorie was at school. Dona told me all about it, and it was quite romantic. They'd have seen more of each other only, after the armistice, his regiment was ordered out to India. He's home on leave now. He wrote to Marjorie all the time he was away, regularly. She's tremendous friends with his sisters, and they asked her to join them on this tour. Looks suspicious, doesn't it?"

"Rather! I hope it will really come off," answered Peachy, looking sympathetically at the attractive pair whose chairs always seemed to gravitate together. "She's pretty! And his brown eyes are the twinkliest I've ever seen! Yes! I'm prepared to give them my blessing! I only wish he'd get on with it. Why doesn't somebody give him a push over the brink and make him propose? He's marking time, and for two cents I'd tell him so myself. I guess his eyes would pop out, but I shouldn't care! Don't be alarmed! I promise I won't interfere. But onlookers see the most of the game, and with an affair like this under my very nose I'll be mad if they don't fix-it up."

Captain Preston was hardly likely to conduct his love-making under full fire of inquisitive eyes, but he generally managed to appropriate Marjorie on walks or excursions; they strolled out together to admire the moon, hunted for orchids on the hills, searched the beach for shells, and saw enough of one another's society to satisfy the most ardent matchmakers. It was an established fact that these two should always sit together in boat or carriage, but the rest of the party revolved like a kaleidoscope. Lorna sometimes found herself escorted by Stewart or Angus, sometimes by Charlie or Michael Foard, the friends who were staying with them, and oftener still by Vincent Beverley, whose fair hair, blue eyes, and merry face—so like Irene's—specially attracted her. She was so unaccustomed to have a cavalier at all that it seemed wonderful to her that any one should take the trouble to carry her basket, pick flowers that grew out of her reach, help her up difficult steps or hand her into a rocking boat. This new aspect of the world was very sweet. Insensibly it affected her.

"Lorna's growing so pretty," commented Peachy to Irene. "She's a queer girl. At school she goes about looking almost plain and as dreary as an owl. She's suddenly jumped into life here. Anybody who hadn't seen the two sides of her wouldn't believe the difference. When she's animated she's nearly beautiful."

"I don't think she's ever been really appreciated at the Villa Camellia," replied Irene. "Mums likes her immensely. She says there's so much in her, and that she only wants 'mothering' to bring her out. As for Vin, his head's turned. He's made me vow faithfully to engineer that he sits next to Lorna in the boat to-day. Are you going with Stewart? Well, I've promised Michael if he's a particularly good boy I'll let him row me in the little skiff. I dare say Charlie will be angry, but I can't help it. The Foards are as alike as buttons in looks, but the younger one is so infinitely nicer than the other."

Tuesday, Wednesday, and Thursday had slipped blissfully by. Except for the few hours daily during which the steamer from Naples visited Capri, with promenade deck filled with tourists, the little island was wonderfully quiet, and by keeping away from the Marina Grande or the highroads it was possible to avoid other holiday-makers. If they were not on the sea "the clan," as the whole party liked to call themselves, generally went up the hills to escape civilization. The natives had begun to know them, and though they might be offered oranges, figs, or dates by street vendors they were not continually pestered to take carriages, engage guides or donkeys, or buy picture post-cards or long strings of coral. Irene loved occasional excursions into the white town on the rock. The strict rules and convent seclusion of the Villa Camellia had given her no opportunity of sampling shops at Fossato, so, except for her half-term holiday at Naples, this was her first experience of marketing in Italy. The unfamiliar money and measures were of course confusing, but the quaint little cakes, the lollipops wrapped in fringed tissue paper of gay colors, the sugar hearts, the plaited baskets, the inlaid boxes, the mosaic brooches, the beads, and the hundred and one cheap trifles spread forth on stalls or in windows fascinated her, and drew many lire from her purse. She only knew a few words of colloquial Italian, but she used these to the best advantage, and made up the rest with nods and smiles, a language well understood by the kindly people of Capri, to whom a gesture is as eloquent as a whole sentence. Vincent, whose talents ran more towards prowess at football than a gift for languages, would often escort his sister, and conducted his bargaining by pointing to what he wanted and counting the price in lire on his five fingers, an operation that caused fits of amusement to the shopkeepers, with whom the fair young Englishman became quite a favorite. As long as Vincent could see what he wished for on sale and indicate it with a finger he got along all right, but matters grew complicated if he tried to explain himself. One day his mother, having run short of methylated spirit, for her teakettle, sent him with a bottle to buy some more. He looked the words up in a dictionary, entered a chemist's, and demanded "alcohol for burning" in his best Italian. The assistant seemed mystified, but suddenly a light flooded his intelligent face, he flew to a series of neat little drawers behind the counter, rummaged about, and in much triumph produced an "Alcock's porous plaster," which he vehemently assured Vincent would be sure to burn, and was a real English medicine, imported with great trouble and expense, and certain to cure the ailment from which he was suffering. How Vincent would have got out of the tangle, or convinced the chemist's assistant that he was not in need of medical aid, is uncertain, but at that moment Irene, who was walking with Lorna in the square, spied him through the window, and brought her chum to the rescue. Lorna's Italian was excellent; she soon unravelled the matter, returned the porous plaster to the disappointed assistant, and explained to Vincent that the local name for methylated spirit was "spirito," and that it was generally procured from an oil colorman's.

"How was I to know?" grumbled Vincent dramatically. "A fellow goes by the dictionary."

"It's always called 'alcohol' in Rome, and in some other places," pacified Lorna, who was still laughing at the mistake, "and I've bought it at a chemist's myself in Naples. Come along round the corner and we'll find the right shop. I had my own bottle filled there yesterday, so I know where to go."

On the Friday, Mrs. Cameron, who by universal consent had constituted herself organizer of the various joint expeditions, sent out invitations for a grand gathering of the Clan to go and view the ruins of the villa of Tiberius. This was one of the principal sights of the island, and, as the Preston party were not staying over the following week, it would have seemed a pity for them to miss it.

"It's a case of taking nose-bags and going for the day," said Stewart, delivering his messages at the various villas. "Meeting-place, the piazza in the town. Those who like to come up by the funicular can do so. We'll wait for them. I think the Mater will take the train and save herself some of the climb. She doesn't like these endless steps, and it's certainly a pull from our place to the town. It's worth while walking down to the Marina to get the railway."

Mrs. Beverley, Mrs. Roper, and Joyce Preston joined Mrs. Cameron in taking advantage of the little "Ferrovia Funicolare" that connected the harbor with the town, and arrived on the piazza cool and fresh compared with those who had preferred to toil up the steep path.

"I told you to come with me, Renie child," chided Mrs. Beverley. "Look how hot you are already. You'll be quite overdone before we get to the summit."

"Oh, Mums darling, I'm not tired! I've saved the fare and bought this swanky little cane instead. Look! Isn't it dinky?" protested Irene, proudly exhibiting her newly purchased treasure. "It has a leather strap and a tassel and a knob that one can suck."

"You baby," laughed her mother. "We shall have to buy you a tin trumpet. I don't believe you're out of the nursery yet."

"Tin trumpet, Mums darling? Oh! You've given me such an idea," purred Irene, running to Michael Foard and whispering some communication into his sympathetic ear, which caused him to walk back to a certain street stall and purchase nine tin whistles, with which the younger members of the party armed themselves and immediately began a desperate attempt to reproduce "The Bluebells of Scotland," hugely to the entertainment of the natives, who flocked to their doors all smiles and amused exclamations.

"Bairns! I think shame of you," declared Mrs. Cameron. "They'll take us for a wandering circus. Put those unmusical instruments in your pockets till we're clear of the town. I never heard a poor Scottish air so mangled. You may practice your band on the hills and scare the goats. Don't play it in my ears again till you catch the proper tune."

The musicians, after their first burst of enthusiasm was expended, were glad to save their breath for the climb. When houses were left behind their way wound between high walls, up, up, up, along a paved pathway among orange groves, till at last the allotments disappeared, and they were on the open hillside, among the low shrubs and the rough grass and the beautiful flowers. Irene, running up a bank in quest of bee-orchises, broke her new cane into four pieces, but was somewhat consoled by a stick which Michael cut her from a chestnut tree.

"It hasn't a knob to suck," he laughed, "but I'll tie a stick of peppermint on to the end of it if you like."

"Don't tease me, or I'll throw a squashy orange at you."

"I thought you were fond of peppermint."

"So I am, and if there's another of those creamy Neapolitans left in your pocket I'll accept it and forgive you."

"Right you are, O Queen! There are two here. Does your Majesty prefer a purple paper or a green?"

The ruins, which formed the goal of their expedition, were the remains of a once splendid villa erected by the Emperor Tiberius, and used constantly by him until his death in A.D. 37. Most of the party were disappointed to find them, as Peachy expressed it, "so very ruiny." It was difficult to picture what the original palace must have been like, for nothing was left of all the grandeur but crumbling walls, over which Nature had scattered ferns and flowers. At the very top some of the old masonry had been used to build a tiny church; this was closed, but, peeping through the grille in the door, the visitors could catch glimpses of blue-painted roof and of little model ships, placed as votive offerings by the sailors in gratitude for preservation from danger at sea. Outside this chapel was a great stone monument built so near the edge of the cliff that, when sitting on its steps, one could look down a sheer drop of several hundred feet into the blue waters below. The view from here was magnificent, and as the Clan, in turns, scanned the neighboring coast of Italy with field glasses, they believed they could even distinguish the Greek temples at Pæstum. The girls described the glorious excursion they had taken there from school.

"You were lucky to be able to go all the way by char-à-banc," commented Mrs. Cameron. "Dad and I went there on our honeymoon, years and years ago, and traveled all the way from Naples by a terrible little jolting train that carried cattle-trucks and luggage-trucks as well as passenger carriages. I shan't ever forget that journey. We had to leave the station at 6.30 and when we came downstairs we found it was a pouring wet day. It was only the fact that the sleepy looking waiter at our hotel must have roused himself at 5 A.M. to prepare our coffee, and that we did not like to ask him to do it again another morning, that forced us to set off in the rain. I never felt so disinclined for an excursion in my life. Dad said afterwards if I'd given him the least hint he'd have joyfully relinquished it, but each thought the other wanted to go, so off we set. All the way to Cava it simply streamed, and we sat in our corners of the carriage secretly calling ourselves idiots, and wondering how we were going to look over temples in a deluge. But our heroism was rewarded, for just as the train crossed the brigand's marsh the rain stopped and the sun shone out, and the effect of blue sky and clouds was simply glorious. We had a great joke at Pæstum.

A mosquito had stung me badly on one lid so that I looked as if I had a black eye. It was most uncomfortable and painful, I remember. Well, a party of French tourists were going round the temples, and as they passed us they glanced at my eye and then at Daddy—a husband of three weeks' standing—and they murmured something to one another. I couldn't catch their words, but quite plainly they were saying: 'Oh, these dreadful English! He's evidently given her a black eye, poor thing! That's how they treat their wives!'

"The French people went on to the second temple, and Dad and I sat down to eat our lunch. We were fearfully annoyed by dogs that sat in front of us and watched every mouthful, and barked incessantly. (Did they trouble you too! How funny! They must surely be the descendants of our dogs who've inherited a bad habit.) Dad got so utterly exasperated that he said he must and would get rid of them, so he seized my umbrella, shook it furiously at them and yelled out 'Va via' in the most awful and blood-curdling voice he could command. Just at that moment the French tourists came back round the corner. They turned to one another with nods of comprehension, as if they were saying, 'There! Didn't I tell you so! See what a brute he really is,' and they cast the most sympathetic glances at me as they filed by. Isn't that true, Daddy?"

Mr. Cameron lazily removed his cigarette.

"It's a stock story, my dear, that you've told against me for the last twenty years. I won't say that it's not exaggerated. Go on telling it if you like. My back's broad enough to bear it. Shall I return good for evil? Well, as I walked through the town to-day, waiting till you came up by the funicular, I saw one of the Tarantella dancers, and I engaged the whole troupe to come to the house to-night and give us a performance. You said you wanted to see them. Will our friends here honor us with their company and help to act audience?"

It seemed an appropriate ending to such a delightful day, and all the party readily accepted the invitation. After twilight fell they assembled at the

Camerons' villa and took their places in the salon, which had been temporarily cleared of some of its furniture. The Tarantella dancers, who were accustomed to give their small exhibition to visitors, brought their own orchestra with them, a thin youth who played the violin, a stout individual who plucked the mandolin, and an enthusiast who twanged the guitar. The performers were charmingly dressed in the old native costumes of the country, the men in soft white shirts, green sleeveless velvet coats, red plush knickers, silk stockings and shoes with scarlet bows, while the girls wore gay skirts, striped sashes, lace fichus, and aprons, and gold beads round their shapely throats. They danced several sprightly measures, waving tambourines and rattling castanets, or twining silk scarves together, while the musicians fiddled and strummed their hardest; then six of them stood aside and the two principal artists advanced to do a "star turn." "Romeo" sang an impassioned love song, with his hand on his heart, while "Juliette" plucked at her apron and appeared doubtful of the truth of his protestations. Then the "funny man" had his innings. He sat in a chair with a shoe in his hand and tried to smack the head of a humorist who knelt in front but always managed neatly to avoid his blows, the whole being punctuated by vigorous exclamations in Italian, and much energetic music from the orchestra.

A pretty girl sauntered next on to the scene, and sang — in a rather peacock voice — a little ditty lamenting the weather, at which a velvet-coated cavalier came to the rescue, and chanting his offer of help sheltered her with a huge green umbrella, under which they proceeded to make love, and finally executed a dance beneath its friendly shade. The whole of the little performance was very graceful and attractive, savoring so thoroughly of Southern Italy and showing the courteous manners and winning smiles to the utmost advantage. The dancers themselves seemed to have enjoyed it, and stood with beaming faces as they bowed their adieux and thanked the audience for their kind attention.

"Aren't they just too perfect," commented Peachy.

"I want to wear a velvet bodice and a green skirt with a yellow border. I want to dance the tarantella with a tambourine in my hand."

"Won't a two-step content you?" said Angus. "Mater says since the room is cleared we may just as well finish with a little hop ourselves. May I have the pleasure? Thanks so much. Mrs. Beverley's going to play for us. It's a beast of a piano but it's good enough to dance to. We mustn't notice if the bass is out of tune."

CHAPTER XXI

The Blue Grotto

Very early on Saturday morning Mr. Carson returned to Capri in a sailing vessel, having taken advantage of a night crossing and arriving with the dawn. Lorna had bidden her friends a temporary good-by for the week-end, refusing all kind invitations of "bring your father to see us," or "tell him he must join the Clan." She felt that her excuses for him were of the flimsiest; she said he was tired, unwell, and needed absolute rest and solitude, and begged them to forgive her if she spent the time with him alone, and, though they replied that they could understand his desire for quiet, she was conscious that they thought she might at least have volunteered an introduction. Lorna knew only too well that, if her father was aware there was the slightest danger of meeting English people, he would probably insist upon taking the next boat back to Naples; it was the consciousness of complete isolation that gave the value to his holiday. She told him indeed that she had met some of her school friends and had taken walks with them, but she mentioned that they were staying down below, nearer the Marina, and that they were not in the least likely to come up to the Casa Verdi.

"Let us take our books, Daddy," she suggested, "and go and sit on the hillside as we did last Sunday. It was quiet on that ledge of the crag, and away from everybody. The rest did you good, and I'm sure you enjoyed it."

Lying on the cliff among the flowers, with blue sky above and blue sea beneath, poor Mr. Carson allowed himself a temporary relaxation. He smoked his pipe and read his paper, and for a little while at least the hard lines round his mouth softened, and his anxious eyes grew easy. He finished his Italian journal, lay idly watching the scenery, chatted, dozed, and finally stretched out his hand for one of Lorna's books. It happened to be an Anthology of Poetry which Irene had lent her, and which contained one of the ballads that Mrs. Cameron had recited to the assembled Clan. It had struck Lorna's fancy, and she was trying to learn it by heart. Mr.

Carson turned over the pages, read a few of the pieces, and was closing the little volume when his eye chanced to light upon the name written on the title page. Its effect upon him was like a charge of electricity.

"David Beverley," he gasped. "David Beverley! Lorna! Great Heavens! By all that's sacred, where did you get this?"

"Why, Dad! What's the matter? Irene lent me the book. It belongs to her father."

"Her father! You don't mean to tell me your friend's father is David Beverley?"

"Why not, Dad," whispered Lorna, looking with apprehension into his haggard, excited face.

She guessed even before he spoke what the answer was going to be.

"David Beverley is the man who ruined my life!"

The blow which had fallen was utterly overwhelming. For a moment Lorna fought against the knowledge like a drowning man battling with the waters.

"Oh, Dad! Surely there's some mistake. It can't be! Isn't it some other Beverley perhaps?"

"I know his writing only too well. There's no possibility of a mistake. Besides, I saw him in Naples—at the end of February. I haven't forgotten the shock it gave me. Why," turning almost fiercely upon Lorna, "didn't you tell me your schoolfellow's name before? Have you all this time been making friends with your father's enemy?"

"I thought I'd often talked about Renie," faltered poor Lorna. "Perhaps I never mentioned her surname. Oh, Dad! Dad! Is it really true? It's too horrible to be believed."

Lying in the soft Capri grass, with the pink cistus flowers brushing her hot cheeks, Lorna raged impotently against the tragedy of a fate which was changing the dearest friendship of her life into a feud. Irene!—the only one at school who had sympathized and understood her, who had behaved with a delicacy and kindness such as no other person had ever shown her, who had taken her into her home circle and given her the happiest time she had ever had in her shadowed girlhood; Irene with her merry gray eyes and her bright sunny hair, the very incarnation of warm-hearted genuine affection—Irene, her roommate, her buddy, her chosen confidante. How was it possible ever to regard her as an enemy? Yet had she not vowed a solemn oath to hate all belonging to the man who had so desperately injured them? Oh! The world seemed turning upside down. Loyalty to her father and love for her friend dragged different ways, and in the bitter conflict her heart was torn in two.

Mr. Carson, haunted to the verge of insanity by the terror of discovery, was now obsessed with the one idea of escape from Mr. Beverley. He no longer felt safe on the island. Any moment he dreaded to meet faces that would betray recognition of his past. The calm and content of his visit were utterly shattered, and a sudden violent impulse urged him to return to Naples.

"Capri is not large enough to hold myself and David Beverley," he declared. "We'll go back by the night boat, Lorna. Meantime we'll borrow Signor Verdi's skiff and paddle about among the rocks. I feel easier on water than on land. I like the sense of a space of ocean round me. You can't suddenly meet a man when you've plenty of sea-room, can you?"

"No, no, Dad!" said Lorna, trying to soothe him. "We can walk down the steps to the cove and get the skiff, and be quite away from everybody once we are on the sea."

She was ready to humor his every whim, for in the blackness of her trouble nothing seemed at present to really matter. The whirling eddies of her thoughts rushed through her brain in a perpetual series of questions and answers. Must hate strike the death knell of love? Surely the only thing to do with an injury is to forgive it. Would revenge wipe out the wrong or in any way solve anything? No, there would only be one more wrong done in the world, to go on in ever-widening circles of hatred and misery. Curses, like chickens, come home to roost, and "getting even" may bring its own punishment.

"Our only chance is to go away and start afresh in a new country," she sobbed. "At the other side of the Pacific we might forget—but no! Renie! Renie! If I go to the back of beyond I shan't forget you, and all you've been to me. The memory of you, darling, will last until the end of my life."

Mr. Carson found Signor Verdi working in his allotment, obtained leave from him to use the skiff, and climbing down the flight of steep steps cut in the rock, reached the cove where the boat was beached on the shingle. He had been an expert oarsman from his college days, and understood Neapolitan waters, so in a short time he and Lorna were skimming gently over the surface of the blue sea, keeping well away from rocks and out of currents, but within reasonable distance of the land. Sometimes they rowed and sometimes they drifted, hardly caring in what direction they steered so long as they circled round the island. Their only object was to stop out on the sea, and, as they had brought a picnic basket with them, there was nothing to urge their return until sunset. In the course of the afternoon they had coasted below Monte Solaro, and found themselves approaching the entrance that led to the Blue Grotto. In the mornings, when the steamer brought its crowd of tourists, there was generally quite a little fleet of skiffs to be seen here, but now, with the exception of a solitary boat, the famous cavern was deserted. To avoid passing too near to even this one craft Mr. Carson steered away from the shore, but turned his head in consternation, for loud and unmistakable cries of "help" were ringing over the water, and the occupants, frantically waving handkerchiefs, were evidently doing their utmost to attract his attention. Common humanity demanded that he must at least go and see what was the matter, so he reluctantly altered his course.

In a boat close to the entrance of the grotto were several young people, and Lorna instantly recognized Angus, Stewart, Jess, Michael, and Peachy.

They appeared in much anxiety, and directly they were within hailing distance they called out their news:

"Mr. Beverley and Vincent and Irene have gone inside the grotto, and they don't seem able to get out again. We can hear them shouting for help."

The party, in their British imprudence, had not brought a boatman, and they were uncertain what to do. Their own barque was too large to go through the narrow opening into the cavern, and they looked hopefully at Mr. Carson's little skiff.

"We don't know what's happened," gulped Jess.

"They went in to explore the Roman passage."

"Just by themselves."

"They've been gone such a long time," volunteered the others.

"Listen," said Peachy.

For from out the low entrance of the grotto floated a faint far-off echoing ghost of a shout.

Lorna glanced imploringly at her father. He did not hesitate for a moment. The man who had injured him was inside the cavern, perhaps in deadly danger, and he was going to risk his own life and his daughter's to save him. And risk there undoubtedly was. A breeze had arisen and agitated the surface of the water, so that the ingress was smaller than ever and more difficult to compass. When waves lashed the tideless Mediterranean even the Capri fishermen shunned entering the grotto, for they knew its perils only too well. Telling Lorna to lie flat on her back Mr. Carson took the same position, and with infinite difficulty managed to maneuver the skiff into the rocky entrance. There was barely room, for each wave bumped it against the roof, but by clinging to the chain he worked his way along and shot through into the lake within. On the right of the cavern three figures, holding a light, stood on a kind of landing-place, while a skiff drifting far off in the shadows told its own tale.

Mr. Carson rowed at once to retrieve the truant boat, and towed it back to its owners.

"We thought we had tied it securely," explained Mr. Beverley. "We were utterly aghast when we came back and found it had drifted. It would have been a horrible experience to stay here all night. If the sea rose we might even have been imprisoned for days. We were fools to come, but I didn't realize the danger."

"The sea is much rougher already," said Mr. Carson. "It'll be a ticklish matter to get out again, and the sooner we do it the better. Will you go first and I'll follow on after?"

"It's like you, Lorna, to come to rescue us. I always called you my good angel," choked Irene, as she entered the skiff. "I thought just now I was never going to see you again in this world. Let's get out of this horrible place as fast as we can. It's like Dante's Inferno. I've never been so frightened in all my life."

One after the other the two skiffs started on their risky exit from the grotto, scraping and bumping against the roof with the water on a level with the gunwale; one wave indeed overflowed and soused them, but the next moment they sighted the sky and grazing through the entrance they gained the open water.

It was only when, in the clear afternoon daylight he turned to thank his rescuer that a flash of recognition flooded Mr. Beverley's face.

"Cedric Houghten! You! You!" he stammered, as if almost disbelieving the evidence of his own eyes.

"Yes, it is I; but having seen me, forget me," returned Mr. Carson, his dark face flushed and his hand on the oar. "It's the one favor you can do me for saving you. Let me vanish as I came, and don't try to follow me. I only hope we may never cross each other's paths again."

"Cedric! Come back!" yelled Mr. Beverley, as the skiff shot away. "Man alive! We've been searching for you for years. Don't you know that we've proved your innocence! Come back, I say, and let me tell you."

It was late that evening, after a very long talk with Mr. Beverley, that Lorna's father explained to her the circumstances that had cleared his name.

"David had no more embezzled the money than I, and, thank God, he has no idea I ever distrusted him. When a further sum went, Mr. Fenton set a trap, and discovered to his infinite grief that it was his own son who had been robbing the firm. It practically broke him, and he has retired from all active share in the business now. They packed young Fenton off to New Zealand to try farming instead of finance, but he's not doing any good there. Mr. Fenton, it seems, was most anxious to find me and right the injustice done me, but I had hidden myself so well under an assumed name in Naples that it was impossible for them to trace me. They advertised in the Agony column of The Times, but I avoided English papers, so never saw the advertisements. My efforts to escape notice were only too successful, and, although I didn't know it, I was actually defeating my own ends by my caution. If, as I intended, I had started for a new continent, I might so completely have broken all links with my old life that I might have gone to my grave in ignorance that my innocence was proved. It was only the marvelous chance of this afternoon's meeting that cleared up the tangle. I can look the world in the face again, now, and not fear the sight of an Englishman. Oh, the joy of having got one's honor back untarnished! Next best to that is to know it was not my friend who had wronged me. The belief in his treachery was half the bitterness of those dreadful years. Capri has been a fortunate island for us, Lorna. It's truly called the 'Mascot of Naples,' and I shall love it to the end of my days. I can take my old name again now and be proud of it. You're Lorna Houghten in future, not Lorna Carson. What a triumph to write to our relations and tell them the glorious news. I feel like a man let loose from slavery."

226

To Lorna also this happy consummation of all their troubles seemed a relief almost too great for expression. That Irene, her own Renie, should be the daughter of her father's favorite friend, and therefore a hereditary as well as a chosen chum, was a special delight, for it welded the links that bound them together. The future shone rosy, and she felt that wherever her life might be cast the Beverleys would always remain part and parcel of it. Perhaps the triumph she appreciated most of all was the introduction of her father to the Cameron Clan. No more hiding in out-of-the-way corners and avoiding the very sound of a British voice; henceforth they might hold up their heads with the rest and take again their true position. She was proud of her father: now that the black cloak of despair had dropped away from him, his old happier nature shone out and he seemed suddenly ten years younger. To present him into the intimate circle of her friends realized her dearest wish.

"It's been a wonderful week-end," said Peachy, standing with her girl friends on the quay to wave good-by to the Monday morning steamer that bore some of their relations back to Naples and business. "Here's Lorna with a new name, and Renie with a fresh cousin. Haven't you heard? Why, Captain Preston popped the question last night, and he and Marjorie announced their engagement at the breakfast table. Not the most romantic place to glean up congratulations, but, of course, that's just as you think about it. When I get engaged it shall be announced by moonlight, so that I can hide my blushes. I don't ever want the holidays to end. Capri's the dandiest place in Italy, and if Dad doesn't buy a villa here I'll never forgive him. You want one too, Lorna? Hooray! We'll make a Colony of Camellia Buds on the little island and spend the summer here. We may be globe-trotters and all the rest of it, but I vote we get up a good old Anglo-Saxon League and stick together for better or for worse. I'll buy a Union Jack to-day if the Cameron Clan will promise to wave the Stars and Stripes, and sing 'Yankee Doodle' with 'Auld Lang Syne.'"

"We've welded America already into the clan, dear bairn," smiled Mrs. Cameron. "No other visitor keeps us alive like you do."

"Pronounce thy wishes, O Peach of the West," laughed Stewart. "We rechristen thee Queen of the South."

"Then I summon you all some day to come back to this, my kingdom by the sea. School is school and I've got to have another term there, but I want to feel this happy island is waiting for us to return to it. You promise? Thanks! Here's a new version then of the old song—composed by Miss Priscilla Proctor, please!

H'm—a poor thing, but mine own!"

"There are two of us at any rate who won't forget to come back," said Lorna, linking her arm fondly in Irene's as they walked away from the quay.

THE END.

Milton Keynes UK
Ingram Content Group UK Ltd.
UKHW010704260923
429409UK00004B/343